I0590423

THE INDIAN STEPS

AND OTHER

PENNSYLVANIA MOUNTIAN STORIES

METALMARK BOOKS

The Indian Steps

AND OTHER

Pennsylvania Mountain Stories

By Henry W. Shoemaker

Author of "Pennsylvania Mountain Stories," "More
Pennsylvania Mountain Stories," etc.

" . . . . thro' the green land,
Vistas of change and adventure,
The gray roads go beckoning and winding."

Illustrated

COPYRIGHTED

PUBLISHED BY

The Bright Printing Company, Reading, Pa.

1912

INTRODUCTION

NCE upon a time the author received a letter which said in part, " I didn't write half that was on my mind last night, so this is the second volume." These words are about the best apology for the publication of the present collection of mountain legends, if any is needed. After the appearance of " More Pennsylvania Mountain Stories" last March there were so many yet unwritten which the author felt were equally worthy, or unworthy, as the case might be, to be brought before the public that he decided to start the work immediately and prepare a new collection. The edition of " More Pennsylvania Mountain Stories" was entirely exhausted within a month after publication, and the author decided that it would be better to prepare an entirely new book than to bring out a second edition of the other volume, as was done with the earlier work, " Pennsylvania Mountain Stories." What was said in the Explanatory Preface of the last book holds good for this one. The stories are equally true; at

least they came from sources equally reliable,
and those which were the author's personal
experience more or less he can certainly vouch
for. He much appreciates the kindly recep-
tion from press and public which was so generously given to " More Pennsylvania Mountain Stories." That is another reason for
the appearance of this book. In it, as
in the previous volumes, the author strives
to show the variety and scope of Pennsylvania folk-lore and tradition and through
them hopes to give fresh vitality and interest to the localities where they occurred.
There is no spot of ground a hundred
feet square in the Pennsylvania mountains that
has not its legend. Some are old, as ancient
as the old, old forests. 'Others are of recent
making or in formation now. Each one is
different, each is full of its own local color.
There are some stories in this book which contain more human interest than folk-lore, but
they are included in order to give romance to
certain places where older legends have not
been secured. Any story which relates to
human beings will sooner or later become folk-

lore. It is only when it is "new" that its presence in a volume like this may be questioned. The people of to-day who live, love and suffer will fill the pages of the history and literature of the future. A glimpse or two at present day residents of the Pennsylvania mountains ought to have almost the same call on the reader's attention as tales pertaining to those " who lived and loved a thousand years ago." The Indian Steps from which the present volume receives its name is an interesting landmark in the Tussey Mountains, not far from Pennsylvania Furnace, in Centre County. The Steps were made, so tradition states, to enable Indian warriors from the southern part of the State to quickly cross the mountains when they invaded their northern rivals. In this vicinity was enacted, about the year 1600, one of the bloodiest battles recorded in the annals of the Redmen. It only lasted for a day, but it ended by the southern Indians being driven out of the Spruce Creek Valley and across the mountains, their warriors being nearly annihilated. It has been a matter of general note among the historians that shortly before the advent of the Whites, the Indians were greatly decreased in numbers by pestilences and warfare. Had this not been the case, the first white settlers would have been so out-numbered by the Indians that they might never have been able to effect a permanent settlement. The passage of years, but more especially the running of logs, have pretty well obliterated the Indian Steps, but enough remains to serve as a marker of the frightful conflict between the combined tribes of what we shall call the Kishoquoquilas and the Susquehanahs. Many pleasant acquaintances were made while securing the material for the story of the Steps, the night spent recently at Baileyville having been one of the happiest of the author's life. Mr. John H. Chatham, who taught the " Glades" school forty-three years ago, accompanied the author on the trip and met many of his old time friends and pupils. It is the author's hope that these and the many other charming acquaintances gained through the preparation of this and the earlier volumes may be continued. He certainly owes to one and all a debt of grateful appreciation. A love of the Central Pennsylvania mountains is and always will be the passport of his affections; he knows of no finer bond.

HENRY W. SHOEMAKER.

New York City, July 12, 1912.

INDEX

ILLUSTRATIONS

I

THE INDIAN STEPS

T was at the foot-races between the Indians south of the Tussey Mountains and the Indians north of these mountains, which took place on the " plains" near what is now Pine Grove, that Silver Eagle, ruler of the Kishoquoquilas, or Southern Indians, saw his cousin, the beautiful Princess Meadow Sweet. He had not laid eyes on her since she was carried away when the Northern Indians, or Susquehanahs, overran the Southern country and killed her father, King Yellow Thistle. She had been a nominal captive since her sixth year, and she was now sixteen. Ironwood, the mighty warrior and King of the Susquehanahs, who invaded the Southern country, had adopted her, and her beauty and intelligence made him lavish on her more affection than on his own children. At his death his eldest son, Pipsisseway, or Prince's Pine, inherited the

11

rulership of the vast domain which included
all the territory now known as "northern,"
"central," and "western" Pennsylvania. He
greatly admired his exquisite-looking foster-
sister Meadow Sweet, who in turn looked up
to him on account of his sterling character,
intrepid military skill and giant strength. The
young monarch had always called her his
"little sister," and looking upon her as such,
romantic impulses were not stirred within him
as early as they might otherwise have been.
When old Ironwood was dying he begged his
sons to see that Meadow Sweet received a
dowry on her marriage. Pipsisseway promised
the expiring ruler that she should have "all
the lands which lay east of Spruce Creek, south
and west of the Susquehanah and north of
Jack's Mountains." There was a smile on the
aged chieftain's lips when he heard this, and
in another hour he was dead. None mourned
him more than his foster-daughter, for there
was a deep sympathetic bond between them.
Pipsisseway carried out his promise, which
made Meadow Sweet possessor of a domain of
singular beauty and natural wealth. And this

territory became speedily known under the
poetic title of " The Land of Meadow Sweet."
Thus it was described in Indian oratory
and in agreements with distant tribes. There
may have been a " love motive" back of Pipsisseway's generous suggestion,' as it would
seem unusual to present a foster-sister with a
territory comprising some of the richest land
in what is now Central Pennsylvania. It even
included the royal camp-grounds, burial
grounds and pottery works which were located
in what is now Wayne Township, Clinton
County. This beautiful retreat, known to the
first white settlers as " Patterson's Town," had
been the favorite headquarters for the great
chieftains for centuries, and unless Pipsisseway
intended marrying Meadow Sweet he would be
forced to move the royal lodge-houses and
abandon the graves of his ancestors if she became the wife of another. It may have been
her extreme youth that prevented his open
love-making, or some secret understanding between the girl and himself that the betrothal
was not to be announced until some future
date. The princess was treated with the great-

est deference by Pipsisseway and his three
brothers, Checkerberry, Red Pine and Moon-
seed. Most of her time was spent at the royal
encampment by the Susquehanah, where she
was attended by a score of maidens, the daugh-
ters of noted war-chiefs. Wise men, from beyond the Allegheny Mountains and from the
far South, instructed her in all the arts and
sciences known to the redmen. She was taught
the use of the bow and arrow, and dart. The
mysteries of woodcraft were explained by the
greatest hunters that could be summoned for
that purpose. Her life was a happy one, surrounded by congenial company, and, living in
a beautiful region, she had little to wish for.
During important religious ceremonials or
sporting events she accompanied Pipsisseway
to different parts of his domain. It had hitherto been deemed wise not to encourage any
athletic competitions with other Indian kingdoms, but the Kishoquoquilas had challenged
so repeatedly that the Council of Wise Men,
after grave deliberation, advised Pipsisseway
to allow it to be accepted. These Wise Men
knew that in their realm resided the fleetest

runners, jumpers, wrestlers, and weight-
throwers, and no challenging party would
stand any chance against them. They considered it would be humbling to the pride of
their opponents to give them a decisive defeat
in the field of sport and make them feel less
likely to stir up warfare. This was logic, but
they omitted to figure in the effect of the presence of Princess Meadow Sweet, stolen in her
early childhood from the Kishoquoquilas, upon
the horde of warriors from the South. The
great athletic meet took place the latter part
of May, when nature was at her loveliest. The
" plains" where it occurred were just north of
the mountains which formed the boundary between the two rival kingdoms. They had been
formed by fires frequently burning the timber,
which had eventually fallen down, and the
ground pastured smooth by vast herds of buffaloes, elks, moose, and deer. The sports were
to continue during four days and at night love
feasts were to be held for the visiting redmen
to become better acquainted with their neighbors. The greatest precautions were made to
have everything pass off pleasantly. Pipsisse-

way, who was a diplomat as well as a warrior, called all the athletes before him in a
private audience, urging them in no case to
defeat a Southern Indian by a wide margin.
Every finish was to be close, and if it looked
as if the Susquehanahs were to roll up a huge
score of points against their competitors, some
events must be purposely lost.   This was a
slightly different program from the one advised
by the Wise Men, who urged that the Northern
athletes give a decisive beating to their rivals.
The weather was ideal for the tournament, and
the number of Indians present far exceeded
anticipations. They came from every direction, marshaled by their chiefs.   It was twenty
years since the last contest of this kind had
taken place. The Susquehanahs had been vic-
torious by a wide margin, and the Kishoquoquilas had returned across the mountains in
an ugly frame of mind. On several occasions
they had sent expeditions to the North, which,
though always repudiated by King Yellow
Thistle, inflicted serious damage on unpro-
tected Northern tribes. The direct result of
the athletic games had been King Ironwood's

great invasion of the South, ending with the
killing of Yellow Thistle and the capture of
his young daughter. Ten years had passed,
and the jealousy of the Kishoquoquilas, while
not wholly appeased, was apparently not at a
very acute stage. Embassies protesting friendship and laden with gifts had visited Pipsisseway after his father's death. The first challenge for an athletic tournament had been made
in a friendly spirit. Had it been accepted at
once, the unpleasant features which later
clustered about it might have been averted.
Pipsisseway was young, and referred the matter to his Council. They voted against it un-
animously, so the challenge was rejected. Later
when Pipsisseway heard the disagreeable talk
occasioned he regretted what had been done.
When he discussed it with the Councillors they
told him that the previous tournament had
brought on a bloody and senseless war. This
one would do the same. When a second challenge arrived it was rejected on similar
grounds. Had the third challenge been refused, war would undoubtedly have resulted.
Pipsisseway said if the meet were held and no

ill-feeling resulted, it would show that he was as great a ruler as the greatest of his ancestors. None of them had ever sanctioned an athletic contest with the Kishoquoquilas that had not ended in a war. This was as sure as the sun would rise in the morning. Pipsisseway surely wanted no wars during his reign. He wanted to make an agricultural people out of his subjects; wars and disease had made awful inroads in the Indian population. He would recoup their numbers. He was the first man on the American continent to preach against race suicide. Not that Indians wilfully prevented large families, but the mothers were often ignorant or careless, consequently infant mortality was high. Prizes were offered for large families, and to mothers who were able to raise their children beyond the " dangerous age" where children's diseases were most fatal. Prizes were offered for the largest patches of cleared land, the largest yields of crops, the most substantially built lodges, for the scalps of dangerous animals and the like. Pipsisseway was essentially a " constructive monarch." A description of his personal appearance has

come down to us, and is strangely like that of
the most constructive American of the present
day, Col. Theodore Roosevelt. He was, of
course, darker than the Colonel, but like him
was of medium height, powerfully built, and
with prominent, aggressive teeth. Unlike his
modern prototype, he died at an early age, but
he ranked as the greatest Indian King Central
Pennsylvania ever possessed. He was simple
in his habits, being extremely democratic and
affable. His subjects, who numbered about
fifty thousand souls of different tribal charac-
teristics and residing vast distances apart, all
worshiped him, and would have laid down their
lives for him without a murmur. When he appeared at the "plains," accompanied by his
faithful brothers, and his foster-sister Meadow
Sweet, he was greeted with the wildest enthusiasm. As a personal tribute nothing like it
was known in Indian annals. Many old men
said that the bulk of the vast turnout of people
was due to a desire to see the popular monarch
rather than to witness the contests. Fewer
Indians would have tramped a hundred miles
to see races alone. They had come from the

headwaters of the Allegheny, the Chemung, the
Lycoming, from Chillesquaque, Shamokin and
Mahantango, ostensibly to see a magnificent
tourney, but in reality to show their loyalty to
their King. Unlike other Indian rulers, and
some of lesser rank, Pipsisseway did not travel
in a litter. He walked every foot of the way
from the Susquehanna to the Spruce Creek
Valley. His brothers also walked, but insisted
that Meadow Sweet ride in a litter. She reluctantly consented, as she had absorbed her
foster relatives' democratic spirit. Horses
were unknown in those days, but sometimes
the priests rode elks and moose in religious
pageants. As these animals were only ridden
on sacred occasions, races between Indians
mounted upon them would have been impossible. The first event was a foot-race from the
head of the plains to the Rock Spring and
return. Two champion runners, one repre-
senting the Susquehanahs and the other the
Kishoquoquilas, started on a signal given by
Meadow Sweet, who waved a bunch of heron's
feathers. The Susquehanah runner leaped to
the front and led his Southern competitor by

several hundred yards. There was silence in
the Kishoquoquilas camp, and not too much
applause among the Susquehanahs, as they had
been warned not to display undue enthusiasm
lest it anger their rivals. The race seemed like
a procession until the last hundred yards, when
the Susquehanah runner seemed to tire badly.
His Southern rival crept upon him amid the
terrifying yells of his cohorts, but the Susquehanah managed to last long enough to win
by a foot. The Southern Indians were delighted with the result, but they little knew
that the Susquehanah runner had only feigned
fatigue, and could have won by several hundred yards, if he wished. The second event
was a twenty-mile point-to-point relay race,
which the Susquehanahs could have won easily,
but they held back and only allowed themselves
to win by a narrow margin. The first day's
sport ending without ill-feeling of any kind,
Pipsisseway felt much encouraged. A magnificent banquet was spread under the white
oaks, which was attended by King Silver Eagle,
of the Kishoquoquilas, his retinue, as well as
Pipsisseway, his brothers, retainers, and the

Princess Meadow Sweet. Silver Eagle was
presented to the princess, whom, as already
stated, he had not seen in many years, since
she was carried off by the conquering invader,
Ironwood. Although she was his cousin,
Silver Eagle fell in love with her instantly.
He was very attentive to her all through the
evening, but she kept him at a distance, being
discreet enough not to want to offend him, but
at the same time not caring to arouse Pipsisseway's jealousy. She was woman enough to
feel that underneath her foster-brother's calm
exterior, there smoldered a deep interest for
her. She admired him, and was only waiting
for him to say the word, when she would gladly
agree to become his wife. Silver Eagle laid
great stress on their relationship, and suggested now that the feeling between his tribes
and the Susquehanahs were so thoroughly
amicable that, accompanied by a proper bodyguard, she be allowed to pay a visit to her old
home south of the Tussey Mountains. She told
him that she would love to do this *some time*,
and felt confident her kingly foster-brother and
guardian Pipsisseway would gladly give her

permission. At midnight the visitors retired
to their quarters, and every one in authority
among the Susquehanahs breathed easier. The
first day's festivities had come and gone, and
everybody was happy. On the next day took
place the jumping contests, and shooting
matches. At high-jumping and broad-jumping
the Susquehanahs excelled, but they were careful not to win too easily from the Kishoquoquilas. The shooting was the most interesting
part of the entire tournament. There were
contests at archery, participated in by trained
warriors, by aged warriors, by small boys and
by women. In all these classes, Susquehanah
prowess prevailed, but only by the narrowest
of margins. The Kishoquoquilas were beaten,
but not disgraced. The Indians from the
South were still hopeful they might win something before the contest ended, and exhibited
no ill-feeling. That night King Pipsisseway
dined a select company under the white oaks.
The only outsiders were Silver Eagle and his
personal suite. He renewed his attentions to
Meadow Sweet, painting to her in lurid colors
the beauties of the Southern Country, its val-

leys, its mountains, its rivers, its population
so intelligent and handsome compared to those
in the North. " They are your people," he
said; " you must mingle with them; you will
love them as much as they love you. You
know how they cheer you every time
you appear at the tournament." Meadow
Sweet continued her tactfully guarded conduct,
and Silver Eagle departed at the midnight
hour, in excellent humor. " You are a born
diplomatist," said Pipsisseway to her after the
distinguished guest had gone. " You were
born to rule over vast dominions. The world
has never seen your equal in womankind."
Meadow Sweet smiled to herself; Silver Eagle's
attentions were arousing the latent fire of
Pipsisseway. Probably the crowning event of
the tournament would be his public announcement of their betrothal. But he hadn't proposed as yet. She knew full well who she
was, and how at a word from herself Silver
Eagle would demand her restoration to the
Kishoquoquilas. But she would remain where
she was for two considerations. Being a
woman, she had no inheritance beside her rank

in her own country; with the Susquehanahs
she had inherited a large territory, and had a
chance of becoming the Queen of King Pipsisseway, if he proposed. With the third day took
place the wrestling matches, the live-bird
shoots, the weight-throwing competitions and
the grand animal drive. The Susquehanah
wrestlers and weight-throwers were the victors,
but their rivals apparently put up good fights.
Ten thousand live wild pigeons and parrots
were shot at in the live - bird competition,
the majority of which were killed by the
Susquehanahs. Then came the animal drive.
A thousand buffaloes, elks, moose, and deer
were released one by one from a corral and
driven across the plains. The idea was to
kill an animal at the first shot. If it did
not fall it scored one against the party who
held the bow. Out of the thousand animals
seven hundred fell at the first bow thrust.
Of these, three hundred and forty-nine were
killed by the Susquehanah nimrods, so carefully had they measured their skill against
their opponents. The Kishoquoquilas had won
an event, so were happy. That evening Silver

Eagle was again entertained at Pipsisseway's
quarters. He was in excellent spirits and
monopolized so much of Meadow Sweet's attentions that Pipsisseway almost felt slighted.
This was especially so when he began talking to
her in his Southern dialect, as if to cut Pip-
sissesway entirely out of the conversation.
Meadow Sweet was glad when he left, and
threw herself at full length at Pipsisseway's
feet, exclaiming, "Oh, how he tires me."
"I'll be glad when this is all over, just
to get rid of Silver Eagle," said Pipsisseway.
The next day's program consisted of several
minor contests, such as a three-legged race, a
race for cripples, and a dart-throwing competition. These the Susquehanahs let the
Kishoquoquilas win. The score of the tournament stood fifty-five to forty-five; the Susquehanahs had "played their cards well." After
these contests, a magnificent barbecue took
place, and the beasts slain in the animal drive
the day before were served up, deliciously
cooked, to the multitude. It was estimated that
ten thousand Indians "partook" of the repast,
but in what proportion seven hundred animals

could go into ten thousand rapacious Indian
stomachs is a question for an expert hotel-
keeper, and not for an historian. A private repast was served under the white oaks by Pipsisseway, as a parting honor to King Silver
Eagle, his retinue, and staff. Antelopes
brought from what is now Kentucky were
served to these dignitaries, as was green corn
and tomatoes preserved in their natural state
from the year before. Silver Eagle was
crouched close to Meadow Sweet while the feast
was in progress, and whispering compliments
in her ears. After the meal was over he contrived to edge her into a quiet corner, where
he could talk to her undisturbed. " I love you,
fairest cousin," he expostulated, " I can keep
back these words no longer. Come with me
to-night; we shall be married with great pomp,
and you shall rule with me over my dominions.
You belong to our people by birth; you are an
alien among the Susquehanahs." Meadow
Sweet fully expected this outcome, and was
prepared to meet it. It was a trying position,
as to give an excuse that would not insult her
admirer took considerable tact. " I am honored

by your proposal, famous cousin," she replied,
" but you are aware that I am a captive, though
a willing one, of Pipsisseway; I am also very
young; my power of choice is vested in him as
my guardian. Ask his permission; I shall be
guided by his noble sense of fairness." Silver
Eagle could not tell whether it was " yes" or
" no," but was not displeased. He took the
maiden's hand in his and kissed it. " We will
go at once to your worthy guardian, Pipsisseway, who is not the man to hinder a cause like
true love." Pipsisseway had been pretending
to be holding a conversation with some of his
chiefs while this little talk was in progress, but
he had been watching the two actors carefully.
He was especially anxious to note any sign in
Meadow Sweet's face indicating that she possessed a lurking interest for her cousin. Being
impressed by her lack of concern, he was determined to outwit the wily interloper. Of
course, he could not be sure that Silver Eagle
had been proposing, but it looked very much
that way. When the Southern monarch and
Meadow Sweet approached, and the retainers
fell back leaving the trio together, he was pre-

pared for any emergency. " Worthy King, I have come to ask your foster-sister's hand in holy marriage," said Silver Eagle. " Gracious ruler, I much regret to say that I have promised her in marriage to *myself*," replied Pipsisseway. This was a stinging blow to Silver Eagle's hope and pride; his black eyes snapped angrily; he staggered like a drunken man. When he recovered himself he said, " Is this true, fairest cousin?" Meadow Sweet, while Pipsisseway had never proposed to her, would have taken him any time if he had, was only too glad to answer, " It *is* the truth." " Then, why didn't you tell me so a few minutes ago, and save me this humiliation?" said Silver Eagle with renewed anger. " I am, great king, as you are aware, only a captive of Pipsisseway's; I could not answer for myself. But I can truthfully say that I love him with all my heart." Pipsisseway smiled at this clever rejoinder, and held out his hand in a friendly manner to Silver Eagle. The Southern monarch put his own hand behind his back, and edged away from him, muttering to himself. Pipsisseway walked after him, but he refused

to notice him. The four days' festivities had
wound up in a quarrel after all. There was no
use trying to pacify Silver Eagle; he had probably been mad all along over the almost con-
tinuous victories of the Susquehanahs in the
tournament, but now had come " the unkindest
cut of all." Early in the morning it was reported that Silver Eagle had broken camp at
dawn, and withdrawn across the Tussey Mountains. There were a number of unpleasant incidents between the Kishoquoquilas and the
Susquehanahs over the breaking up of camp;
several unprovoked murders were committed by
the Southern Indians, and threats of all kinds
passed. Their King's disappointment, though
unknown to them, was evidently telegraphed
to them in some form of unrest, and all the
ugliness in their natures came to the surface
on " moving day." Nothing further was said
about the marriage of Pipsisseway and Meadow
Sweet until they had returned to the royal
camping-grounds on the Susquehanna. There
the betrothal was publicly announced, and fleet
runners sent to all quarters of the realm to
acquaint the various tribes of the gladsome

news. This, coming so soon after the signal victory over the Kishoquoquilas in the athletic tournament, stirred the Susquehanahs into a white heat of patriotism. It would have been a good time to go to war; every one was in a mood to fight for his country. The wedding took place " two moons" after the betrothal was announced, being attended by fully five thousand Indians, as many Susquehanahs who had witnessed the athletic tournament. Ambassadors were present from all the neighboring kingdoms, with the one notable exception of the Kishoquoquilas. This was accounted extraordinary, as Meadow Sweet, being a Kishoquoquilas princess, the daughter of their late King Yellow Thistle, should have married in the presence of some of her own countrymen. A brief honeymoon was taken to Lewis' Lake, a spot sacred to the Indians as having been once the entrance to the Underworld, or realm of spirits. Upon their return, the Council of Wise Men had what they considered bad tidings to relate. Hunters had reported that a vast force of Kishoquoquilas were building a flight of stone steps in Stone Valley, from the

foot of the Tussey Mountains to the summit.
Why this was being built was a mystery, except that it would enable the Kishoquoquilas
Indians, in case they invaded the Northern
Country, to cross the mountains with greater
rapidity. They could make a " flying attack,"
as it were. Pipsisseway looked grave when he
heard this. " Not only that," he said, " but I
believe those steps are being built because they
feel certain they will conquer us after their
invasion, and they want to minimize nature's
barriers. After they imagine they have conquered us, they will expect to finish the steps
down the northern slope of the mountain."
Pipsisseway's abilities as a strategist were
confirmed by spies whom he caused to be sent
out. They returned, saying that Silver Eagle
was assembling a vast army in the Southern
valleys. He was drafting warriors from as far
South as what is now Maryland and Virginia.
From talk they had heard six or seven thousand braves were under arms. The purpose
of the steps was now established. This vast
force of Indians was at present spread out
through the valleys. When the time arrived

they could be marshaled quickly and sent
across into Spruce Creek Valley on a run.
They would appear in this valley so suddenly
that there would be no time to resist. Sweeping northward, they would pillage and capture
everything in sight until they reached the royal
encampment by the Susquehanna. The buildings would be burnt, Pipsisseway and his
brothers surprised and murdered, while the
beautiful Princess Meadow Sweet would be
carried off to her old home in the South. Pipsisseway and his brothers dead, a marriage
could be arranged between the young widow
and Silver Eagle, who would rule over the
largest domain on the eastern slope of the
Alleghenies. The Indian Steps would be a
recognized gateway of travel between the South
and North. The most trustworthy and intelligent chiefs were summoned for conference
with Pipsisseway and his Council. Fifty
chieftains answered the call. It was decided
by them that every male Indian fit for service
should be moved in the direction of the Tussey
Mountains. That was to be the ultimate destination, but they should tarry at all the fre-

quented mountain passes where ingress from the South was afforded. But the rallying point was to be at the northern side of the " Indian Steps." Every brave was to start separately; no two men should travel together. It could not be said that a vast " body" of Indians was moving to the South; they would go as in- dividuals. The chiefs returned to their homes, and ere long the advance began. Among them were Indians from the Chillesquaque country, led by Chief Hidden River; Indians from the Loyalsock region under Chief Mountain Ash; Indians from Nippenose Valley, led by Chief Lock-and-Bar; Indians from the region north of the royal encampment, in what is now Wayne Township, Clinton County, led by Chief Hazelwood; Indians from the Monsey Town Flats, as the country around what is now Lock Haven was called, commanded by Chief Gold Thread; Indians from the Sinnemahoning region, led by Chief Sonicle; Indians from the Bald Eagle Valley, under Chief Mountain Lion; Indians from Penn's Valley, led by Chief Panther Fangs, the grandfather, by the way, of the celebrated Indian Red Panther; Indians

from the Black Forest, famed for their skill
with bow and arrow and spear, led by Chief
Tiadaghton; the Indians residing in Spruce
Creek Valley, under Chief Golden Hour;—all
moving in a common direction by different
routes, each as an individual, silent, loyal, determined.   It was a subject of some discussion
among Pipsisseway and his brothers if Meadow
Sweet be allowed to accompany them.   She
pleaded so hard, and Pipsisseway relied so much
on her judgment, that she went with the royal
party.   This consisted of King Pipsisseway,
his brothers, the Council of Fifty Wise Men,
the royal bodyguard, and household.   Queen
Meadow Sweet was attended by a single
maiden.   The rest of her retinue remained in
the beautiful retreat by the Susquehanna,
watched by one hundred picked Indians of the
home - guard.   The regal camp - ground looked
deserted when they were gone; it seemed a pity
to leave such an ideal spot.   Arriving in the
Southern country the various tribesmen of the
Susquehanahs camped out as individuals and
waited.   Spies who visited Stone Valley and
adjoining valleys under cover of darkness re-

ported that the main bodies of the Southern Indians, or Kishoquoquilas, were camping along what are now known as Shaver's Run, Globe Run, and Garner's Run. This showed that the line of attack was to be by way of the Steps. It was to be the sudden rush of a vast horde of warriors, whose combined strength would sweep everything before. When this information was thoroughly verified, the Indians that were posted near the various points of ingress to the Susquehanah kingdom were concentrated in Spruce Creek Valley. All were ordered to remain in the forests, and it would be impossible to have imagined army lurking at the foot of the Tussey Mountains. Undoubtedly the Kishoquoquilas sent out spies, but not finding any connected bodies of warriors, would imagine that the ones they saw were hunters or fishermen. The Steps were completed in the early winter, and the invasion was expected to follow. The army of the defense was on the alert, but nothing seemed to happen. Days and weeks passed. The forests were banked with snow. The waiting force became restless, hungry, and unhappy. They begged to be allowed to visit their homes and help their families.   Permission was granted in rotation, and when an Indian left on a week's furlough, another would return from his trip the same day. Evidently the Kisho-quoquilas finally received some intimation that a strong force awaited them, and were trying tactics of delay in order to reduce the numbers of their enemies. Some day when the defense was disorganized they would sweep over the mountain and the domain of Pipsisseway would be theirs. But the same dissatisfaction which had reigned among the Susquehanahs broke out among the Kishoquoquilas. It was an outrage to keep them so long without sign of a battle.   Being encamped in compact bodies it was impossible to grant furloughs wholesale.   In consequence there were threats of mutiny and desertion from some of the war-riors from below the Potomac. An advance must be made, or the force could not be held together, was the advice given repeatedly to Silver Eagle by his aides. He would try to show them that the longer it was postponed the better the chance of finding their adver-

saries scattered and unprepared. " Your great
mistake, sire," said Dangleberry, one of his
oldest warriors, " was in assembling your force
before the completion of the Steps. You should
have waited until a year after they were finished; then you would have found our enemies
completely off their guard." " It's too late
now," replied Silver Eagle, ruefully; " we must
do the best we can." The reports of dissatisfaction were so overwhelming that one snowy
morning at daybreak the advance, at double
quick, was ordered. The force, numbering
some five thousand braves, trooped up the
Steps, over the summit, and down the rough
mountain sides, coming on the level at the
" plains." As they emerged into the open
country a terrific fusillade of arrows, darts,
and spears assailed them from the forests on
either side. Some of the more mercenary
quickly retreated into the woods and up the
mountain, but the majority, goaded on by their
chiefs, kept advancing across the plain. The
casualties in Pickett's Charge at Gettysburg
were trifles compared to the harvest of death
in this invasion of Spruce Creek Valley by the

Kishoquoquilas.   Before they were halfway
across the open space, panic began seizing the
entire body, and they ran from side to side,
under the merciless rain of arrows.   Many
dropped into the snow from sheer fright and
lay as dead.   It is related that the entire in-
vading army did not shoot five hundred arrows.
They were overcome with terror too quickly.
All they could do was stagger about, waiting
to be killed.   Out of the five thousand who appeared on the plains, scarcely a thousand
reached the forest on the northern edge of it in
safety.   These, when they came face to face
with their enemies, felt renewed courage, and
drawing their knives and tomahawks fought
desperately.   In a few minutes a thousand
hand to hand conflicts of the bloodiest character were in progress.   Silver Eagle was one
of those lucky enough to cross the plain safely,
and fought with diabolical bravery.   He
hacked his way through a mass of Susquehanahs, swearing that he'd reach the headquarters of Pipsisseway, the location of which
he seemed to know, if he had to kill a thousand
tribesmen on the way.   He probably slew a

score of Indians before he was free to run forward unhampered. In the distance, through
the spaces between the trunks of the giant
white oaks, he could make out a substantial
lodge house built of logs. It stood a hundred
yards from the Rock Spring, the source of
Spruce Creek. " That's Pipsisseway's house;
I'll kill him, I'll kill him; Meadow Sweet will
yet be mine!" As he neared the door he saw
the beautiful Queen emerge, looking weary
and anxious. He waved to her, roaring, " I've
killed your cursed husband; fly with me and
be mine," and redoubled his pace through the
wet snow. Just then a powerful voice rang
out, " Not so fast, ambitious king, not so fast;
I'm far from dead." He looked around and
beheld his arch-enemy, Pipsisseway. He had
not time to raise his tomahawk, for the King
of the Susquehanahs had punctuated his greeting by cleaving his skull. He fell in a limp
mass in the slush, his brains spattering about
like a fox's entrails. Silver Eagle being dead,
Pipsisseway rushed back into the thick of the
conflict, and helped despatch some of the few
remaining Kishoquoquilas. The slaughter con-

tinued all day long, and when night fell it was
safe to say that there wasn't a living Kishoquoquilas north of Tussey Mountains. Even
those who had fallen, panic-stricken, in the
snow on the plains were butchered later when
they attempted to sneak away. The order
went out, "Kill every Kishoquoquilas; take
no prisoners." As Pipsisseway, reeking with
blood, tramped back to his lodge-house that
night his mind evolved a fiendish revenge on
his enemies. "I'll have Silver Eagle's body
thrown into the Rock Spring, and every other
corpse of his followers of high rank that we
can identify. Rock Spring is the source of
Spruce Creek, and Spruce Creek flows into the
Juniata, that runs through the richest territory of the Kishoquoquilas. The putrifying
carcasses of their king and the pick of their
warriors shall taint the water that they drink."
Next morning this scheme was put into effect;
over a hundred scalped and mutilated corpses
being dumped into the Spring. For a full year
the Indians who lived at the mouth of the creek
said that the water smelled rancid even there.
It was deemed unwholesome, and for years the

redmen had an idea it was not fit to drink.
But what was pollution then adds to its
purity now. Just as sugar is strained through
bones, the crystalline source at Rock Spring
flows through bones, the bones of warriors
which time has left unsullied, and bubbles into
the bowl of the spring limpid and sweet as
dew. After the great conflict, which was called
" The Battle of the Indian Steps," the Kishoquoquilas went on the decline. They split up
into small tribes, and were constantly at war
with one another. Pipsisseway did not follow
up his victory, but returned to his beautiful
retreat by the Susquehanna, where he died the
following autumn of chills and fever. Besides
his widow he left a son, named War Bonnet,
who ultimately came to rule over his posses-
sions. The Susquehanah kingdom enjoyed
marked prosperity for nearly a hundred years
after the great battle, only falling into a state
of civil war during the last years of the Seven-
teenth Century. King Merciless and King
Golden Treasure were two rival rulers of a
later date, whose factional fights did much to
disrupt the old kingdom. It seemed a shame

that the passing of the redmen should have practically obliterated the Story of the Indian Steps and the resultant battle. But it is only one of the many historical legends that are fading away.

II.

A REDMAN'S GRATITUDE

ANCASTER was thronged by a wild and noisy mob. It was as noisy as only North of Ireland men can be when something disagrees with their principles. They had come to town vowing vengeance, and no one of this race says a thing without meaning it, or seldom wills without the accomplishment. The Indian outrages had become so terrifying that an example, summary and lasting, must be administered. Unfortunately the real offenders were out of reach, but in Lancaster jail were lodged a score of harmless remnants of the once-great tribal organization, the Lenni Lenape. For half a dozen years they had camped on the outskirts of the town, on the present site of Grand View, although some few of them had their lodges along the

shady banks of Conestoga. They were a sickly
lot, tall, weak-kneed, hollowed-chested. Even
the heralded beauty of the Indian race was
lacking in the women. Children were few;
they seemed on the verge of extinction. The
white settlers had it that they drowned their
offspring, but it was Nature, and not human
nature, that kept down the increase. When
the Indian massacres along the border became
of daily occurrence the most stolid white neigh
bors began to look askance at the little band
of aborigines in their midst. They subjected
them to petty slights; those few who were
willing to work were denied the chance; they
were driven from their fishing grounds, their
corn uprooted, and children fired stones at
them as they stolidly filed along the paths leading to town. They could not have retaliated if
they wanted, they were so outnumbered. But
these persecutions could have been endured, had
they not ended in the murder of some of the Indian women and children. The leaders, thoroughly alarmed, went to see the town burgess, to
beg protection. "Come into town," said Dr.
Adam Kuhn, "and we will lodge you in the

workhouse until the excitement dies down."
This seemed like sage advice, so the entire band
gave themselves over to the local authorities.
Jail life was not disagreeable. They could
smoke in the court-yards, do their own cooking
and were liberally provided with food. Some
of them openly remarked that they could stand
life sentences. But the presence of so many
Indians housed and fed by the authorities in-
censed the more belligerent citizens, especially
those who had tasted warfare with the redmen.
The town officials were lampooned and ridiculed, but they were conscientious men, and felt
a sense of duty towards their helpless wards.
The work-house was a flimsy affair, even though
it was built of stone. The walls were thin; it
looked as if the Quaker architect had never expected it to be occupied by real criminals. It
was like a jail one would see on the stage. The
Indians realized their physical insecurity, but
concluded that they were safer within its narrow walls than in the open country. They also
believed that in case of an attack, soldiery,
what or where from was vague, would come to
their rescue. The burgess, when armed men

rode through the streets and shouted, " Death to every Indian," said he " relied on the natural common-sense of the people to avert blood-shed." The common-sense people were evidently far in a minority, for when the jail was attacked, there seemed to be an unanimity of opinion favoring it. The quarters of the jailer, Ben McKeehan, were in a smaller stone house, separated from the main structure by a narrow alley-way. His wife, daughter and niece, though it was Sunday, were cooking dinner when the attack began. In their domestic duties they were being assisted by Blue Cloud, a boy of the Lenape, about fourteen years old. He was a mild-faced lad, tall for his age, and tolerably well muscled. Katie Bigland, one of the jailer's nieces, about his own age, had taken quite a fancy to him. She was helping him learn the English language, with a top-dressing of North of Ireland brogue, and showing him the intricacies of civilized culinary art. Katie and her sister Maggie, who was a couple of years older, were orphans. Their parents had died in Donegal, in the old country, several years before, and they were being brought up

by their prosperous relatives. Jail-keeping
may not seem a prosperous calling, but it was
an office always held by politicians, and politicians even in those remote days were "well-
fixed." As the Indian boy was useful, his
presence wasn't distasteful; it was lucky for
him that such was the case. The cooking was
half over before the women realized that the
work-house had been broken into, the jailer
overpowered and a hundred brawny, red-
headed Irishmen were butchering the swarthy
captives in true Donnybrook Fair fashion.
Katie was quick to scent danger for her Indian
friend. "-You've got to hide this very minute,
you Blue Cloud. I don't want anything happen-
ing to you." " Where shall I hide?" inquired
the Indian, with stolid stupidity. " In the
chimney," was the girl's quick-witted answer.
The Indian clambered up, sending a trail of
soot clattering down after him. He got out of
sight none too soon. The mob, fresh from
their successful butchery, were already peering
through the windows of the jailer's home. The
women were standing about the cupboard, apparently busy. Their faces looked as if they

knew little and cared less about the massacre
that had just occurred. They looked no worse
than ordinary farmers' wives after a particularly sanguinary butchering. But some of the
mob were more hot-headed than the rest. They
pushed open the doors of the house, and trooped
into the kitchen. They inspected everything,
but did no damage, except with their muddy
boots. After the last man had walked through
the house, the women were left in peace to re-
sume their cooking. There wasn't much heat
in the fireplace, else Blue Cloud would have
resembled a ham fresh from the smoke-house
upon his release. At nightfall Katie took the
responsibility of summoning him down. When
he appeared he looked like a different person.
Formerly he was one of the lightest colored of
the tribe, but now, after four hours up the
chimney, he was one of the blackest. " You
look like a true Lenape now," said Katie. She
had teased him by telling him he had Irish
blood, as he was so light colored; his skin was
buff, whereas most members of his tribe were
sooty black. " Judging from the way the Irish
acted today, I'm glad I don't look like that

breed," said the Indian, sarcastically, in his best English. He was told to sit in the ingle-nook, so to be handy to return into the chimney if a fresh outbreak occurred. He remained there in silence until the jailer himself ap-peared. " Heaven help us," he declared. " that mob of boys from the border have killed every one of the fourteen Indians we had in the jail." Then he glanced at Blue Cloud and said, " You've one consolation, my boy; you now have the distinction of being the last of the Lenni Lenape." Just then Katie spoke up; " Well, uncle Ben, he never did look like one; it would have been a shame to have killed an Irish Indian." At this the entire roomful, in-cluding the " last of the Lenape," laughed. Evidently the lad had lost no relatives in the massacre, for he was still able to smile. Per-haps he was too dazed to know what he was doing. The jailer soon brought him to his senses by telling him he must make his escape to the mountains that very night; there was no chance for an Indian to survive in Lan-caster. He explained that a German trader, who stabled in a log barn in the rear of the

work-house, was starting on a trip to the Blue
Mountains at midnight. He would arrange
with him to secrete the Indian somewhere
among the bales and boxes. "We'll be back
if he won't do this," said McKeehan, "but I
think he will." Dressing the youth as much as
possible to resemble one of the fiery "Paxton
Boys," he escorted him across the alley to
where the old German, by the light of several
tallow tips and rushlights, was harnessing his
spike team of giant roan-colored Conestoga
horses. The old trader liked the lad's looks,
so consented to run the risk, agreeing to carry
him until they reached a spot where he could
be liberated with safety. Just as he was
climbing into the heavy conveyance Katie made
her appearance with a packet of provisions.
"You have all been very good to me," said the
Indian, quite overcome by such an exhibition
of thoughtfulness. "Young lady, I will never
forget how you saved my life; perhaps a day
will come when I can do as much for you.
Good night." This was the longest speech in
English he had ever made. His vocabulary
was exhausted, and if an Indian can be em-

barrassed he felt that way; so he hid himself
forthwith behind the folds of the canvas cover
of the wagon. Once inside he crouched among
baskets of goods. He might have been a bale
of cloth, he doubled himself up so completely.
In the darkness he could thing of nothing
else except the plump, trim little figure of
Katie Bigland, with her round face, frank blue
eyes, and light, wavy, brown hair. She was
his light; he was leaving her and going out
into the darkness in more ways than one.
Katie, to use a local expression, " wasn't worth
much for work" for a full week after the departure of the young Indian. This would have
brought down on her head the wrath of her
industrious aunt at any other time but this.
Now, the jail premises were topsy-turvy, the
jail building was tumbling down, corpses were
being buried, blood, teeth, and hair were being
gathered up in every direction, gruesome relics
of the needless massacre of the Lenni Lenape.
In due time Katie's spirits returned—that is
to a certain extent—but she was never as light-
hearted as of yore. It wasn't the memory of
the massacre that oppressed her; it was the

passing of the first person of the opposite sex
she had liked. Transformed into modern
phraseology, " she had lost her first love." First
loves are lost almost as regularly as " first
teeth," but often the second, third, or fourth
love gets even more devotion than he deserves.
With Katie, she had almost a heart-full of
sincere affection left, which she bestowed, when
in her eighteenth year, on Anthony Stouch, a
sturdy young farmer from Warwick Township.
Anthony had outgrown the civilized conditions
of Lancaster, and suggested that Katie and he
take up a homestead in the vicinity of Muncy
Town. She was only too glad to become an
individual in a new country. She was tired
of being a dependent nobody in a narrow,
provincial town. There were many settlers in
the Muncy region, a medley of Germans, Scotch-
Irish, Quakers, Welsh and Huguenots. There
were too many to suit the preconceived ideas
of Anthony and Katie as to what a truly back-
woods country should be. They traded their
land with a Frenchman named Emile Letort
for a claim far in the wilderness, on the upper
reaches of the West Branch. The Frenchman

accompanied them as guide, and they enjoyed
every step of the journey. It was just what
they wanted; they were going into the track-
less wilds where game of all descriptions
abounded. Elk and deer were innumerable;
there were small herds of buffaloes, and fur-
bearing animals of all kinds. Wild pigeons
darkened the sun by their flights; they could be
easily netted, and made excellent eating.
Immense flocks of parrots sometimes gave a
fresh coloring of green to the leafless trees in
the fall. Nature seemed to make a special effort
to welcome and feed newcomers. The mountains were high and imposing, and covered with
pine trees which appeared to pierce the celestial
canopy. There was an atmosphere of space,
freedom, good health. It was an ideal country
to begin life in. The Frenchman's tract lay
not far from the mouth of Hyner Run, a nice
stretch of rich bottom land, free from stones,
and easily cleared. The young couple were
perfectly happy. They could not have been
better suited had they made the spot themselves, so they said again and again. The
Frenchman, genial soul, was happy because

they were, and insisted on staying with them
until they enlarged the cabin and built a barn.
The happy pair prospered from the start.
Eight children were born to them, good crops
were raised, they enjoyed satisfactory health;
there was little more to be desired. There
was only one disquieting element. Roving
bands of ugly-visaged Indians often camped
in the vicinity of the farm. They were always
asking favors and begging, and acted with ill-
concealed meanness if these were refused.
Rumors of occasional fights between Indians
and settlers often came to their ears, but the
brave-hearted Anthony and Katie felt they
could hold their own against any of them if
they wanted trouble. However, when a family
named McCabe, consisting of husband, wife and
four half-grown children, who lived at the next
clearing two miles further up the river, were
brutally murdered, supposedly by Indians, it
began to look as if they were on dangerous
ground. Then came a period of calm lasting
six months. Anthony Stouch began going on
his hunting trips — buffaloes were becoming
scarce—leaving his wife at home with a loaded

rifle, to guard the premises and the children.
Sometimes upon his return she would tell him
how she had seen a bear skulking across the
upper end of the sheep pasture, or almost ran
into a wolf near the smokehouse, but nothing
worse than that. One overcast, misty morning
in the fall, when Anthony was absent on one
of his trips, Katie was in the garden lot " rais-
ing" potatoes. Everything was quiet about her;
the giant original pines on the edge of the
clearing had temporarily ceased their sighing;
they were an unhappy lot, and probably fore-
saw their total annihilation within the next
hundred years. The river was low, and made
no sound as it ran over the slippery brown
rocks, where at times it roared vociferously.
The children had gone down to the water's edge
to fish—the eldest, named Hamilton, a boy of
seventeen, had developed into an expert salmon
fisherman. The good woman was working
away, humming an Irish song as only a person
with a clear conscience can. The potatoes
were large, as the season, being dry, had
favored the crop. All at once a terrific yell
resounded through the narrow valley. Katie

Stouch knew what it meant. She had been
surprised by Indians. She had become so sure
of herself that she had left the rifle on the
stump fence, and ran after it, as fast as she
could over the rough ground. Before she
reached it, three tall, gaunt savages loomed out
of the fog between her and the fence. She
was cut off from her means of safety. She
resolved to die bravely, and calmed herself by
the thought that the children, on hearing the
war-whoop, had secreted themselves. The
tallest Indian rushed up to her, and laid his
great tawny hands on her shoulders. She
smiled at him, resolving to be unlike a girl she
had heard of near Muncy Town who died of
fright when an Indian laid hands on her. The
Indian's eyes met hers; there was a look of
recognition that was mutual. " Where did I
see you before, lady?" said the redman, in
English that had the merest trace of Irish
brogue to it. There was something in the buff
color of his complexion, so different from that
of any other Indian she had seen, that made
her understand. " I knew you when you were
in the jail at Lancaster twenty-five years ago.

I'm Katie Bigland." The other Indians looked
at one another in disappointment. What
promised to be a bloody butchering affray was
turning into a family reunion. " Yes, you're
Katie Bigland, the little girl who taught me
English and hid me in the chimney and saved
my life. I owe you everything for that. I
beg your humble pardon for my attack on you
now." " Never mind that," said Katie, her
assurance fully restored, and smiling broadly
with her open blue eyes, " I'm glad you came
after *me*. If it had been somebody else she'd
have been scalped; so no harm's done." The
eight children had heard the war-cry and run
to cover; but on hearing nothing further came
out, and with youthful curiosity crept on their
hands and knees to the edge of the potato
patch, where they had last seen their mother.
Through gaps in the stump fence they saw her,
to their utter mystification, engaged in a
friendly conversation with three fierce-looking
savages. They knew it was a pleasant talk,
as they could hear their mother's merry laugh.
Finally Hamilton's head appeared over the top
of the fence, and his mother saw him. " Come

here, children," she called. When they climbed
over the fence with the agility of young Indians, she presented them one by one to the
three redmen.   "Children, this is Mr. Blue
Cloud; this is Mr. Bog Bilberry; this is Mr.
Winter Cress." The young folks were amazed
to meet Indians, about whom they had always
heard such awful tales, on terms of social intercourse. They could scarcely credit their senses;
it was like making the personal acquaintance
of the devil.   They were still more amazed
when they heard their mother invite the Indians to remain for dinner. They all accepted
with alacrity, and sat on the grass until the
meal was ready. Blue Cloud was the only one
of the trio who could speak English, that is,
well enough to be understood, and amused the
younger children by showing them his rifle
and scalping-knife and explaining the " signa-
ture" on the leaves of a liver-leaf plant, while
the cooking went on. By the time the dinner
was over, children and Indians were as friendly
as if they had been acquainted since birth.
" One touch of nature makes the whole world
kin." When they were ready to leave, Blue

Cloud asked Katie if he could have a few
words with her alone. They walked together
to the spring on the hillside at the rear of the
house, where they conversed for ten minutes.
"Why did you become a bad Indian?" said
Katie, thus heading off the redman's probable
efforts to justify himself. "I became a bad
Indian because I had to; I was forced to see
my race butchered unjustly on every side; I
was denied a living, even the right to walk on
the earth. I have seen my friends shot down
at my side in cold blood. I have been present
at massacres of whole villages that would make
that butchery by the 'Paxton Boys' at Lancaster jail appear as nothing. I have seen our
lands stolen, our game slaughtered, our people
misrepresented. It was a case of reprisal with
me; by vengeance alone could I live. If I was
a peaceable Indian I would be a victim of
treachery. If I lived by murder, I had a
chance to survive. If white people feared me I
could keep my distance; if they didn't and
approached me I would surely die. That is
how I am living now, after nearly twenty-five
years of remorseless persecution. In truth,

the Indian has all the right on his side; he did
not draw first blood. He will never have any
historians; his memory will only persist in
vengeance. A few whites are slain, it is true,
but an entire race of Indians is being wiped
out by the white men. I am forced to be what
I am. I am sorry I happened upon you in my
travels, but if it hadn't been you, I would have
scalped woman, children and all. I cared a
lot for you; I often thought of you, but I never
expected to meet you again. Please forgive
me." Katie looked him squarely in the face
and said, " There may be justice in what you
say, but I cannot see things from your point
of view. The murder of any woman is wrong;
confine yourself to the men, if you must kill,
and history will not be unjust. I will forgive
you for your attempt to butcher a defenceless
woman and children if you will promise to lead
a new life henceforth. Go beyond the Allegheny if the settlers won't let you alone here,
but ' sin no more.' I thought you were a right
decent young lad; I liked you in the old days;
don't make me change my opinion." Her voice
was serious and determined, and her words had

their effect. Holding out his hand the Indian took hers and clasped it in the compact. And Central Pennsylvania knew no more of B'ue Cloud.

III

THE FAIRY PARKS

AIRIES in Central Pennsylvania? Why, certainly there are, lots of them hereabouts," said old man Bomeister, as he emptied his corncob pipe against the rock on which we sat under the mountain-ash tree. " Right down the Pike is where they make their headquarters — they've been dancing and playing there now for over fifty years, and they're increasing in numbers as fast as dandelions. Every year they're making new parks, or playgrounds, until now they're more than a dozen of them between the top of Grindstone Hill and where the road dips to go down to Pine Creek." I had often noticed these parks, or circular patches of trees and green sward, and admired their beauty, wondering at their odd form, and apparent immunity from forest fires. Now it was all being explained to me. " The little people

63

make a ring on the first night of the new
moon," the old man continued, "and dance
around it until the moon goes down that night.
After that the fires can't pass their boundary,
the trees grow nicely and the grass stays green.
Travellers like to rest there and pasture their
horses—they always seem to have cool breezes
to spare, for the Fairies have the kindliest and
most lovable feelings towards mankind; they
want to make things pleasant for them. But
on moonlight nights, then's when you see the
fun; the parks swarm with the gay little folks,
but they are so shy it's difficult for a person
to see them first. I don't believe Fairies are
native to America—I never heard tell of any in
Pennsylvania except our little colony along
the Pike. They wouldn't be here if it wasn't
for one old woman; she hated to leave the
Fatherland unless she could bring some Fairies with her. At first her relatives objected,
but she had her way and brought a dozen of
them in a black bag. I've often heard my parents tell the story; they came from the same
village in Wurtemberg as Gran'mam Swartz,
the old lady who fetched the Fairies. When

BUILDING SLIDES

Photo by W. T. Clarke

she was young Lotte Rudesehli, they say that
she was the prettiest girl for miles and miles—
the prettiest blonde that imagination could
conjure up. She was much given to wandering
in the woods, especially on moonlight nights,
and the neighbors would have ascribed this to
sentimentality if she hadn't been so indifferent
to the young men. Some thought she met a
lover in the forest depths, nothing else could
take a girl alone into such secluded localities.
But it was a long time before any one had the
courage to follow her, she seemed so haughty
and reserved. There was a young man in the
village named Wilhelm Swartz, a sort of
country gallant, whom all the girls, except
Lotte Rudesehli, the solitary wanderer, had
loved at one time or another. Her indifference
piqued him to such an extent that he came to
sincerely love the one girl who wouldn't notice
him. Often he had the desire to follow her
on her lonely rambles; he had a jealous impulse to meet her secret lover and drive him
away. But he feared the villagers would see
him follow her into the forest, and twit him
when he came back shame-faced and with hang-

ing head. But one evening, it was the first
night of a new moon, and the silvery crescent
was dancing above the tops of the tall spruces,
as he walked along through the sweet-scented
woods he came upon a place that the path led
down a steep hillside, where a brook tumbled
along beneath the giant trees. Through an
opening in the evergreen boughs he could see
quite a distance ahead of him. To his amazement he saw Lotte Rudesehli seated on a mossy
log surrounded not by one, but by a hundred
admirers. They were not big, stalwart lads
like himself, but tiny chaps, scarcely a foot
high, clad in tight-fitting suits of green and
yellow. They held hands as they danced
about her, sometimes breaking into weird little
songs in a minor key. Many little women,
dressed in bodiced skirts of the same colors sat
nearby on little hillocks or bunches of grass.
Lotte seemed to be their queen, and was as
radiantly happy as her company. It seemed a
pity to break in on such a merry, innocent
scene, and Wilhelm would not have done so
intentionally. In an effort to draw nearer to
obtain a better view he stepped on a dry root

which cracked audibly. Lotte looked up, recognizing him instantly, while the Fairy band scampered out of sight under leaves, stumps, rocks and logs with all the alacrity of chipmunks. Lotte had too equable a disposition naturally, and was in too happy a frame of mind at this particular moment to mind the intrusion, and accepted Wilhelm's profuse apologies with smiling good will. They had known one another, though not well, for a long time, so it did not seem like being too forward when the young man seated himself beside her on the moss-grown log. Nervously plucking a fern he began talking to her as if they had met under the most ordinary circumstances, and not as the result of his breaking up a Fairy merry-go-round. Strange as it may seem, Lotte treated him better on this occasion than she ever had before, or any other man for that matter. He was so good-looking, he had such wonderful expression, and never showed off to better advantage than this night, bathed in ghastly moon-rays. He was tactful enough to make no allusion to the party he had disturbed, and as she made no effort to explain, it

seemed to be the one subject unmentioned during their blissful tryst in the forest. 'What
will my parents say,' gasped Lotte, putting her
hand to her head in a gesture of terror as she
noticed the hands of the village clock pointing
to two as they neared her home. But whether
they protested or not, or even knew when she
got home, is not a part of the story. Wilhelm
had started on a successful wooing; nothing
could stop him now. How far he progressed
that night is also a mystery, but he doubtless
kissed her—who could have protested on such
a beautiful night? It was soon noticed by the
villagers that Wilhelm Swartz always accompanied Lotte on her rambles into the forest.
If she had been meeting some one else previously, clearly that suitor had fallen into disfavor, or it might be she had been meeting
Wilhelm all along. But that couldn't be the
case either; he had been noticed too many
times gazing after her ruefully, cap in hand,
as she disappeared into the shadowy depths.
Her conduct had always been a mystery any-
way; this interest in Wilhelm, so handsome
and strong, was the one normal act of her life.

About this time there was great talk in the
little mountainous community about emigrat-
ing to America. Land could be bought outright very cheap in all the States, especially in
Pennsylvania, which was said to teem with
prosperous Germans. Some few had gone over
already, and wrote back glowing accounts of
the riches of the new country, but above all the
social equality and opportunities which
awaited every one. There were no landlords,
no supercilious nobility, any one could rise
who had energy and a fair share of adapta-
bility. Wolfgang Rudesehli and his good wife
Minne, the parents of Lotte, caught the passing enthusiasm. They began corresponding
with a neighbor who was in Northern Pennsylvania, and that individual, to make sure of
them, had the foreign agents of several land
companies in Philadelphia visit their home,
and paint pictures that can only be described
as glorious. Why the emigrants in the wild
Pennsylvania hills were so anxious that more
of their kind should follow them may be ascribed to two reasons. They may have been
lonesome for more friends from ' home,' or,

like the monkey with his tail off, wanted others
in the same predicament. There was only one
member of the Rudesehli family who objected
to the proposed change of destiny, and that was
Lotte. Her older brothers and sisters thought
the idea a grand one; they were tired of being
branded as ' peasants,' tired of filling a place
in life from which *caste* would give them no
escape. They would go to a land of freedom,
where their children might become Presidents.
Lotte, hitherto the proudest of the family, was
the only one who wanted to remain. ' You
can be a great lady over there,' her brothers
urged; but this appeal to her vanity, once so
potent, was of avail no longer. Wilhelm
Swartz had always cherished a secret hanker-
ing for the ' new world,' and when he heard
the talk in the Rudesehli household, told his
sweetheart he would gladly go along. They
could marry just as well in Pennsylvania as
in Wurtemberg—easier in fact. They did not
publish ' banns' over there, no tests or quali-
fications were required of candidates for mar-
ital happiness in the ' land of the free.' But
to his surprise Lotte said she was not going;

the others could go, but she would remain. It
took some time for Wilhelm to learn her
reason; had she not been so much in love with
him, it would have been impossible—a woman
regards a *reason* as the one secret she can
keep. But finally she confessed why she was
so wedded to the hills of old Wurtemberg. One
night when she was a wee girl, so she said,
she had strayed into the forest. Evening was
coming on, and everything gleamed so clear-
cut in the final cadences of the golden hour.
The pines and spruces seemed to the tiniest
needle carved out of the transparent ether.
The air seemed so sweet it must have been
freshly let loose from realms celestial. She
had sat down to rest by the waterfall, which
created its own little rainbow in the maze of
froth and spray. She was entranced by the
scene—anybody, young or old, would have been
—until she was aroused from her contempla-
tions by the sound of squeaky voices, like old
men talking far away—only these voices were
near at hand. Presently she saw the speakers
—they were a horde of tiny Fairies, nothing
else, clad in tight-fitting suits of yellow and

green. They waved their hands to her, and
made every effort to become acquainted. She
wasn't a bit frightened; there were such merry
twinkles in the little fellows' eyes that they
surely meant no harm. She waved to them,
and they came close to where she sat, and
began conversing in a friendly, cheerful manner. Once they were at their ease, and a troop
of little lady Fairies, dressed in bodiced skirts
of bright colors, came out of the underbrush
and sought the young girl's acquaintance.
Their spokesman explained to her they had
always regretted the gulf which existed between them and the 'big people,' but in her
they had found a 'happy medium.' They
could love her; would she consent to become
their queen? Lotte at that time didn't have
a very definite idea what the word 'queen'
meant, but she had heard that there was one
in Wurtemberg, so high above her subjects that
many doubted she was of the same clay. Yes,
she would become their queen gladly, if it
would do them any good. The Fairies were
delighted; they joined hands and danced
about her singing gayly. When she returned

home she had difficulty in explaining to her
family what had kept her so long in the forest
—she had lost her way, that was the best
excuse her childish shrewdness could invent.
After that it was difficult to restrain her from
wandering in the forest. Threats of punishment were unavailing; she was naturally a
headstrong girl and the family pet, so she
knew her family really meant nothing. As she
grew older the family began to realize that
her solitary strolls were harmless; they had
heard of people ' loving nature,' their daughter
must be one of these strange creatures. But
it was her duty as Queen of the Fairies to go
among her subjects as often as possible. She
made a gracious queen, as she grew in loveliness and charm with each succeeding year.
But love for a mortal had come into her life,
and her family wanted to emigrate to America.
Her lover was also anxious to go to the new
country—everything seemed to point to her
departure from her Fairy kingdom. She was
unhappy now for the first time in the eighteen
years of her life; her brow, formerly smooth
as marble, now showed lines of thought. She

was sure she loved Wilhelm dearly; her family
had always been good to her, but how could
she leave the 'little people' who had elected
her their queen? Wilhelm's pleadings prevailed; after shedding a few tears she resolved
to go. She was not a sneak nor a coward; she
resolved to break the news to her tiny subjects
before starting on the long journey. One night
in June, when the new moon had appeared, she
went to the Fairy rendezvous accompanied by
Wilhelm. Calling her beloved subjects about
her she explained to them the step she was
about to take. Her voice was choked with
sobs, but every one of her audience understood
why her love for her sweetheart and family
should be the controlling motive in her life.
Just when she finished talking one little shrill
voice piped up, 'May I go with you?' Immediately all the others clustered about her, taking up the same refrain, 'May we go along,
may we go with you?' They held Lotte's hands
tightly, and some clambered all over Wilhelm,
striving like squirrels to hide themselves in
the pockets of his velveteen jacket. Their demands were so sincere and importunate that

the young girl smilingly declared that she
would take as many Fairies with her to America as she could carry in a wool-sack. There
was a cheer from the little people; they would
follow her to the ends of the earth, they insisted. But a process of selection must be
made—which Fairies should go, which should
remain. It was decided to draw lots with
twigs of hazel after Wilhelm would come back
with the wool-sack. He started to the village,
returning with a sack of black material such
as was used in those days. The lots were
drawn; a long twig meant 'go,' a short one
'stay,' until the bag was filled. Twelve Fairies,
six men, six women, were chosen, and hid their
smiling faces in the hot, stuffy sack.   The
others kissed the fortunate ones 'goodbye,' and
with no recriminations, danced away to their
homes under the rocks and roots. Wilhelm
saw to it that air-holes were provided so that
the little voyagers would not be smothered—
for Fairies are in a sense human—they are
like us except that there are no diseases among
them—they are in a sense immortal.   Two
days later the Rudeschli family, accompanied

by the faithful Wilhelm Swartz, began their
tedious journey to the 'land of promise.' It
was fraught with untold inconveniences and de-
lays in those days. By 'diligence' and goods
train, interrupted by frequent changes of conveyance, they proceeded to Paris. Wilhelm
and Lotte had many adventures with the wool-
sack, to be sure. To the old folks and inquisitive brothers and sisters it contained kit-
tens, rabbits, white rats, Fairies, anything—to
the baggage and customs officials, vegetables,
meats, clothing, whatever seemed advisable.
Wilhelm was well provided with money, but
it ate into his store to 'tip' every one into
silence who might question the well-filled wool-
sack. Many complications would otherwise
have arisen, especially in France, where none
of the party knew a word of the prevailing
language. It was a critical trip for Wilhelm;
he had promised Lotte to see that her little
friends reached America in safety; he could
not disappoint in his first real effort to aug-
ment her happiness. The party embarked on a
sailing vessel at Havre, and were three months
at sea, alternately becalmed and tempest-

tossed. Lotte kept the 'little people' in her bunk by day, but let them out at night, to scamper about the decks, sometimes scaring the other passengers, who thought the ship bewitched. But they were too agile to be captured, or even be wholly seen by outsiders. They were fed with what Lotte and Wilhelm could snatch from the mess, and also with nuts, berries and roots, their favorite food, brought along for this purpose. The customs officers at old Castle Garden couldn't have been very alert at that time, for the mysterious black wool-sack passed through unmolested. It is said that an 'O. K.; U. S. Customs' was tied on it. It may be that Fairies are providentially lucky; they have to be if they are immortals. Outside the imposing building one of the old neighbors, Carl Aeschlimann, who had lived near the Rudesehli's in Wurtemberg, was waiting. He greeted them with a wild burst of delight. Here were people, his people, who had actually seen his beloved hills and vales and waterfalls, in dear old Wurtemberg, a little less than four months ago, while he had not seen them in sixteen long, toilsome

years. There was also a representative of the
real estate company at the landing; he would
help pilot and install them in their new home
in Pennsylvania. Then they were escorted up
Broadway, marvelling at the wonders of New
York, across the waters of the Hudson in a
ramshackly ferry-boat, and aboard a train for
Philadelphia. At the City of Brotherly Love
they spent the night, starting away the next
morning, changing cars three or four times until they reached a place called Antes Fort, on a
railroad which they were told had just been
completed two months before. The engines
were wood-burners, and moved slowly enough
through the country, so that they could admire its fertility and grandeur. They marvelled at the number of persons who got in the
cars, who looked like Americans but who spoke
a dialect that sounded like German. At Antes
Fort two teams were waiting to convey them
on the last stage of their journey, to the un-
cleared tract of land on the Pike which they
were to make 'blossom like the rose.' Most
of the way the road led through a virgin forest
—the trees were even taller than in the Father-

land, the waterfalls wilder, the silence more
intense. At length they came to a small opening in the forest, made by cutting the trees so
that they fell against their standing neighbors.
In the centre of it was a log shack—they use
it now for a woodshed--here the Rudesehlis
were to stay until they cleared more land and
built a more respectable abode. The tract they
had bought comprised one hundred and sixty
acres, ' more or less,' so the deeds ran. It was
past dark when they arrived, so that they could
not tell whether they were pleased or not, but
they were probably too tired to care. Soon a
new moon appeared, shimmering between gal-
axies of unstable stars. Wilhelm and Lotte
had noted a cozy little nook along the road—
it was near a waterfall and a spring—where
they decided to liberate the Fairy band. After
partaking of a light supper, they were too excited to eat much, they started down the Pike,
carrying the bag between them. When they
reached the pretty spot, they emptied the sack;
the little people shouted in treble ecstasies of
joy, and began dancing merrily. They formed
a circle and danced about the couple who had

safely carried them so far. The young couple
had much work ahead of them, so they probably
took less notice of their surroundings henceforth than the Fairies. The 'little people'
were immensely pleased; it was *their* Black
Forest over again, but on an amplified scale.
Lotte intended visiting them each night, but
she felt so tired she postponed it a week. One
night the family heard an awful screaming and
wailing in the wilderness; it sounded like some
frail woman in distress. They were all for
running out with torches to find her, until
Carl Aeschlimann who was still stopping with
them, explained that it was a panther, or as he
pronounced it a ' pon-tare,' an animal bigger
and more rapacious than the traditional lions
of the Bible. All the family except Lotte were
satisfied by this explanation, but it only made
the girl more uneasy. ' I'm afraid,' she whispered to Wilhelm, ' that it has eaten my little
people, and enjoying them, has come to devour
us.' Next night she went in fear and trembling
to the Fairy abode, and called to the little
colony. To her surprise they all responded,
and danced and sang about her gleefully. ' I

feared you were all eaten by that awful mon-
ster which screamed around our cabin last
night. I never expected to see you again!' The
Fairies laughed outright; 'Panther eat us?
Never fear, it *did* chase us, but we were too
quick.' Lotte was reassured, and on succeeding nights when she heard the panthers' wail
and wolves' call she knew her little friends
were safe. They thrived in their new home;
children were born to them—for Fairies are
partly human—they were happy. Lotte married Wilhelm the next spring, but continued
her visits to the Fairy home, even after her own
children were born. Occasionally, Wilhelm accompanied her. At times she would say she
would go back to Wurtemberg for a visit before she died, and take the Fairies along, but
for some reason they didn't enthuse; it can
only be surmised that they were not sentimental. Fairies own no Fatherland. As she
grew older and especially after Wilhelm's
death, Lotte became known as Gran-mam
Swartz, and her connection with the Fairy
colony was generally acknowledged. Even her
children admitted she was a trifle queer, and

her grandchildren were even more positive of it. But she pursued the even tenor of her way, a good wife and mother, hard-working and plodding, until in her seventieth year, from the infirmities of age, she passed away. She was buried in the little mountaineers' cemetery on Grindstone Hill, and her grave is marked by a rough slab of mountain brownstone. They say, and I'll admit I've seen it myself once, that on a certain June night, when the young moon first comes up from behind the Bald Eagle Mountains, the Fairy band, old and young, congregate there and dance daintily — which seems to be their only form of worship—about the ivy-grown mound."

IV

A HERMIT'S SECRET

 N walking trips I always liked to spend a night with old Jackson Everhard at his comfortable cottage on the hill back of Cammal, where the road branches off that crosses Bendel Point. I enjoyed my brief visits with the old hermit; he possessed so many original ideas, which he thought out during long periods of solitude on the mountain top. My fondness for hermits, which began in 1900, when I met old Pierre Bayle, who lived at the foot of one of the famous Knobs of Clearfield County, seemed to grow with the years. I could readily understand the point of view which drove them into the wilderness. It is hard to pursue an idea or stick to one subject amid the turmoil of the city. Persons cherishing a bitter disappointment, or bent on solving some intricate problem, can best indulge themselves far from the

habitations of men. A man who does not
think, or one dependent upon petty gossip or
excitement, can never fully cut himself off from
the world. A possessor of beautiful thoughts
can do so readily, as they grow and develop
amid quietude. Jackson Everhard claimed
that he was a hermit because he wanted to
watch his coal lands grow into value. " If I
lived in Williamsport or Sunbury I could
never estimate their true worth; some one else
would reap the benefits." It was his belief
that his six-hundred-acre tract of land was un-
derlaid with the most valuable coal deposits
in Northern Pennsylvania. " Those rich people
who own the land all around mine aren't selling
theirs off; I may as well watch mine, and open
it some day myself." He had estimated the
coal to be worth at least a million dollars, and
had drawn up elaborate papers for the in-
corporation of a coal company capitalized in
the six figures, of which he was to be president,
and which would take him from obscurity and
make him a man of affairs. But this wasn't to
be done until the long-discussed railroad which
was to penetrate the coal fields became a

reality, or the "rich people" who owned the surrounding territory made a move to operate. Meanwhile the old man, who had moved to the mountain top at the close of the Civil War, had sacrificed first the saw-timber, then the props, and lastly the ties, to keep alive until he opened "his gold mine of coal." He was also writing a book to show the fallacy of religion, how it had hampered the work of civilization and enlightenment. This was a much-worn theme, except that it was discussed from Jackson Everhard's point of view, which was decidedly original. He occasionally read me choice excerpts, but his favorite quotations were from the preface, which explained why he had turned against the teachings of the church. It was during the Civil War when he was on picket duty in Tennessee. At the next post, the sentry was a young theological student, who enlisted as a moral duty to help save his country. Near his post was a spring, and one dark night a lurking confederate made a desperate effort to get a drink from it. Crawling on hands and knees as silently as he could, he was within a few feet of the refresh-

ing source, when the alert ears of the churchly
sentry heard the cracking of some twigs. He
shouted in the direction from whence the faint
noises came, but received no answer. He put
his rifle to his shoulder and deliberately fired
into the thicket where he imagined the in-
truder was hiding. There was a groan and a
shriek; he had evidently hit a living object.
Hurrying down the hill he found that he had
shot a young confederate soldier through the
throat, and that he would be dead in a few
minutes. Stooping down on his knees beside
the dying man he gave him the last consolation
of the church. " That was too much for me,"
said the hermit, "A system that in two thousand years hasn't gotten humanity above such
barbarous conduct deserves to be blotted out;
it's hindering human progress; it's the cause
of all our scallywags." We had heard this
and much worse before, but I was convinced of
one thing—Jackson Everhard was true to his
ideals; he was honest, truthful, honorable—
I had never met a man of purer life. His pets
consisted of a family of bluebirds, which came
annually to occupy a box which was nailed to

the top of a tall, swaying pole by the garden
fence. " Blue birds prefer poles that swing a
bit in the winds; its more like the tree-tops."
A man who could watch birds for hours, and
make them his companions, was surely a being
of simple, unspoiled nature. No man who
loves birds can be bad. I asked him why he
had never married—a wife of the right sort
might have lived comfortably on the summit.
Instead of a two-roomed shanty, a commodious
square mansion, like those on Oregon Hill,
would probably have occupied the site. Instead of five acres cleared, two hundred acres of
the tract would now be under cultivation, I
suggested. " Yes, the right sort of woman
could have done all that, but where could she
be found?" Then he told me that he had never
enjoyed what other men call a " love affair."
He was too short and homely, he said, to be
attractive physically to the girls. They preferred taller and handsomer men. Sometimes,
if homely men were rich they got married, but
they never had their wives' love. " Being poor,
no woman could be attracted to me by anything except my personality, and that wasn't

the kind that the dear girls wanted." To my
eyes, the old man wasn't homely at all. He
was short, probably four inches shorter than
I am, but he had a large and well-shaped head,
steady, transparent blue eyes, a nose inclined
to the aquiline, and quantities of light brown
hair that the weight of seventy years had not
diminished. He wore a long beard, which was
brown and curling. Many men grow beards
after they have been disappointed in love, so
I have read. But we were many hours together, and the true story of his life was eventually, little by little, revealed to me. Finally I
was able to piece it together. In reality he
blamed the Universe for not giving him the
same success in love that it had to most every
other man. The story of the theological sentry,
with his gospel of blood and absolution, was
only a blind to his true sentiments. His dream
of vast riches originated only in his desire to
look successful in the eyes of *one woman* who
had turned cold to him long years before in
old Jacobsburg. He had known her from
earliest childhood, and loved her as far back
as he could remember. She was very beauti-

ful, that is, beautiful for Jacobsburg, I suppose; was really intelligent and cultivated.
But she never paid much attention to the undersized Jackson Everhard when handsome
men were around. He felt his physical limita-
tions keenly, and tried to ease his wounded soul
by seeking the society of other young girls.
But the result was always the same; he was
tolerated until handsomer men appeared. He
tried to dress as well as he could afford, read
books, think pure thoughts, cultivate his
powers of conversation, but he was *hopeless* in
the eyes of the women. He only went to the
war to make himself heroic. The one girl's
indifference pained him most. It seemed so
unjust of nature to treat him so roughly. This
was accentuated when she married the village
rake, a tall, handsome fellow, with no morals
nor means of support. This marriage was the
crowning blow. His war record was unavailing, everything was useless, so he decided to
quit the unappreciative world. From relatives
he borrowed enough money to buy the six-
hundred-acre tract on the remote mountain
top; land was cheap then, and there he retired

in 1867.   He knew before he left that his
sweetheart's marriage was most unhappy, and
her sorrows bowed him to the earth. They
mattered more to him than they did to her, for
she had the physical possession of a handsome
man she loved; he had nothing but a phantom,
which he did not possess. But he was sure
he had located on land of vast mineral wealth.
It would some day make him one of the finan-
cial powers of the Commonwealth. His *only
love* would realize how unkind she had been to
a really remarkable, sagacious man. But
nature loves to deepen wounds. Years went
by, and no railroad nor development appeared
to bring the coal into market. He refused to
let outsiders prospect it; he would not discuss
terms of sale to various capitalists who might
have bought it on speculation; he would do it
his way, and become richer than them all in
time. But it would take time. The girl back
in Jacobsburg had been a mother and a grand-
mother on quite a few occasions; her life was
drifting on, yet he hadn't made his strike to
impress her. " The veins are deeper on my
property than anywhere else on these moun-

tains," he would say. " They taper down to
thin seams when they reach the land owned by
those rich people. I will make more out of
my six hundred acres than they will from their
six thousand. I don't expect to ever see my
old sweetheart again, but I want her to know
I've done well in this world." It certainly required much patience to wait until a turn of
events would bring him into prominence, but as
Jackson Everhard's life had brought him nothing, he could easily wait for something. Last
summer Bill and I tramped up the mountain
road one hot afternoon in August. The route
would have seemed long had we not overtaken
old Martin Hampe on the way. He told us
about a small flock of wild pigeons that nested
on the steep mountain facing Pine Creek, and
every day visited Morris English's fields below
Cammal. He would surely trap the whole lot
of them for us next Spring. He knew what a
wild pigeon was; he had trapped them by the
thousands in Tioga County in the old days.
Almost before we knew it we came in sight of
Jackson Everhard's home. We told our companion we'd stop a while with our old friend.

" You know Jack?" he asked; " it's too bad he's
feeling so poorly this season; guess it's a general breaking up of the system; he's well up in
seventy." Instantly the thought flashed
through me that something had gone wrong between him and his lost love; when I left him
the year before, he was spry-looking, calm, hopeful. We went around to the back door where
we usually found him sitting on the steps on
afternoons watching the blue-birds with their
buff breasts, dodging in and out of their tiny
home on the top of the swaying pole. The old
man was there, but what a change was wrought.
His eyes were faded and expressionless, his
calmness gone, he looked dejected and sad. He
tried to greet us with his cheery manner, as of
old. " The railroad's sure to be built next
spring, boys, *Morgan* himself's back of it;
they'll have to buy my land to make it pay.
You know I've a million dollars worth of coal
in sight." But there was a tremble to his
voice, that betrayed false gaiety. It seemed
harder for him to carry on a connected conversation. " Take a drink of this cool water," he
continued; " I just brought it from the spring

a few minutes ago. The wood-robins are singing away there at a lively rate; they're your
favorite birds, I haven't forgotten." In the
past it had been a pleasure to stop with the
hermit—on this occasion it was a duty. Just
before the " golden hour," when the air is
purest and every leaf is rigid and clear cut in
the cloudless atmosphere, Jackson Everhard
and I took a stroll down to the spring. Bill
tactfully remained at the house, to drive a
nail out of one of his shoes, he said. When we
reached the spring the wood-robins were silent,
but we heard the plaintive melody of a far-off
cow-bell. Why is it a cow-bell sounds sweet-
est on a mountain top in the late afternoon?
We sat down, each on a flat rock, by the gurgling ever-running pool, and for a time were
silent. " I suppose you see the change in me?"
said the hermit. " I think you look all right,"
was my evasive reply. But as a friend I was
interested to hear the finale of his love story.
I was sure there must be one. " I stood the
winter better than I had in thirty years; I
was full of hopes, and happy. That's the way
folks always feel before ' a bolt from the blue.'

The first day of trout season an old fisherman
stopped and asked if he might have supper
with me. He had walked all the way over from
Laurel Run. I said I would be glad to accommodate him. He said he was from Straubstown, five miles down the valley from my old
home. We got to talking about old times, and
of people who were prominent in that section
forty years ago. While I'd never met the
fisherman, he was twenty or more years
younger than I, I knew his family very well.
He asked me if I knew that Jacob Eppler was
dead. A strange, uncanny, exultant thrill ran
through me at these words—Jacob Eppler was
my old sweetheart's husband. I said it was
news to me, I didn't hear very often from Oak
Valley. ' Yes, he's been dead over a year; the
fisherman went on; ' he was a great sport and
drinker; what a dance he led his poor wife
until the end. Everybody thought her health
would improve after she buried him, but no;
she sank right away, and died in January; the
doctors said it was from a broken heart over
losing him.' My heart stood still; my old
sweetheart dead—the planning and hoping of

years was naught. She had died without a thought of me; I was of less consequence than when I struck out for the wilds in 1867. I lost all interest in getting supper that night. I was so slow and my hands shook so much, that the fisherman thought I needed a bracer, so he gave me a drink from his whiskey-flask. This steadied me, and the meal was served, but I guess it was my poorest attempt. I wonder if it was nature, that I have been abusing so long in my writings, that sent that fisherman up to this mountain top to give me the final thrust. I've never felt like myself since that night. Even when I met a party of surveyors, and they assured me the railroad would be surely built into the coal fields next year, I cared nothing. All my coal is so much black dirt to me now. What do I care for being a man of affairs under such conditions. I'd rather die a hermit. I've burnt the manuscripts of my book on nature and religion. Nature is too powerful for a homely little man like me to fight. I'm only one of her discards; I was not meant for marriage or happiness. She likes to revenge herself on imperfect specimens. I've been here forty-four years. I'll sit on these coal beds until it's all over." I could see a tear in each of the hermit's faded blue eyes. We drank our tinfuls of water, and wended our way silently back to the shanty.

V

THE LONELY GRAVE

HEN the log-train on the Mc-Murray's Run Railway backed into the lone section-hand Tom Kane, and the log-loader mangled him beyond recognition, it was thought that his relatives would order his remains shipped to his old home at Dunnsburg for interment. But his brother, who hurried to the scene after the disaster, said the family plot was overcrowded and suggested that his burial be beside the tracks where he was killed. Laid out in a box of rough pine boards he was lowered to rest in a shallow trench, and an itinerant preacher, who worked in the camp, recited the last words. The accident occurred early in May, and so busy was the lumber operation that it would have been entirely forgotten after Memorial Day had it not been for a strange incident. Tom Kane had a devoted admirer, although he never

knew it while he was alive. Maybe when his
spirit was released into cosmic wisdom, he understood, but it was then too late. But this
admirer was only a little girl of fourteen, and
if she had ever been seen talking with him, all
the boys at the camp would have said he was
"running after a child." Ada Costikan was
the little girl. She was the daughter of a
shiftless woodsman, Phil Costikan, whose
tumble-down shanty stood near the tracks, at
a distance of about a mile from where poor
Tom was killed. Ada was a pretty girl, with
bright, dark-colored eyes, rosy lips and a smile
she seemed always trying to suppress. She
was plump and well-developed for her age. Beyond her secret interest in Tom, she apparently
cared for no other man. She never gave her
parents any trouble, and they were proud to
say she had not " the makings of a flirt." Phil
Costikan, her father, was descended from the Indian fighter of that name, one of John Brady's
heroes, that was the sole family tradition.
After him had come four generations shrouded
in ignorance and obscurity. The mother was
Sugar Valley Dutch, stolid, amiable, and

naturally industrious but for her husband's
example. Ada saw Tom Kane nearly every
day, but always at a distance. Whether the
impression he made on her at a hundred yards
was as the man really looked is doubtful—he
was just far enough off to be invested with a
halo of ideality. Actually speaking, Tom was
a fine specimen of manhood, tall, stalwart, good
natured. Until he was twenty-five he had
worked in the bark-woods in summer and in
the pine forests in winter, punctuating the time
between the quitting of one job and taking up
another with debauches of two weeks' standing
in Lock Haven, Emporium, or Driftwood.
These were his sole recreations, his star of
hope during the weary months of toil in the
wilderness. He had exhausted life as it appeared to him by the time he was twenty-five,
and decided to " settle down." To many, marriage and home would have been the panacea,
but he declared he was too " case hardened"
for that; he was too honest to try to play the
" reformed rake." Drifting out to McMurray's
Run one spring when they were building the
log road he joined the construction gang. The

boss was an old friend, so when the line was
completed as far as was needed he was re-
tained as section hand. When the work was
heavy he picked up a couple of Italians to help
him, but he was generally able to handle it
himself. On many occasions he noticed Ada
Costikan around her humble home, but to him
she was a unit of humanity, a child, that was
all. He had settled down for good. If he
lived long enough to become too old for work
he would become a hermit—that was his type.
No inexperienced man ever became a hermit.
Even the hermits of the days of faith had
pasts ramified and horrible. Tom Kane was
the joy of Ada's life—at a distance. Tom's
work and rest at night were the only goals he
knew. " He must get lonely," thought the girl;
" I wish I knew him and could make things
brighter for him." On the warm spring evening when Phil Costikan came home and told
his family that Tom Kane had been backed into
and cut to pieces by the log train, Ada wept.
It was the first time since she was a tiny girl,
and her parents were dumbstruck by this show
of emotion. " He's better off dead," was the

mother's comment, " He was pretty much of
a bum," said the father, but Ada couldn't see
it that way, and kept on weeping. She
wandered, half-hysterical, into the woods back
of the shanty, and lay down against a log,
among the skunk-cabbages, wake robins,
anemones, and immortelles, until her grief was
spent. " If she takes on like that over a
stranger, I don't see how she'll get through the
world," remarked her mother, as she noticed
the disconsolate figure, with a drooping wake
robin in her hand, returning homeward. " I've
a good mind to lick you for such a fool exhibition," she growled at her, as the girl came in
the door. Life was a stern reality to the
mother; tears belonged to the upper classes,
who had no actual trouble. On Memorial Day
Ada walked up the track with a girl friend,
Clara Ganson, to where Tom Kane had been
buried. Already the spring rains had almost
flattened out the mound, which made it look
doubly desolate. " Too bad he has no flowers,"
said Clara, thoughtlessly. Ada had thought
the same thing, but it meant too much to her
soul to mention it. " In another year," it ran

through her mind, " I'll go to work in some
factory in Lock Haven; I'll save enough money
to buy some flowers, and I'll decorate that
grave all right." She always had a vague desire to go to work; now that she had an ideal,
it would be hard to prevent her purpose. As
a means of passing the time, all the woodsmen
strolled up to Tom's grave and looked at it.
Some of the shack-dwellers came down from the
mountains and looked at it. More persons
visited it that Memorial Day than viewed the
tombs of some distinguished patriots. With
the advent of summer the grass grew thick on
the grave. It would have been hard to tell
where it was were it not for a stone that one
of the trainmen put at the head of it when he
saw how nature was trying to hide her dead.
On several Sundays that summer Ada visited
the grave in company with her young friends.
She was indifferent to most boys, but if they
suggested a stroll on the track, she gladly
assented. She felt it her duty to pass by Tom's
grave. " It must be terribly lonely at night,"
she often reasoned, " but he has the whip-poor-
wills, the crickets, the katydids, the wind in

the gum trees, the roar of McMurray's Run;
he must have liked those sounds else he
wouldn't have been living in the woods." These
were some of the semi-morbid ideas she had
when she cried herself to sleep. Ada's fifteenth
birthday took place early in December. After
Christmas she went to Lock Haven, ostensibly
to visit her cousin, Bessie Swope, but mainly
with the idea of getting work in a silk mill.
Instead of finding a position there, she secured
a more satisfactory offer to do housework in a
handsome brick mansion on West Church
Street. Hired girls were hard to find, house-
wives were willing to offer them almost anything. Many girls refused to go into service
because they wanted their "evenings free,"
Ada, not having a lover, did not care whether
her evenings were free or not. She worked
faithfully all winter, and her employer declared she had never met with such a willing
girl. Never once did she express a desire to go
home on a visit, but she sent a part of her
wages to her parents each month. These
worthy people were far from pleased when they
first heard she had gone to work. The ancestral

pride of Phil Costikan was suddenly aroused;
he recalled his grandfather telling him that
the old Indian fighter not only kept negro
slaves, but white servants as well. He called
Ada's conduct a " come-down." But when the
first postal order arrived he capitulated. Ada
did not spend much on clothes or finery. Apart
from what she sent home she saved considerable
of her modest stipend. " I will cover poor
Tom Kane's grave with flowers" was her con-
stant thought. About the first of May she
asked her employer if she might go home for
a few days over Memorial Day.   She had
worked so conscientiously that the request was
cheerfully granted. But Ada was not going
home, at least not to the shanty where her
parents resided. The day before the holiday
she went to the florist's on Bellefonte Avenue,
and bought a number of cut-flowers, roses,
carnations, jonquils, violets, and lilacs. These
were put in a large, flat, pasteboard box, like
dressmakers use. With the cut-flowers were
put two scarlet flowering geranium plants,
with the roots moistened and wrapped in
tissue-paper. Carrying the box, which though

bulky was not heavy—although she would not have minded if it was—the girl started on foot for McMurray's Run. A liveryman who was going after a trout fisherman met her on the road and carried her part way. She left the highway several miles below the mouth of the run, so as not to be observed by anyone who knew her, and struck boldly up the face of the mountain. Night was upon her before she reached the summit of the ridge which rose above the hollow where the lumber camp was located. There was a deer-hunter's shack near an old runway, and in it she spent the night. When a great flare of crimson appeared over the eastern mountains, betokening dawn, she crept down the mountain side carrying her box of flowers. On the way she heard a meadow-lark singing. " *Everything is beautiful, but oh, so sad,*" it seemed to say. Arriving at the lonely grave, she covered it with a quilt of bloom. She planted the two geraniums, one at the head and the other at the foot. She pulled up all the weeds and wild-grasses. Then she slipped back among the underbrush, and up the hill, and returned on foot to Lock

Haven. She was in the kitchen in time to
wash the supper-dishes, much to the surprise
of her employer. " You didn't stay away
long," said the lady. " I had my visit; that
was all I wanted," was the girl's reply. There
was consternation that morning among the
train crew, the loggers, and the backwoodsmen
when they saw the grave banked with costly
flowers. No such mystery had been known in
the retired valley of McMurray's Run, so the
natives made the most of it. The summer cot-
tagers from River View came and marvelled.
Various were the conjectures, and the story
spread in all directions. But no one guessed
anywhere near to the right solution. It remained a mystery. Ada felt satisfied with her
labor of love; she resolved to do the same thing
next year. For five more years, on Memorial
Day, the lonely grave was found buried beneath flowers. Several times watchers arrived at daybreak, but she was prepared for
these, and the last three years the decorations
were arranged at midnight. The fame of the
lonely grave spread all over the county. Ada
had never seen a soul until the sixth year—

while thus engaged. On the night of her sixth
visit, she was on her knees finishing the spread-
ing of the flowers and blossoms over the mound,
when she heard footsteps on the ties of the
log-railway. Some one was close by her, before she had time to hide herself. She was
caught in the act, and resolved to stand her
ground bravely. The stranger, who was more
surprised to find her in this lonely spot than
she was to be discovered, was tall and powerfully built. He wore a soft hat, and the canvas
garb of a fisherman. He carried a fishing-rod
in a canvas cover, while his wicker fish-
basket was slung over one shoulder. "Good
morning," he said, as he came to a halt beside her. He lit a match and took out his
watch. "It's twelve ten; I knew I was right
when I said 'good morning.'" By the flicker
of the match, Ada had a good look at his face.
She had seen the counterpart of that face before, but at a distance. It was the face—and
the figure—of Tom Kane. The image she had
worshiped in the spirit all these years while
she developed from girlhood into womanhood
stood before her in the flesh. And the voice,

it had the same cheery tones as Tom's used to when he would call out "Good morning" to her father as he tramped along the ties. Ada was slow in taking up the conversation, but she had gotten up from her knees, and was smoothing her skirts. The match went out, and the pair stood together in the darkness. She was not afraid; it was as if Tom, risen from his grave, was with her. "I've fished this stream for the past six years," said the young man, "ever since the first year this grave was decorated. I used to wonder who did it. No one could tell me. Little did I think I would find out for myself. I had actually forgotten I was so near it, when I made you out in the darkness." "Yes, you are the first person to find out who decorated the grave. I wanted to keep it a secret to the end." "I'm very sorry," said the fisherman. "Was the man who is buried here a relative or merely a dear friend?" "He was no relative; I never met him; I only saw him at a distance." Ada was shocked when she had said these words. She was telling too much, perhaps, but an uncontrollable desire to set herself right with this

new acquaintance led her to unveil the whole
truth. " It is certainly very good of you to
remember this poor unfortunate. He was
killed by being crushed by the log-train, wasn't
he?" " He was cut to pieces, as you say. I
have done this, not because I was sorry for
him, but because I liked him." The fisherman
felt something like a knife-thrust in his heart.
" What did he look like?" he stammered, like
a school-boy lover. " I think he looked just
like you," said Ada. After that the young man
was comforted, and the couple talked together
for over an hour. Then the man realized the
lateness of the hour, and said she had better
hurry home to bed and get her beauty sleep.
" No bed for me this night," said the girl;
" I'm going to tramp back to Lock Haven."
" Do you live there?" inquired the fisherman.
" I work there," said Ada. " I'm headed for
town myself; may I accompany you?" The
girl was delighted, and the long walk seemed
as nothing. Her employer was opening the
outside doors when she saw the girl coming
down the street accompanied by a tall, handsome man, who had all the marks of a gentle-

man. He tipped his hat to her when they
parted at the gate, and she ran around to the
side door with a lightness of step that seemed
unnatural to her. "That's a good-looking
young man you had with you, Ada; who is he?"
queried the lady, whose curiosity had brought
her into the kitchen. "He's a railroader; he's
one of the Despatchers on the Pennsy." The
lady said no more; she was surprised to think
of her hired girl moving in such good company.
And she kept wondering where they were coming from at such an early hour. Towards evening she could stand it no longer. "Where
were you coming from with the young man?"
"We walked to town together from McMurray's Run." The answer was so spontaneous
that the lady had to be satisfied. In a few
days Ada began receiving letters postmarked
Sunbury. The lady eyed them critically before she handed them to the girl. She never
recollected her getting letters in men's handwriting in all the six years she had been with
her; this affair with the Despatcher must be
something new. One night she heard that the
girl was seen at the station, meeting a young

man who came up on number one. Another
night she went driving with a man. And so
events shaped themselves until one day Ada
told her employer that she was going home.
Asked if she meant to get married, she replied
that she " couldn't tell just yet." After she
had been gone a month the lady read in the list
of marriage licenses granted at the local court-
house the names of " Thomas McNary, Sunbury, aged 32 years, and Ada Costikan,
McMurray's Run, aged 21 years. Inquiry
showed that her former hired girl was marrying a Pennsylvania Railroad official. The next
Memorial Day dawned on the lonely grave on
McMurray's Run and it was undecorated. The
train crew, and the loggers and the shack-
dwellers repined. The chief glamor, the only
mystery of the sequestered valley had departed.
The grave was never again decorated. Ada's
faith had been rewarded by finding her ideal
in the flesh. And surely the calm spirit of the
mutilated section - hand could not have be-
grudged the happiness that was hers.

VI

THE JOCKEY'S SISTER

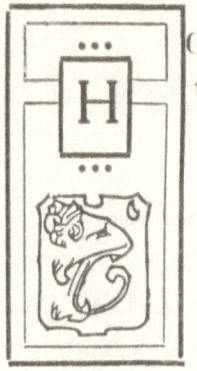

OW Moroni, estwhile champion of the Chicago suburban tracks, landed on the Pennsylvania County Fair circuit might seem considerable of a mystery. Perhaps it was because racing was legislated out of existence in the neighborhood of the windy city, but most probably a chronic case of change of owners had drifted the old horse into the hill country. In Chicago they used to say that Moroni originated the term "one best bet," for whenever he ran he was sure to get a place. Wiseacres who took friends or country relatives to the races for the first time endeavored to do so on days Moroni ran, so they could pilot the neophytes to play the old reliable and bring home some "easy money." On days when the tracks were deep with mud, and fields were marred by "scratching," Moroni was sure to start, and it was said he could swim faster

than he could run. His name being the same
as the angel of Mormon fame was hinted to be
the reason why so many missionaries of the
Latter Day Saints were in evidence along the
rail at Hawthorne, Roby and Harlem. With
such eclat, one would expect to see a handsome
horse, or a big horse; but Moroni was neither.
He looked more like an undersized trotting
stallion than a runner, especially as he carried
a long tail at a time when all the other racers
wore theirs banged. In color he was a faded-out
bay, with a vague white spot on his broad forehead. He had bad hocks, and when he started
three times in a week his ribs showed plainly.
But he always got a place, so his friends were
legion. It was Ammon Holtzclaw that owned
him when he was unloaded from a box-car at
Straubstown the night before the fair opened.
Peering out into the darkness as he held his
lantern aloft, the young owner's eyes rested
on the expansive and sympathetic features of
William Green, a bow-legged colored boy of
indeterminate age. The negro took the hint
quickly, and started to help " unload" regardless of first striking a bargain. When Moroni

and several trotters that shipped with him were safely on *terra firma,* Holtzclaw beckoned the colored lad to come with him to the end of the car, where he held up the lantern and showed him a name written almost illegibly on the wall. It read: " Eleanor Wittgenstein, Straubstown, Pa." The darky rubbed his head, as Holtzclaw spelled it out for him. " Do you know of any such girl here?" he said, impatiently. " I sure do," replied the darky, " and say, she's all right." Holtzclaw smiled visibly; he had decided to ship to Straubstown at the last minute just because he had seen that name written in the car. He had been helping his friend Levi Kessler load his harness horses, when he saw it, and now he felt his move was worth the effort. Moroni had been a failure in his hands; he was going to take him back to the farm in Centre County and turn him out, but he would have to run one more race to help him meet the girl who wrote her name in the box-car. " Her brother's de leadin' jockey in town," continued William Green. " Why, she's great on horses herself; dey jest caint keep her away from de stables; she out dere

ebery mornin'." Ammon Holtzclaw locked
Moroni in his box and went to the Mansion
House for the night so as to be able to look
" spick and span" next morning. Usually he
slept in the box adjoining his horse, but in
those days there was no one with the magical
name of Eleanor Wittgenstein to cause him to
brighten up. Ammon had never been sentimental, but his continued ill success in his
racing ventures, coupled with the fact that he
could interest himself in nothing else, made
him long for a change of some kind in his
career. His father, a prosperous farmer, had
offered him many inducements to prepare for
State College or go into business, but he
spurned the chances when he thought of the
allurements of the track. And yet he wasn't
happy racing; it was an ignoble existence, and
was merely a false mode of expression for his
vagabond nature. It might have come out in
making him an artist or a strolling poet. The
name in the box-car was an *open sesame* to
something new, yet something still more in
harmony with his inclinations. The next
morning at daybreak he was at the Fair

Grounds, while his exercise boy, Leo Quailey, breezed Moroni. The old horse did not seem stiff after his twelve-hour ride in the car, and bounded along with his head held low, and legs moving as precise as clockwork, as was his wont. After he had been cooled off and put in the stall, Ammon sat outside on a bench, gazing abstractedly at the clumps of trees, the rolling country, and distant ranges of blue mountains which rose above the row of frame houses and sheds beyond the infield. The summer was not too far spent for the birds to have lost their zest for song, and there was occasional chirping in the tall maples behind the sheds. The sky was blue, save for some round steel-colored clouds. Ammon could not put himself in accord with his surroundings. He lacked the sentiment to do so, but his nature was too well developed to accept it with dull animal resignation. He must have sat there a long while, for he began to feel pretty hungry. He considered for a minute before deciding to forego breakfast. If he went to the hotel for an hour, Eleanor might come to the track and be gone before he returned; to

surely meet her he must wait. It was a wise
decision, as it was not long before a number of
visitors appeared in the neighborhood of the
stables. Although the boxes were tightly
closed, the country curiosity-seekers had hopes
of getting a look at the horses before the racing
began. Some few were acquainted with owners
or trainers, and these were accommodated, as
the parties in authority were found easily, all
huddled together gossiping in the stalls,
curiously avoiding the bright sunshine. Pretty
soon Leo Quailey approached, accompanied by
several other boys. Leo introduced them to
Ammon, one by one, as if he were some great
personage. This made little impression until
he mentioned the name "Adam Wittgentsein."
" I've heard of you," said Ammon with quick
interest, " you're quite a rider, they say."
" Well, I do ride some," replied the boy, " I
won a good race down to Point Breeze with
Pennlyn on Decoration Day, but I do most of
my riding around home." " Have you got a
mount for this afternoon?" queried Ammon.
"No, I haven't; that's why I wanted to meet you
most. I heard you've got a pretty likely

runner." " I don't know about that, but he'll
try his best." An arrangement was made, and
Adam Wittgenstein seated himself beside
Ammon, and felt a part of the establishment.
Leo, though too heavy to ride in races, had a
good deal of *esprit de corps,* and brought out
the racing colors, grass green and white, to
show to the newly-engaged jockey. This
brought several idlers to the scene, eager to
look at anything bright or showy. It was during the exhibition of the colors that Ammon
noticed a young girl approaching the stables,
wading as best she could through the tall grass
in her tight skirt. She wore a big black hat
with white ostrich plumes, which hid her face
until she was very near. Then she looked up,
and her dark eyes met his. She was very
pretty, very unlike Adam Wittgenstein, but
who else could she be but his sister? Adam
made no attempt to introduce her, though she
linked her arm in his, which caused Ammon to
think for a minute it wasn't the jockey's sister
at all, but his sweetheart. But a second glance
showed that, though much darker in coloring
and with more regularity of features, there

was a certain fullness of the lips and length
of nose which revealed consanguinity. Ammon
looked at her so hard and then at Adam
that the lad realized something was left
undone, so he said, "Eleanor, this is Mr.
Holtzclaw, the owner of the horse I'm to
ride." That was enough; Eleanor and
Ammon were now friends. Among persons
naturally congenial, or as the sentimental-
minded would say, "intended for one another,"
preliminary acquaintance is unnecessary. It
is so much so one would almost imagine that
all that had happened in previous existences,
or states of mind. We know our ideal so well,
that we do not have to find out about her after
meeting her. Ammon's abstracted, discon-
tented manner vanished in an instant. He
was geniality, thoughtfulness, politeness itself.
Tipping his hat, he begged permission to show
off old Moroni to his new acquaintance. He
had Leo unblanket the horse, and lead him
out into the sunlight, where he could be seen
to advantage. The old campaigner, while lacking a good deal in inches to make him what
horsemen call a "picture horse," had to a

marked degree that kindly and intelligent expression so noticeable in *entire* horses, made
up to Eleanor as quickly as his owner. She
stroked his mouse-colored nose, and over his
eyes, and he tried to lay his head on her shoulder. " He surely will win this afternoon," she
said, as she smiled into Ammon's honest blue
eyes. " I know he would if you had anything
to say about it. I thank you very much for
your kind words. I appreciate them." The
girl's sincere manner and gentle voice meant
everything to the young horseman. Lack of
sympathy in his family and continued ill-luck
made him hunger for appreciation of a kind
he never expected to receive. A kind word for
his horse, hopes that he might win the race,
these were expressions, if received before, might
have given him a courage that would have resulted in greater success in his undertakings.
" I think your brother will ride a good race;
that's the best any one can do." " I'm sure
he will. He'll ride the best race of his life
to-day," replied Eleanor, enthusiastically.
When lunch-time arrived Ammon and Eleanor
were so mutually interested in the preparations

given Moroni for the race that they were loath
to spare the time necessary to visit the refreshment tent on the far side of the grand-stand.
William Green, the colored boy who had told
Ammon about Eleanor Wittgenstein the night
before, happened on the scene at the opportune
moment. He looked so happy when he saw the
young couple together, that Ammon gave him a
dollar bill to go and get them some sandwiches,
pop-corn, and sarsaparilla, and said he might
keep the change. Lunch was served on a trunk
in an empty box adjoining Moroni's stall, being
enjoyed more than an elaborate repast at the
Bellevue-Stratford. The colored boy seemed to
take a paternal interest in the pair, and was
assiduous in his attentions. Moroni was a
quiet horse, and while they ate did not thrash
about with his heels as do mettlesome racers
before a contest. The repast was so enjoyable
that Ammon and Eleanor did not notice that
the sun had become obscured, and the oppressive atmosphere betokened showers. When
they came out, the first heat of the harness
races had already begun. Five horses were
shooting around the turn in a cloud of dust.

During the next heat thunder and lightning were apparent, and soon a heavy rainfall ensued. Ammon and Eleanor, who had gone no further than the rail to witness the races, sought refuge in the box-stall. Eleanor sat on the trunk, while Ammon occupied a camp stool before her. The rain was short-lived, but the young couple enjoyed being together too much to venture forth to see the sport. Besides the secretary had appeared and told them that the first heat of the running race would not be run until after the last heat of the two harness events. That meant that Moroni would not appear under silks until at least five o'clock. Ordinarily Ammon would have become angry, and demanded that the first heat be run earlier, but on this occasion he smiled and said nothing. The harness races waxed as fast and furious as harness races can, and Ammon and Eleanor were left to their own devices in the cozy box-stall. It did not take them long to discover they were lovers, or to confess that with both it had been a case of love at first glimpse. Ammon had told her how he had seen her name written on the wall

inside the freight car the morning before, while
helping Levi Kessler load his harness horses.
He liked the sound of the name; it had induced him to ship Moroni in the same car, because the destination Straubstown was the
address written below the name.   Eleanor
told how one Sunday afternoon a month previously, in company with several other girls,
she had seen the empty box-car lying on the
siding by the freight house.   In a spirit of
fun they went in it, and one of the girls dared
the others to write their names on the wall.
None of them cared to do it except Eleanor,
and she had repented that night and determined to erase it next morning.   She was at
the station before six-thirty, but the freight
car had gone.   Now she was glad she had not
erased it.   She was unhappy at home; had
disliked working in the pants factory, had
quit, to her mother's disgust, and was hoping
for a new life.   In the midst of these pleasant
self-revelations, William Green, who had been
apparently acting as guardian of the portal all
afternoon, came in to say that it was half-past
four, and time to saddle Moroni for the first

heat of the running race. Reluctantly Ammon
arose from the camp-stool, and Eleanor followed him. " Who is that colored boy, any
way?" Ammon whispered to her. " He seems
powerfully interested in our welfare." " His
father, old Mose Green, is porter at the hotel,
and lives next door to us; the whole family
have a sort of interest in us; I think he likes
to see us together." Ammon, Leo and William, as well as Adam, who had been wearing
the gay jockey suit all afternoon, attended to
the saddling of Moroni, and when the bugle blew
he was the first at the post. Adam made a
good appearance, riding with an English seat,
and horse and rider were favorably commented
upon as they paraded by the stand. There
were eight starters, an unusual number, but
they were a cheap-looking lot. Of course, there
was a favored horse, which Ammon learned
afterwards was owned by the starter's brother. He was such a painful apology for a racer
that his presence was scarcely heeded. The
starter, however, seemed determined to give
his favorite the best of the start. It was sick-
ening to watch his futile efforts to make the

wretched beast break in front. The creature
was inert, and his jockey, a big blonde farmer
boy, dug him with his spurs, jerked his mouth,
and beat him unmercifully to get him to run.
Every time the starter dropped his flag Moroni
was in the van, with the rest barely moving.
The man with the advance flag always sent
them back, until the crowd became impatient
at the delay. The noise on the stand became
so loud that at one of the breaks where Moroni
was standing with his head towards the stables,
both starters let their flags fall, calling it a
" go." Adam Wittgenstein, well and favorably
known in Straubstown, had many friends in
the crowd, and they howled vociferously when
they saw the way in which he was treated. But
Adam needed no sympathy. He quickly turned
Moroni; plying his whip vigorously, he urged
the old thoroughbred on in pursuit of the field.
He " collared them" at the first turn, which
made the crowd yell with delight. He raced
them to a standstill along the back-stretch,
until each of his seven competitors quit like
dogs. Around the last turn Moroni was coming at a common canter, with the rest, like in

Eclipse's day, "nowhere." There was genuine
enthusiasm in the crowd; it was good to see
the local boy in front. When he finished an
easy winner, a swarm of friends climbed over
the fences and poured through the gates surrounding him when he rode back to the judges'
stand to ask permission to dismount. But he
was to be robbed of his victory. The starter
and his assistant, who had been engaged in a
whispered consultation after the finish, hurried
into the judges' box and assured the officials
that they had made a grave mistake in ringing
the bell, as the advance flag had never been
dropped. The judges at first insisted that they
could believe their eyes, but the starter, who
was also the son of the heaviest stockholder
in the Fair Association, wanted to know who
was running things, so they lapsed into docile
silence, fearing to lose their jobs. Ammon and
Eleanor, who had been watching the race from
the last row of seats in the stand, and were
naturally in a happy frame of mind over the
victory, began wondering why the result was
not announced. Jockeys and horses were still
on the track waiting for the announcement;

something must be wrong. Finally the announcer raised his megaphone to his lips and called out that that race was " no heat," owing to the horses starting before the advance flag had been dropped. Fifteen minutes rest was to be given the horses. " Never mind," said Ammon, " we'll clean them up next time," so Eleanor and he began munching peanuts until the race began. It seemed more than fifteen minutes before the heat was called. It was just long enough to give the rain another chance. That was what the clique in charge of the program wanted, so they were quick to call the races off for the day. When the announcer made this discouraging statement a look of inexpressable sadness came into Ammon Holtzclaw's face. " What makes you look so sad?" inquired Eleanor, with a woman's intuition. " I'm sad because everything I try remains unfinished. I can't seem to round up anything." " Oh, yes you can," said the girl; " what's this one race in a lifetime? You'll surely win out in everything else you try." The crowd was rapidly leaving the stand, but the young man made no move to go nor speak.

Eleanor sat by him patiently. At length he
broke the silence. " You say I can do everything else, even if I wasn't allowed to win that
heat?" " That's just what I said," answered
the girl. " There's a train leaving here at
eight-fifty to-night for Lewistown that con-
nects with the West. I've wanted to go into
the Shades of Night country in Indiana for over
a year to take charge of a little farm I inherited from an uncle. They say it's a lovely
little place. Will you come with me? I know
everything *will* turn out right with me if you
do. But if you come along we'll never come
back. It will be a new life for both of us. We
will have time enough in Pittsburg to-morrow
to be married. I'll have my friend Kessler
see that my horse is started to-morrow, and
then have him ship the outfit out to the farm
in charge of Leo Quailey. It's now six-
thirty," he continued, looking at his watch,
" what do you say?" " I said you'd surely
win out in everything. Why shouldn't I go
with you?" Ammon put his arm around her
and kissed her, as they sat there on the top row
of seats in the deserted grandstand. Then he

A GROUP OF BARK-PEELERS

Photo by W. T. Clarke

remarked calmly, " Let's find a little supper, and tell friend Kessler what to do to-morrow. Then we'll have just about enough time left to stroll over to the station to board the eight-fifty."

VII.

THE DESPATCH RIDER

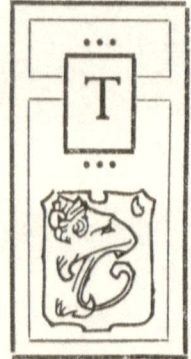HE little 'Red Hornet' was pretty badly fagged. There seemed little use in going ahead with him unless I wanted him to drop under me. The sun was coming up frightfully hot, making the air oppressive with the scent of the sweet ferns. Ahead of me the pale green ridges exuded humidity, save where clumps of yellow pines looked cool and green like the palms of an oasis. But there was no time to stop, the hoofbeats of my pursuers' horses could be heard in moments of especial calmness. We were in the bottom of a deep ravine, where a small stream flowed, when I felt the gallant little pony's forelegs giving way. Quick as a flash I swung out of the saddle and stood beside him. All his superfluous flesh had been worn away in the wild race, and froth and foam ran from his flanks and belly like rivulets. Poor little fel-

130

low, he gazed at me appealingly with his blood-
shot, prominent eyes, as with legs spread apart
to support his weight, he rested, and coughed,
and panted. Just then I fancied I heard the
swish of horses running through the ferns. I
had to decide quickly. I cut the saddle-girths
and bridle so that they could not be used again,
tossed them behind a tall fire-blackened stump,
gave the pony a slap to set him going somewhere, and started running myself down the
ravine, with my left hand held over the pocket
containing the precious despatches. I hadn't
eaten since three o'clock the afternoon before,
so I had to stop and drink out of a puddle in
the stream. But I kept up a steady gait, and
soon had put a mile between me and the abandoned pony. I began fancying that I was in
too great a hurry until the sound of hoof-beats
again echoed in my ears. It was no illusion;
it was plainer than ever. My pursuers must
now be at the top of the ravine where I had cut
loose from the pony. I redoubled my efforts,
but was careful to make as little noise as
possible. Once I scared up a kingfisher from
a pool of dead water, and my heart sank lest

his " rattle" as he rose high in the air would
give a clue to my whereabouts. As the bird's
chattering died away I was sure I heard the
splash and pounding of horses' hoofs back
along the bed of the stream. Where I was the
creek made a sudden drop, forming a waterfall
that sent a jet or flume across some decaying
logs and downward a dozen feet. Below that
the hollow widened out, but just enough to
make room for a log cabin and a little garden,
which seemed to be mothered by the encircling
hills and a great, white-armed buttonwood
tree. The front door, made of boards and
painted light blue, was shut. I supposed the
house was empty. I pushed into it, thinking
I would race out the back door, and that would
throw my pursuers off the track for a few
minutes, as if they saw me entering they
would stop to search the shack. Instead of
the house being empty I found a good-looking
young woman of about twenty, dressed in a
black and white checked frock, seated in an
armchair sewing complacently. Though I
wore no military costume, there was something about my wild eyes, long hair, and hag-

gard face that connected me with the army.
Though she was not stout, there was a certain
development or fullness of line in her that made
me feel that I had happened upon somebody's
wife. We looked at each other, and the feeling that each produced was that the other was
not unattractive. Her eyes were dark brown,
her hair brownish, tinted with gold. She appeared to be sensible and quick-witted. On
seeing her my plans changed; I wanted to remain where I was, and told her so. 'The
Johnny Rebs have been after me since six
o'clock last night; I wasn't a mile and a half
ahead of them when I had to cut loose from
my horse. It's only a question of a half hour
until they get me, unless you can hide me here.'
' My husband's a soldier in the Confederate
army, and a Virginian by birth, but I'm a
Pennsylvanian and we're on Pennsylvania soil,
so I guess it's the least I can do to give you a
chance.' She led me to the back door and out
to where cellar steps seemed to burrow under
the cabin and into the side hill. We were
both calm, but acted quickly. In the capacious
cellar, which was larger than the floor-space of

the house, was a running spring, all except the
mouth of which was overlaid with slabs. On
the top of these was piled considerable fire-
wood. At the opening of this covered rivulet,
deep in the water, were numerous crocks and
bottles, and I slipped into the water, and lay
with my nose out like a carp in the gloomy
recess. The crocks and bottles were replaced,
a few sticks of wood were thrown carelessly
across the aperture. It was chilling cold, and
my teeth shook, but I worried more lest the
water seep through my leather wallet and destroy the valuable papers, than I did about my
contact with the spring water. It seemed I
was in my watery retreat so long that I began
wondering whether after all I was being pursued, or had thrown my enemies into dismay
somewhere further back. All was silent upstairs; at times I imagined I could hear the
ticking of a clock. Once I heard a rooster
crowing. Everything was still, and the looked-
for incidents not occurring, I began thinking
about myself, how cold I was, how hungry I
felt. I was tormented by these ideas to such
an extent that I was thankful when the excite-

ment began. First of all I heard the racket
of the horses' approach, then the voices of the
riders. I listened to hear the young woman's
voice, but could not detect it. Somehow I had
a perfect trust in her, even though she was the
wife of a Johnny Reb. We hadn't spoken
much; I knew nothing of her past character,
but there are some women we instinctively believe in, and she was one. Just when my faith
was truest, I heard the cellar-doors open, and
the tramp of heavy, booted, spurred feet on the
loosely-laid plank stairs. My three pursuers
were in the cellar, and were apparently looking
around. Then I could make out a woman's
voice whispering with one of the men, and then
they all went up the stairs. Some one shut the
doors with a bang. I had forgotten I was
cold or hungry; my trust in my fair young
protector had put into my life a new force
which dulled the physical sensations. I became oblivious to time; I kept thinking of the
young woman upstairs calmly sewing, the
sculptured contour of her face, her dark eyes
and brown-gold hair, her black and white
checked gingham dress. It was late at night

I calculated when I heard the cellar doors open softly, and the trip of gentle steps upon the stairs. She got down on her knees before the hidden rivulet, and called to me to come out ' if I was alive.' 'Alive? I surely am alive, and never felt better in my life. You have performed a miracle and saved my life.' She had no light with her, but to me she was so beautiful and so good that I saw her plainly in the darkness of the cellar. It was dark in the room upstairs, save for the red glow from the stove. ' I am afraid to light a tallow dip,' she said. ' While I'm sure they've gone, they might see a light in my window even from a great distance.' On a chair were some dry clothes; I could go upstairs and change them if I wished. This I did quickly, and when I returned down the ladder, a warm supper had been laid out on the table. The glow from the stove was light enough, and never did I enjoy a meal as much. As I ate she told me what a close call I had, and it is only as the years pass that I realize how near I was to death. My three pursuers had arrived, angry and tired, vowing vengeance. They had found the rider-

less horse, and knew I must be close by. To
her surprise she found one was her husband, a
corporal, whom she imagined was far away in
Northern Virginia. She said that if she had
known he was one of the party she would never
have secreted me; but on this point I am in-
credulous. But the fact that her husband was
in the party saved my life. Evidently he felt
the same faith in her that I had, for when she
told him she had not seen me, and that I was
nowhere on the premises, he believed her, and
only came into the cellar in a perfuntory manner to satisfy his comrades. They had waited
long enough to have tea served, to feed their
horses sparingly, and made off in different directions, promising to capture me by sundown.
But the sun set defiant and red, dusk softened
into night, and she knew that they had not
found a trace of me. When the meditative old
clock struck twelve; she felt there was little
danger of their return that night, so she had
come down and invited me out. ' I am afraid
I have committed a grave sin to have deceived
my husband, but after hiding you away, I could
not bring myself to deliver you up and maybe

have you butchered like a dog. I will never be
happy again for my vile act, but I am thankful
I have not the betrayal of two on my soul.'
When she finished talking I took out my wallet
to examine the integrity of my papers. The
outer covering was water soaked but the price-
less dispatches entrusted me by Colonel Huide-
koper were as clean and strong as when they
were delivered to me. In the case I found a
small photograph of myself in uniform taken
the day before I left Harrisburg for my regiment. I had intended sending it to a sweetheart back in Hopple Hollow, but had never
gotten the chance. I reached to the window
sill, where by the stove-light I detected a pen
and ink. On the back of the picture I wrote
my name and address, " Edwin Garth, Hopple
Hollow, Pa." Below I put the date, " June 28,
1863." I handed it to my deliverer, who looked
around for a place to hide it, finally secreting
it under the sill of the window frame. Outside the windows the landscape became sea-
gray, daylight was crowding into the tents of
night. ' I must be going, thank you ever from
my heart; write to me some time'; I said, as I

clasped her warm hand. I shut the blue door
softly, and retreated up the hollow, in the direction I had come when I abandoned the horse.
I marvelled at the stupidity of the Rebels;
several places I saw my footprints in the muck
by the stream. It was light when I reached the
tall blackened pine stump where I had hidden
the saddle. I found it untouched, but could
locate the pony nowhere. I knew it would be
safer to strike for my destination on foot; a
horseman is always noticeable, but I hated to
lose the Red Hornet, as I had captured the
little stallion from a Rebel cavalryman in one
of our raids into Northern Virginia. But my
disappointment over the missing pony was only
the outward expression of my grief about parting from the young woman who had saved my
life. But she had given me something more to
live for, an added reason to serve my country
well. I was just as brave but not as reckless
in the hours which followed. I travelled fast
across the ridges, and I knew not such a thing
as hunger or fatigue. Just as the sun was
setting calm and golden I was halted by the
sentry at Colonel Wister's camp. In another

five minutes he had my despatches, warmly
commending me for safely getting through such
a perilous country. I had many other ex-
periences and hair-breadth escapes while the
war lasted, but they all sunk into common-
place after they were over. The adventure of
the log cabin and my fair deliverer was the
one living issue of my life. When I was
mustered out, highly commended for my conduct on a dozen occasions, and set out for the
pine-buried depths of Hopple Hollow, I had
another reason to cause me to travel fast, apart
from the desire to be reunited with my family.
It was the hope of finding a letter from my
deliverer. I always thought of her by that
name; I never mentioned or thought of her
by any other. My meeting with the family was
a happy one; they were proud of my record,
but I think I cut the greetings short a trifle
when I asked that time-worn question,' Is there
any mail for me?' ' Yes, quite a few letters
and papers,' replied my white-haired father,
as he brought forth the bundle tied with pink
string from the drawer of the old walnut writing desk. I went through the packet carefully;

there were letters from friends, relatives, and
old-time sweethearts. Every handwriting was
familiar, but no word from 'my deliverer.' I
fear I looked a little sad when I laid the letters
down, and one of my sisters said, 'Ed, I'll
wager you've got a girl down South.' But my
disappointment, though lengthened out, was
not destined to be final. In April, 1867, after
a winter spent working in the woods, I came
home, and at the close of the usual greetings
asked for my mail. My sister smiled broadly
as she hurried to the writing-desk. " There's
only one letter, and something tells me it is the
one I am sure you want.' I don't know why
she said this, but sisters are often intuitive. I
opened it, and my face assumed a serious mien.
I know it did, for my mother called to me and
said I ought to look at myself in the glass. It
was dated March 1, the same year. 'My dear
friend," it ran, " I now feel impelled to take
my pen in hand. I have wanted to do so ever
since the war was ended. My husband never
returned, and his regiment counted him a de-
serter after 1863. He never wrote to me after
he went away that night I hid you in the

spring house in our cellar. I sometimes
thought you met and killed him, but that
cannot be. I wanted to be honorable to
him until I felt there was no chance of
his coming back. I am sure of it now,
and take pleasure in pening these lines.
Write to me soon, and come to see me if ever
in this part of the country. I often look at
your photograph. The date you wrote on the
back, ' July 28, 1863; changed the whole meaning of my life. But I must close. Answer
soon to one you called ' your deliverer'.' Did
I go to see her in the South Mountains and
make her my wife? That would have been a
happy ending to the romance, and would have
sounded well in your next volume of " Mountain Tales.' I did not. When I read that
letter a blind, burning instinct, such as compels us to run before it like a forest fire, told
me in letters of pain that the rebel corporal
was still alive; that he knew when he came to
the house that his wife had hidden me in the
cellar, but with the chivalry of a true Virginian would not brand her as false, nor make
himself the laughing stock of his comrades.

Yes, sir, she did write me again, but by that time I was married happily to my old-time sweetheart in Hopple Hollow."

VIII.

ON BLACK MOSHANNON

OME few years before the middle of the last century there were three substantial log-houses on the "grass flats" of Black Moshannon. The stream is wide, and there is considerable "dead water" at this point. But for its limited acreage this would have made an admirable farming and dairying country. Unfortunately there was not more than three hundred acres suitable for clearing, and these were taken up by three families. These three families were as dissimilar as can possibly be conceived. On the farm furthest down the stream lived the Mc-Caleb family, fresh from the north of Ireland; their old home had been in Donegal. At the next farm lived the Bower family, staid Pennsylvania-Germans from Berks County. At the "upper" farm resided a young couple named de Trzebon, lately arrived from Bohemia. Be-

yond these three farms was the dense, unbroken
forests, where the wolves and panthers held
full sway, and not even a hunter's shanty was
to be met for miles. Old Alexander McCaleb
was the only one of the three settlers who
might be called prosperous. He combined
rafting with farming, and also worked up quite
a respectable fur business. His entire family
were so busy that they did not mind the loneliness of their habitation. They were a less
sociable family than the Bowers, but the
Bohemian couple, the de Trzebons, were the
strangest and most aloof of all. They spoke
English much better than did the Bowers, were
hospitable, so that pride was not the cause of
their reserve. According to old McCaleb, they
had a past. This mattered little to the Bowers, as they accepted people at their "face
value." But to the McCalebs, with the strong
Presbyterian tendencies which they carried
into the wilderness, any divergence from the
straight and narrow path deserved ostracism.
Besides, Elsa de Trzebon had powers of second
sight. She could foretell disasters, unsuccessful hunts, or love affairs, and rafts that would

be wrecked. She knew what people were doing
at every hour of the day and night, even if they
were hundreds of miles away. Her husband,
Alois de Trzebon, was an expert rifle shot, and
that made him the few friends he possessed.
These were wandering hunters whose hunting
shanties had antedated the three log farm-
houses on the "grass flats." They came back
regularly and slept in the settlers' barns, and
furnished a link with the outside world. Every
season a panther would feel too much at home
on the flats, and a hunting party would be
organized to lay him low. Alois de Trzebon
was even more adept at slaying these monsters
than the native shots, and the party would invariably wind up by presenting the carcass to
McCaleb. This was the one annual act of
social intercourse. The old Irishman would
stuff it with leaves and set it up on his raft,
and attract much attention all the way from
Karthaus to Marietta. His pleasure at having
a stuffed panther on his rafts was the one human thing about him. Apart from this he
was moody, brusque, severe. Michael Bower
was a jolly old fellow; he didn't care much for

hunting, but if his farm paid, he was supremely happy. He had a wife and nine children, just one more child than had his neighbor McCaleb. The de Trzebons had none at all. Childless couples were rare in the mountains; they were always supposed to have *pasts*. Bower's eldest child was a daughter, Arminta; McCaleb's was a son, Nicholas. Arminta was blonde and pretty, quite unusual in coloring for a Pennsylvania-German girl. Nicholas McCaleb was tall and slight, with " Irish brown" hair, which is neither red nor ash. He was an agreeable young fellow. Though he had missed being born in Pennsylvania by three years, he was entirely like an American, and utterly unlike a Calvinistic Irishman. He was fond of rafting, and looked upon farming as a mere necessity. But hunting was his chief pleasure, one which he had not much time to indulge. His stern father kept him at his tasks continually, and had he not been such a happy-go-lucky, genial soul, he would have rebelled. He took a decided liking for Arminta Bower, which was fully reciprocated. Old McCaleb said he disapproved of " mixed marriages." " You

can go with that Dutch girl if you want, but
when you marry, it must be one of our own
stock." Nicholas was shrewd enough never
to answer his parent on this question. When
it was possible to slip away from home the
young woodsman was invariably with Arminta.
Their favorite walk was along the path by the
creek to the de Trzebon home. They liked to
meet the wandering hunters who visited there,
and Nicholas often tested his markmanship
with them. Next to Alois de Trzebon he was the
best shot of all. Sometimes he would match
his skill with hunters from Buffalo or Philadelphia, and often with Indians from the reservations. It was a picturesque concourse at the
de Trzebon home. All kinds of hides would be
displayed—panthers, bears, wolves, wild cats,
catamounts, wolverenes, fishes, otters, red and
grey foxes, beavers, martens and raccoons.
When play was over the hunters repaired to
the McCaleb residence and sold their furs,
but they lingered longest in the congenial
atmosphere of the de Trzebons. Of all
the men who came to the Bohemian household, Elsa de Trzebon admired Nicholas

McCaleb most. " I hate his father, but I
do like him," she often told her husband.
While she was always pleasant to Arminta
Bower, she never treated her with the same
degree of cordiality that she did her lover.
On several occasions she took Nicholas into
the house and gave him exhibitions of her
powers of second sight. Once she told him
that his uncle's distillery in Donegal was being destroyed by fire. He told his father, who
scolded him and quoted scripture by the hour.
Several months later he learned it was the
truth. Another time she told him where six
elks were hiding in a ravine only a couple of
miles from the flats. A party was organized
and the elks slain. These mystic confidences
made Arminta a trifle jealous. But she always consoled herself by the thought that the
woman was married, therefore *harmless*.
Nicholas laughed when once she confided her
unhappy feelings to him. " But you must admit she's pretty," urged Arminta. " She's
pretty," replied the young man, " but not the
kind of prettiness I like; she's not pretty like
you." But jealousy once aroused can never

be downed except by the death or disappearance of the person feared. At the same time
the de Trzebon home was an interesting place
to stroll to, and Nicholas showed in every way
he could that his interest lay wholly with
Arminta.   One afternoon when the gifted
woman confided to him that the raft on which
Bill Erskine, a young man with whom he had
quarrelled over some girl, would be wrecked
going through the chute at Muncy Dam above
Montgomery's Ferry, with the loss of four lives,
including Erskine's, she also related the story
of her life. There wasn't much to it. If there
had been it couldn't have been told quickly
enough to keep Arminta, who was waiting outside, from becoming impatient.   Elsa de
Trzebon, so she stated, had been born twenty-
two years before at the ancient castle of Neu-
haus, in Bohemia. She was the youngest child
in a large family, being the daughter of a
younger brother of the Count von Rosenberg,
who owned the estates and castle. It was an
historic family, proud and aristocratic. But
their chief glamor was having produced a
world-renowned ghost, the famous *White Lady,*

who had such a penchant for appearing before
members of the German royal families shortly
before their deaths.   In each generation some
member of the family possessed supernatural
gifts; in this generation she was the one.   But
it was strange that these gifts never developed
until after some tragedy in the life of the seer
or seeress.   Elsa von Rosenberg had led an
uneventful and monotonous life as a poor dependent in a rich house until she was eighteen.
Then a marriage was arranged for her with
one Nebo Salamonski, son of a wealthy banker
in Breslau.   Breslau meant as little to Nicholas as Shanghai, but he remembered the name,
and repeated it later.   She didn't like the
proffered husband from the start; she detested
him when she compared him with Alois de
Trzebon, a youth of gentle birth, who acted as
a sort of over-gamekeeper and hunting companion to the occupants of the castle.   The wedding journey was to be made partly by carriage, with Paris as the ultimate destination.
The first night was to be spent at a picturesque
inn, in a mountain pass about seventeen miles
from the castle.   The hotel was built against

the side of the mountain. In front was a road,
a ravine, and a waterfall. There was a back
door which opened on the mountain, and here
the bartered bride made her escape while the
bridegroom was superintending the un-
harnessing of his handsome horses. Alois met
her on the mountain top, among the dense firs,
and knowing every path, they baffled detection,
and ultimately sailed for America, from a
French seaport. A land company in Philadelphia sold them the farm on the " flats." That
was the story of Elsa von Rosenberg-Salamon-
ski-de Trzebon to date. She had suggested that
Nicholas keep the story to himself, but as he
considered Arminta and himself as " one," she
heard it from him. He had often told her that
since he met her " his life was an open-book."
To have concealed this interesting story from
her would have broken an otherwise spotless
record of " confidences." Whether Alois and
Elsa were happy together was a question often
discussed by Nicholas and Arminta. " I don't
see how they can be," Arminta would say,
" with the memory of that man she deserted
hanging over her." But as no one in the grass

flats region had seen the deserted Salamonski, the merits of the case could not be adjudicated. Elsa seemed happy enough, although Arminta was about her only woman caller. The other women in the Bower household, though friendly enough, had too much work to cultivate her acquaintance. Arminta being in love was granted more liberty of movement. Among the visitors at the de Trzebon home were, as stated previously, Indian hunters from the northern reservations. The most conspicuous of these was Bob Sunday, a full-blooded Seneca, of colossal proportions. He appeared at the flats regularly twice a year, spring and fall, and always had a stock of choice furs. One spring, after selling his stock to old McCaleb, he urged Nicholas to go north with him on an elk hunt. " I know where there are a hundred elks. No one else knows, and we might as well kill them as any one else. You can be back in time to start on your rafting trip." This was said in the old man's hearing, but he could not protest, as Nicholas was nearing his twenty-third birthday. If he returned in time to help run the logs to the Big Moshannon, and man the

rafts from that point, he could not complain.
"I'll let you know in the morning," was
the young man's final reply before he went
to bed that night.   When he awoke, after
dreams of the chase, he was full of enthusiasm for the hunt.   It was the consensus
of opinion among old hunters that elks were
getting scarce in Pennsylvania.   They could
not last much longer.   They would soon go the
way of the buffaloes.   It wasn't the right
season, but they would kill them just for their
tongues and hearts.   Before breakfasting he
hurried over to the Bower home to tell Arminta
of his intention.   He had gone on many hunting trips before, and his rafting excursions had
taken him hundreds of miles from home, so
there was no reason why the girl should object.
But one can never be sure how a woman will
take anything.   Arminta burst into tears, and
ran into the house without saying "goodbye."
Nicholas was angered by her "baby conduct,"
as he called it, and made no effort to find her.
He joined the Indian, striking out for the
north across the mountain trails.   Once in the
Black Forest they followed Canoe Run to-

wards its headwaters, which were in an im
mense swamp. It had been burned over the
year before, and that, together with the back-
wardness of the spring foliage, made it easily
surveyed from the surrounding hills. The elks
were nowhere to be seen, but two other hunters
with their faces almost hidden by black beards
were skulking about the eastern boundary of
the lowland. " I thought no one knew of this
place but myself," said the Indian, dejectedly.
" Never mind, Bob," said the young hunter,
" we'll get the elks; they won't have a show
at them." Night coming on, a fire was built
and camp started. After a brief supper it was
decided that one of the party go to sleep, and
the other stay on watch, as they sort of dis-
trusted the two hunters they had seen during
the afternoon. They drew lots, and it fell to
Bob to go on watch, and for Nicholas to sleep.
About midnight two rifle shots were heard, and
both men jumped to their feet. The strange
hunters had fired on them from ambush. But
they had miscalculated. Bob and Nicholas
shot off their own firearms, but nothing more
happened until morning. Then the actual hunt

for the elks began. The mysterious adventure
of the night was almost forgotten. Five miles
to the north, on the waters of Brown Bear Run,
the herd was located. "They're feeding and
playing now," said the Indian, "at sundown
they'll start travelling up the hollow, to spend
the night on the summit." Behind a windfall
the hunters awaited their quarry. The hemlock glade was always dark, but there were
signs of increasing gloom as sundown approached. True to prediction, the noble animals started up the glen in single file. How
different they looked from the western or
northern elks we see to-day in our zoological
gardens. Long, rangy, low-bodied elks they
were, almost approaching the drab or slate
color, dappled, with nothing of the tawny hue
we associate with *cervus Americanus*. They had
almost the conformation of reindeers. As they
drew near the hunters, their leader, a bull with
many-tined antlers bursting through the velvet,
stopped and sniffed the air. Then he began
snorting and grunting. The other elks began
running in different directions. Just then
rifle shots rang out from behind. Bob and

Nicholas toppled over, lost their balances, and
fell into the bed of the stream, mortally
wounded.   Then all was silence.   Stealthily
two forms crept down from the mountain and
rifled the pockets of the dead.   Bob Sunday
had over fifty dollars, and Nicholas almost as
much.   Nicholas had a silver watch; both
hunters had rifles and ammunition.   Taking
everything, the mountain outlaws crept up the
hill, and disappeared.   Next morning the herd
of elks on their way down the ravine came
upon the dead bodies of their would-be slayers.
The bull elks, great, heavy, long-bodied brutes,
drab of color, and spotted like hyenas, trampled
the human remains until they were unrecog-
nizable.   All the other elks walked over them
and sniffed at them as they filed onward to the
playgrounds.   That morning Arminta awoke
after a night of troubled dreams.   She had had
confused visions of elks, horns, and men with
horns; all was horrible and complex.   " Something has happened to Nicholas," were the first
words that came to her.   She had to help w.th
breakfast.   It seemed interminable until the
repast was cooked and eaten and the dishes

washed. She was trembling from head to foot
as she ran down the path to Elsa de Trzebon's
home. The Black Moshannon was much swollen
by spring rains. Alois was digging garden
and waved his hat as she passed. Inside the
house she found Elsa in a white dress walking
up and down like a caged wolf, muttering to
herself. "Has anything happened?" said
Arminta with alarm. Elsa glared at her and
said, "I'm finding that out now; I'll tell you
in a minute." For a minute more she continued walking up and down. Suddenly she
stopped in the centre of the room and put her
hands over her eyes. "I see it all now," she
gasped. "Nicholas is lying there—he is dead
—yes, he is dead. Bob Sunday lies beside him;
he, too, is dead. I see the elks; there must be
a hundred of them—great, rangy, low-bodied
elks, drab in color, and spotted with black,
trampling, marching, galloping over, mauling
the dead bodies." Arminta could scarcely believe her ears, and sank into a chair. "They
were murdered last night by two men," continued Elsa; "I see them, I know them;
they've been here as our friends. Oh, Nich-

olas, my love, my love; I can never see you
again in this life. I loved you, Nicholas, Nicholas, my love." Horrified to hear her lover
mentioned as being beloved by another, and
unable to stand the terrible news, Arminta ran
to the garden to warn Alois of his wife's condition. Hardly had she gone when Elsa ran
out the front door and down the path in the
direction of Black Moshannon. She climbed
out on the stump of an old black birch which
overhung the deep water, and plunged in.
Alois and Arminta spied her, but it was too
late. She rose to the surface a couple of times,
and they called to her. The last time she
seemed to shake her head, and disappeared forever. Alois was in the water after her, being
within a few feet of her when she sank for the
last time. Arminta, terribly unnerved, but
bearing up nobly, hurried home, and her father
and brothers in dugouts were soon paddling
around and sounding the water with poles for
the body. It was not recovered. Most probably some current from the spring rains running along the bottom of the dead water carried it to the swift water beyond, where it

lodged among logs or drifts between there and
the Big Moshannon. But could a spirit like that
of Elsa de Trzebon find rest in death? Far
from it; she must expiate her own sins and
the sins of her race. On dark nights Alois
fancied he saw the luminous figure of a woman
all in white walking on the water, near the
far shore. The entire Bower family saw it;
only the McCalebs did not—but they were too
grief - stricken over the loss of their son to
notice anything. Alois moved away first;
he said he must have city life. He was last
heard of in Pittsburg in 1860. The Bowers
were next to go. Arminta was all broken up
by the murder of Nicholas; she needed change
of scene. They returned to the old home near
Friedensburg, in Berks County. The McCalebs
soon followed. " It doesn't seem the same place
since Nicholas has gone," was their excuse.
They found more congenial surroundings in
the Spruce Creek Valley. But the luminous
female figure all in white, that walked upon
the waters on dark nights, remained. She
seemed to thrive on loneliness; stillness
brought her into bolder relief. If she has a

special " mission," as they say in ghostly circles, doubtless she is waiting to see if the
murderers of her lover, whom she recognized,
will return. Hunters and fishermen quickly
pre-empted the three deserted farm-houses, but
they could not be happy in them and just as
quickly vacated them. One and all saw the
silent, silvery figure, more like moonlight than
a woman. The sight of her was depressing;
it made strong men shudder and gasp. " She
must be horribly unhappy to make us feel this
way," said one bold mountaineer. Perhaps
that was the reason why some one burned the
three houses to the ground one August night
in 1891. The burning of the cabins, or the
" lessening of her environment," as the
spiritists say, made the white spirit more
transparent, filmy and vague, but there are
traces of her still discernible on the dead water
on particularly calm nights.

IX

THE DANCING CHAIRS

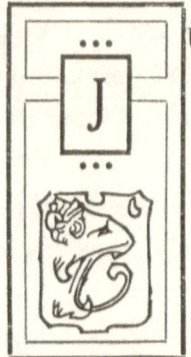

UST as readily as one can tell on sight a Catholic priest, or a physician, or a church edifice, or a schoolhouse, a haunted house can be differentiated from its fellows. One could feel certain that the old weather-beaten mansion at Kern's Store, that had once been painted red, was haunted, even when first seeing it from across the valley a mile away. It was not because of the sign "no haunting" scrawled in crooked characters on a board nailed to a tree in a wood as one emerges from Wolf Gap that makes us feel we are in ghostly territory; it is the aspect, terrible, lonely, bleak, of the old house on the Pike. The shutters are so tightly closed, the path running to the side door is so overgrown with weeds, and the dead pear trees in the yard so dilapidated, that it would appear like a house deserted were it not for the uncon-

trollable feeling of the presence of a ghost.
Under the eaves run a row of tiny windows,
storm stained and rusty paned, that look like
eyes that have cried and dried their tears and
cried again, veritable eyes of the ghost. The
front gate is tied with a string, a string so
musty, that it would seem it had not been
untied for years. Visitors when they came
respected the tied gate, and made ingress
through the barnyard. There remains no living foliage around the haunted house, but on
a windy, chill afternoon in April it looks barer
and more forbidding than ever. It is six years
since I heard the story of the old house. My
informant was reluctant to tell it, and probably
would not have done so at all, had it not been
that we were driving one dark night from
Loganton across the mountain to Stover's, and
it came as natural to discuss " hanting" as it
would to discuss blossoms in an orchard in
May-time. The ghost of the old mansion at
Kern's Store dates back to Civil War times, a
period rich in the production of a new crop of
wandering spirits. The Civil War days loosed
more restless shades upon the countryside than

any other force since America was discovered. It did for our ghostly history what Cromwell did for the ghosts of Ireland, the Wars of the Roses for ghostly England, and the Thirty Years War for continental ghosts. As one old Irishman put it, " Were it not for Cromwell we would have precious few ghosts in Ireland." Ghosts are born of injustice, and unrighteousness; no one ever heard of a ghost admitting a square deal before or after dissolution. Ghosts are disappointments personified, wrongs perpetuated. The haunted house figuring in this story was built less than sixty years ago, but it looks as old, and sad, and lonely as if it had stood for centuries. It looks so old that its architecture might be of any period, so long as it was old. Its builder, Samuel Kern, was a prosperous lumberman and farmer of Timber Valley. Later he built a general store at the X-roads, and the post-office, the first in that end of the valley, was named for him. The store prospered, as did his lumbering and farming enterprises, so he erected, a hundred yards from the store, the great frame mansion which now goes by the name of the " haunted house."

Old Kern was happily married and had a
numerous family at various periods of his life.
But children's diseases ravaged his home on
several occasions, eventually leaving to his devoted wife and himself one daughter, Esther,
to grow to maturity. It was not the ghosts
of these children that haunted the house. They
were well cared for and much beloved. When
they died they were happy; those of them who
were old enough fancying they were going to
an even happier abode. If there had been no
Civil War the mansion might have escaped its
ghostly affiliations, and succeeding generations
of occupants renewed religiously the red paint
that was generously slapped over it when it
was built in 1855. Esther, Samuel Kern's surviving child, was seventeen the day President
Lincoln issued his first call for troops in 1861.
It seemed fitting that the one active period
of her life should be indissolubly linked with
the war. Before the war broke out, nothing
definite can be learned concerning her except
that she was " a sweet little thing." After the
war she became as colorless as does any other
dweller in a haunted house. A mile further

down the Pike, on the farm now occupied by
Moses Smitgall, in the shade of Francis Penn's
Bethrothal trees, lived Azariah Hartline, also
a prosperous farmer. He, too, had been blessed
with a devoted wife and a numerous progeny,
and Providence was kind enough to spare them
all. The oldest boy, Gibson, was just two years
and one day older than Esther Kern, and he,
too, waked into full consciousness with the outbreak of the war. Had he not during the
winter just coming to a close learned to take a
deep interest in Esther, he might have been one
of the first boys in the valley to head for the
county seat to enlist. The deer-horns and bear-
paws nailed to the barn-doors showed his skill
as a rifleman, and he would have been promptly
detailed as a sharp-shooter. He often discussed the war with his young sweetheart, but
Timber Valley was so remote in those days
before the L. & T. was built that it seemed to
them as an echo rather than a call to arms.
All through the summer of 1861, Gibson saw
Esther at regular intervals at the simple social
gatherings in the valley. She seemed to have
thoughts of no other boy, and he surely favored

no other girl. But in between there was much
hard work on the farm, which kept the young
farmer's ardor from boiling over. When the
hunting season opened there was more time
for play, and Gibson's luck became proverbial
among his friends. Esther, pretty, brown-
haired, and with brown eyes with little spots
of red in them like those on the sides of a
mountain trout, often attended the post office
and store, when her father or her cousin David
Owens, who had a brother in the army and
acted as postmaster, were absent. Gibson
would always contrive to wind up his hunting
trips at the head of the lane back of the store,
and stop in for a few minutes to exhibit a
string of black squirrels or wild pigeons or
tell of a big buck he had shot and left in the
woods. Esther would lean over the counter,
and listen eagerly to every word he had to say.
She looked so winsome in her simple frock
and sateen black sleevelets, with her hair plainly
brushed back and kept in place with a net.
She had such pretty, even teeth and red
lips and her manner was so engaging that
Gibson, who was an excellent Bible student,

often recalled the lines in Solomon's Song,
" Thy teeth are like a flock of sheep that are
even shorn; thy lips are like a thread of scarlet,
and thy speech is comely." With the ensuing
winter the young couple maintained their
friendly intercourse, and even when a soldier
boy would appear at the sociables or pro-
tracted meetings, he could not be a hero in the
eyes of Esther, comparable to her sturdy Gibson. And so during the year following the
romance pursued the tenor of its way. Out in
the mountains where, if one survives the diseases of childhood, life is long, and a primitive
sense of honor keeps lovers true to one another,
there was not the feverish haste to consummate
a love affair like in the cities, or even exists in
many of the rural districts to-day. Gradually
the young couple become aware that they loved
one another and would marry. Open declar-
ations of love were rare. Esther and Gibson
understood that they would marry. On one
occasion Gibson said that they would set a
date after his twenty-first birthday. Esther
trusted him, and never asked any further questions; she knew that he would be twenty-one

on April 14, 1863.   Gibson on several occasions discussed the question with his father.
Old Azariah Hartline had married at twenty-
one; it seemed perfectly natural his son should
do likewise.   There was a log-house near the
Hartline home; sometimes it was occupied by
a tenant farmer, but being vacant at that time,
the father said he would put it in good condition
for his son's occupancy. Provided with a home,
and true love, only hard work remained to make
the union lastingly successful.   But in January, 1863, just before Gibson intended outlin-
ing his plans to his sweetheart, old Samuel
Kern, while sledding logs, was kicked by one
of his horses as he fastened the chain traces,
and died without regaining consciousness forty-
eight hours later.   When, some days later, the
young lover confided his plans, Esther thanked
him, but suggested that after their marriage
they come to live with her mother in the mansion.   It would be a shame to start housekeep-
ing a mile and a half away, and leave a half-
sick woman alone in the big house.   Gibson
approved of this idea, and that night an ap-
proximate date was set for the wedding.   It

was to be " after harvest." Everybody in both
families would have time to come to the ceremony, and they could take a honeymoon trip
to visit relatives at Williamsport and Lewisburg. Esther was very happy. She was to
marry her first love; that was a sublime
thought; it assuaged the grief she had felt
over the shocking taking off of her father.
When not working in the post office or helping
her mother she was busy preparing her trous-
seau. It would seem a simple affair, but to her
it was a vast undertaking. Sometimes she
employed Katie Angstadt, a crippled girl who
lived nearby, and an excellent needlewoman, to
help her. With the advent of spring, and with
the wheat sprouting as it was in the fields,
harvest time, and the happy marriage seemed
near at hand. Then came the news of the invasion of Pennsylvania by the Confederate
forces under General Lee; the attempt of
General Gordon's Cavalrymen to cross the
Susquehanna at Wrightsville, and a train of
alarming episodes. Peaceful Timber Valley
was now thoroughly aroused. The roar of
battle came to it no longer as an echo, but

as a call to arms. Gibson ever since
President Lincoln's first call in April, 1861,
had confided to Esther that he felt he ought
to enlist. Now he could resist no longer; it
was not a question of choice; he must go and
do his duty. Esther never faltered, she loved
him as a home-maker, she loved him even more
as a home-defender. It would not be for long;
he might even be back in time to marry her
" after harvest." On the very eve of Gettysburg he spent his last night with his beloved
before leaving for the front. It was too grand
a night to remain indoors; they spent it in an
old box-swing that hung between two tulip
trees growing along the fence at the west side
of the yard. The lilac bushes, boxwoods, and
Irish junipers shielded them from view of any
one passing along the Pike, but it is doubtful if
anyone passed that way on that night of nights.
Esther's pretty head rested upon her lover's
shoulder; they were in full harmony with
themselves and with the world. Time becomes
as nothing to those really happy; it was nearly
two o'clock in the morning when they clasped
hands in a reluctant goodnight. " Stop in to

see me for a minute," said Esther, " as you pass
by in the morning." " I would love to, dearest," replied Gibson, " but there is a superstition in our family that it is bad luck to say
goodbye twice. I could not feel content if I
defied it." Esther understood. The blending
of races in the valley, German, Scotch-Irish,
Huguenot, had woven their superstitions into
the fibres of every soul. They were, whether
they seriously believed them or not, an integral
part of existence. Gibson did not look back
when he left her at the gate, but kept his eyes
straight ahead as he plodded the mile and more
to his home. It had never occurred to him to
say, " Esther, be true to me, while I am away."
His belief in himself was so perfect, there
seemed no earthly reason why he should ever
waver, that he could not imagine his sweetheart
meeting a man able to divert her for an instant.
Parting on any other basis would have been
painful in the extreme; under present conditions it was sublime. Esther would love him
until he returned and they were married. She
was the one woman in the world for him; he
was the one man for her. Could ever embryo

defender of his state have a nobler profession
of faith? At daybreak next morning he bade
good-bye to his parents and younger brothers
and sisters. Mounted on the best colt on the
farm, with two younger brothers on older
horses riding abreast of him as admiring out-
riders, he started for Robertsburg, where he
would take the stage for the county seat. The
War Governor's home was at that " seat of
justice"; for that reason it was a mecca for
patriotic-minded youths. The sun was up
early; July was to be ushered in with hot
weather. Not a misgiving stirred his soul as
he rode along the smooth, unshaded Pike. Confidence was the keynote to his self-poise. Esther
was also up at daybreak. She recalled the
superstition regarding double farewells, and
was careful not to go out in the yard so as to
make the avoidance of waving " goodbyes" to
Gibson, in case she saw him, impossible. Yet
she had a longing to see him just once more.
She had not a doubt but that he would return
in safety, but women are always on the look-
out for uncertainty. They invite it. To see
him without his seeing her she climbed into

the attic and posted herself at one of the tiny
eye-like windows that commanded a prospect of
the Pike for half a mile to where it ran up to
the top of a hill, and disappeared abruptly on
the other side. She had not waited long until
she heard hoofbeats on the limestone road, and
soon perceived the three young horsemen. Gibson was riding in the centre, with one of his
younger brothers on either side.   All three
boys seemed silent and thoughtful. Gibson's
head was down most of the time, except when
he would pull himself together to rein in his
spirited mount. She gazed long and lovingly
at him, noting every feature of his firm, manly
face. His tawny hair was long, and hung in
loose, curly strands from under his soft hat.
There was an aquiline curve to his nose, a firm-
ness of the lips, bespeaking the courage of his
soul.   Esther could not keep her eyes off him,
and watched him transfixed, growing smaller
and smaller until he was lost to view where
the Pike descended the further side of the steep
hill. Even then she could not leave the window.
He must have been almost to Robertsburg when
she abandoned her vigil. She doubtless did

not realize that it is as bad luck to watch a
loved one out of sight as to say goodbye twice.
She was downcast and moody all day, but her
mother did not chide her.   The sewing remained untouched in the basket on the sitting-
room table. She was mentally following her
lover to the county seat. There in the stir of
events while he was re-embarking for Harrisburg the " mental wires" relaxed, and next day
she felt better. She spent that morning sewing, gradually resuming her simple, grave, useful life. That night rumors of a great battle
on Pennsylvania soil reached the little post
office, which was densely crowded with agitated
mountaineers and farmers. Outside long lines
of wagons and saddle-horses were tied to every
available fence and tree. All the county papers
came in the morning following, making the
post office continually popular as a place of
resort. Parents who had sons in the army
were especially eager for news, and the mail-
carrier was nearly mobbed answering questions. Esther, known to have a sweetheart
who had recently enlisted, was an object of
much interest, and she handled the large and

inquisitive crowd with tact and cheerfulness.
The throng having begun to thin out a trifle,
she left the office in charge of David Owens at
about eleven o'clock and hurried down to the
mansion to tell her mother the latest news and
help prepare dinner. The news of battle made
her blood run hot; she felt an exhilaration she
had never experienced before. She was more
keenly alive than at any time in her life. In
her ears she seemed to hear the roar of cannons,
the strains of martial music. Before her eyes
flags seemed waving. As she was cutting potatoes and gazing out of the window of the summer kitchen she noticed far down the pike,
in the direction of the Red Hills, a horseman approaching. It wasn't Gibson; he
was far away, in Harrisburg most likely. This
man rode a powerful bay charger; Gibson's
mount was a sorrel colt. She had seen it led
homeward riderless the evening he left; she
had gone inside and shed tears about it. The
horseman drew near. He wore a military suit
and there was a heavy white bandage across
his forehead. He stopped, dismounted and
tied his horse at the post in front of the man

sion. When he put his feet on the ground, he showed a very decided limp. Dragging himself around to the kitchen door, he was about to knock when it was opened by Mother Kern. " Please excuse this intrusion," said the young soldier, doffing his hat, " but isn't this the Kern mansion? I'm on my way home to Milesburg. Tommy Owens, who is related to you I believe, and was in my company in the 14th Cavalry, said I should stop here and say that he's feeling well and sends his love to all." There was nothing else to do but to invite the polite warrior to rest and remain for dinner. Esther joined in the conversation, and seeing the soldier's physical disabilities ran out and led his charger to the barn to be fed. When she returned to the house, the stranger was sitting comfortably on the kitchen porch fanning himself with his felt hat. By this time dinner was announced, and during the meal the visitor explained that his name was Linn McNight, that he had served eighteen months in the cavalry, had been wounded twice, a sabre cut on the forehead, and a bullet in the thigh, that his present term of enlistment being over, he

was going home until he felt all right, when he
would re-enlist. He had been in twenty-one
battles, and had four horses shot under him.
He felt badly he could not have participated
in the big battle at Gettysburg, about which he
seemed to know everything; nothing could
have kept him out had his physical condition
been such that he would have been accepted.
After dinner Esther invited him to come into
the parlor, which was cooler. He sat down on
the horse-hair sofa, and began telling more of
his military exploits. While other soldiers
had returned to Timber Valley since the outbreak of hostilities, Gibson had always been
near, and they had not interested the young
girl. This soldier was the only one in sight to-
day; he had been wounded twice defending his
country, was young and handsome, but so different from Gibson Hartline. In the first
place he was very tall; Gibson was not over
five feet eight. He had a decided stoop, or
hump on his shoulders, which was not altogether attractive, but his nose was even longer
and more aquiline than Gibson's, his lips thin-
ner and more compressed. His eyes were coal

black, as was his long dank hair. Esther felt
something snap inside of her; it was the birth
of a new interest. It was pleasing to hear him
talk, and he was even planning to write to
her or come to see her again when the tall
clock in the hall chimed *four*. " I must be
going; I can't get much further than Madison-
burg by dark unless I hurry." Before she
could stop herself Esther exclaimed she was
sorry he had to go *so soon*. Then she heard
something else snap inside; this time it was
her conscience, her memory of her own soldier
boy struggling away somewhere with the weary
routine of the first days of enlistment. She
was rather reserved when she said " good afternoon." David Owens had come to the house
after dinner, but did not like to break in on
the stranger and Esther in the parlor. " He's
taking a good rest,"Mrs. Kern explained. David
was at the gate with the soldier's horse, patting
it on the neck and saying what a beauty it was.
It surely was a handsome animal; McNight
said that it was his charger; it had developed
foul hoofs and he had bought it " off the gov
ernment" and was taking it to his home " to

live in peace the balance of its days." What a noble sentiment, thought David and Mrs. Kern. Esther thought nothing; her conscience was troubling her because she had allowed a handsome stranger to make a temporary impression. Now she hated the sight of him, hump-back, limp and all, but it was too late; for a few minutes her fidelity to Gibson had wavered. God help her! David became very friendly with the stranger in the few minutes he tarried at the gate, especially as he claimed to know his brother, and he waved goodbye a dozen times as he rode away. At the post office a score of idlers called to him and asked him if he had been near the great battle, but he shook his head and rode on. Esther lay awake all that night. She was in torment, but there was nothing to be done. Before morning she satisfied herself that she meant nothing by the temporary flicker of interest in another man. She promised herself to forget the incident, and say nothing about it to Gibson, if he returned. Why do some women adopt the route of cowardice and deception; it must be that men treat them too harshly when they are frank.

During the remainder of the six months while
Gibson was absent serving out his enlistment,
Esther was true to him in thought and deed.
Of course, Linn McNight did not write to
her; he probably forgot her when he met the
next doting and admiring girl; but if he had,
his letter would have been thrown into the
stove unopened. Gibson wrote frequently, and
every few days Esther sent him tender, loving
missives. Other soldiers stopped at the post
office, some of them handsome and winning,
but Esther did not heed them. They were as
logs of wood to her. But in her heart of
hearts rankled the memory of the hours spent
with Linn McNight, fascinated by him, and
utterly forgetful of her lover. Gibson was
never able to get in a battle. Gettysburg was
a thing of the past, and General Lee in retreat
when he was mustered in at Harrisburg. He
was put at guard duty on the battlefield, being
present when President Lincoln delivered his
immortal address at the dedication of the
soldiers' burying ground. When Esther received word that he was coming home she was
at once happy and sad. Glad though she was

to see him, she would have felt happier had her conscience been clear. With her lover's family she drove in the big farm-wagon to Robertsburg to meet him. Christmas was near; he was to be her Xmas gift, she said. When he got out of the stage, she saw that he was accompanied by Tommy Owens. Instantly the image of Linn McNight, the destroyer of her spiritual happiness, rose up before her. How terrible it seemed to her to think of that man the same instant she laid eyes on her lover after a separation of over six months. But she had the thought of the stranger none the less; it added to the weight of her oppressed conscience. There was a cordial greeting between the lovers, and they had a delightful ride back to Kern's Store. All the family had questions to ask, which Gibson answered in his straight-forward, modest manner. He had no battles nor wounds to boast of, his annals were brief, and he barely mentioned hearing the great Lincoln's speech. With due consideration his family allowed him to get out of the wagon at the Kern mansion; he was to spend his first evening " home" with his beloved. Mrs.

Kern and Esther made every effort to please
him; in turn he seemed so gracious and happy
to be with them. It was arranged they were
to marry the next week. After supper, the
young people adjourned to the parlor, where
Gibson seated himself on the horse-hair sofa,
in the same corner that had been occupied by
Linn McNight on that unfortunate afternoon.
When she looked at her lover, Esther could see
the long, lank form of the other man. She
shuddered. Gibson asked her if he should put
some more wood in the stove. She said she
felt comfortable; externally she may have been.
Why she did it, she could not tell, but she
began saying how loyal and true she had been
to Gibson during his absence. There was no
reason for this, for he had never doubted her
for an instant. If he had, his army experience
would have been hideous. " I never noticed a
man while you were gone," she went on to say;
" I could not muster sufficient interest to talk
to them; I could hardly be polite. I thought
of you all the time." As she said these words
the heavy walnut centre table began to rock
from side to side. " Men naturally never came

to see me, but if they had I would have turned them over to mother." With these words the giant walnut dresser in the corner of the room began to bounce about on its castors. " I never thought of any other man while you were away." With these words the heavy chairs began dancing about as if bewitched. " I'm afraid I'm sick," whispered Gibson from the sofa. He held his hand to his head, he strained his eyes, he could not be dreaming, the furniture was *moving*. Esther herself was terrified and moved over and sat beside her lover. As she did so the sofa toppled over on them, and they lay in a sprawling mass on the floor. When they got up, they fled from the room, spending the rest of the evening in the kitchen. Gibson went home that night thoroughly perplexed. The weird happenings, about which he feared to speak, took the wire-edge off the happiness he supposed he would feel at seeing Esther again. The next night, when they attempted to sit in the parlor, the furniture carried on outrageously. The heavy dresser eventually fell over, smashing the marble top of the centre-table and breaking the lamp. A conflagration was narrowly averted. Mrs. Kern was awakened by the racket, and accused the young couple of horse-play in the parlor. A third night they attempted to oc cupy the bewitched room, but when the chairs began to climb over one another they ran from the apartment before anything more serious would happen. "What can it all mean?" Gibson asked many times. A voice within Esther told her it was some unseen and potent "god of love" showing his displeasure at her trying to entertain her lover in a room where she had flirted with another. By keeping away from the parlor all went smoothly. As the day of the marriage drew near Esther began wondering whether she dared risk having the ceremony performed in that parlor, or invent some excuse to have it elsewhere. Her fears were active, so when she confided them to Gib- son, he agreed it would be a nice compliment to his parents to have them married in their home. Rev. Speece united them, and the cere- mony went off without a hitch. The wedding trip was harmonious, visits being paid to Will- iamsport, Sunbury, New Berlin and Lewisburg.

Upon their return they took up their residence
in the Kern mansion. All went well until one
evening they decided to sit in the parlor. Instantly the chairs began to dance and hammer.
They were, indeed, glad to beat a retreat. At
other times they attempted the same thing, but
the furniture always rebelled against their
presence. Esther hit upon the idea of putting
the walnut furniture in the attic, and buying
a new set in Bellefonte. After this was done
they sat in the parlor to their hearts' content.
But when the furniture was exiled, the love between Esther and Gibson began to cool. There
was a shadow across their path; the shade of
a .deception and an untruth; it was a barrier
to complete union. Gibson felt ill at ease with
his young wife; he knew not why. She seemed
devoted to him, yet in her heart she felt as
uncomfortable as he. Each felt that they were
acting a part; something was being left un-
said; sincerity was no more. Gibson, naturally a home-loving man, invented business trips
that took him frequently to Robertsburg,
Logansville and to the county seat. When he
returned, sometimes the worse for liquor,

Esther would complain that she had heard the old walnut parlor set dancing away in the attic. Sometimes when she was alone she would vow to tell him how she had admired another man soon after he left to enlist, yet it seemed a very little thing after all. But always when she had that high resolve he would come home partly intoxicated, and she feared to confess. Before they were thirty their neighbors, and even relatives, declared they were eccentric. Old Mrs. Kern died suddenly, and that cut them further off from the world. The farm was beginning to run down, and David Owens had no one to dispute his sway in the post office and store. One night while Gibson was driving home from Robertsburg his horse shied at something—maybe a ghost, and he was thrown out fracturing his skull on one of the projecting limestone rocks by the roadside. He never regained consciousness and died forty-eight hours later, as had his wife's father exactly ten years before. This ended the career of Gibson Hartline, civil war veteran, aged 31 years. Esther, left to her own devices, shrunk even more within herself. Some predicted she would marry again; she was good looking, well off, and under thirty. But she never let a man except the preachers get inside the house. Crippled Katie Angstadt was engaged to live with her, but she left, and more than hinted about hearing strange noises in the attic. Other women held the position from time to time. No one stayed very long. A hired man came daily to do the work at the barn. Once in a while visitors would come to spend an evening out of pity for the poor, lonesome creature. In the midst of pleasant conversations an awful banging would arise in the attic above. Esther would always excuse herself, and when she came back the noise was no more, but she would be deathly pale. On still nights late passersby along the Pike would hear the bang, bang, bang, like falling chairs, away up in the top story of the mansion, in the room with the tiny windows like evil-eyes. Latterly, Esther Hartline has few visitors. She is getting more taciturn, less genial, less gentle. The noises in the attic are louder, and she has to stay upstairs longer to quell them when they interrupt her company. She

has a haunted, hunted look, as if borne down
by a host of sorrows. Like a cancer grows
from an infinitesimal germ, unhappiness,
wretchedness, grief, springs from a petty deception, a small lie.   Growing day by day.
gripping her with tentacles of remorse and despair, it will some time choke into gloom and
death the remnants of her suffering conscience.

X.

MY GIPSY SWEETHEART

HERE was a grove of giant white oaks, black oaks, a few walnuts and a couple of original white pines on the hill which sloped gradually down to the river bank. It was here that I used to sit on the clear summer mornings watching the Gipsy caravans trailing along on the opposite side of the river. The dust-begrimed drivers, horses and dogs all seemed to have spirit and action at the distance from where I viewed them, and the worn-out paint on wheels and wagon trucks gleamed bright in the morning sunlight. As I sat admiring and musing over the distant pageant, the intervening river seemed to typify the gulf which separated me from the life I wanted to lead. Small boy that I was, I loved to imagine that some of my ancestors were Gipsies, or vagabonds of some kind; gentle, friendly wanderers over the face of the earth.

190

But that was all the further it got; with each
passing band went my hopes of the free, un-
circumscribed life, and I sent a part of my
spirit after every cavaran. Though a railroad
ran through the valley a mile further inland
from my vantage-ground, which connected with
the large cities east and west, my idea of seeing
the "big world" seemed to be through the
means of a Gipsy caravan. When I thought
of some distant mountain, or river, or quaint
city that I had read of in my beloved geogra-
phies, I always imagined reaching it through
aid of the Gipsies. I would have scorned the
chance to go in a stuffy sleeper. It must have
been the fresh air, and the human side of
travel, that made Gipsies appeal to me so
strongly. They did what they wanted to;
there was no rule, no schedule to their pil-
grimages; if I travelled by train there were
time-tables to follow, picturesque spots would
have to be passed unscanned; even eating and
sleeping was regulated, narrow, and overbear-
ing. I often wondered why the Gipsies never
came on the side of the river where I lived.
It would have been an ideal place for them to

camp, under the ancient oaks. The old folks
said it was because it was off the main line of
travel; they disliked the trouble of crossing
the old rope ferry; but others said it was because a band of these people had been ill-used
in our hamlet fifty years before, and Gipsies
never forget. People on the other shore liked
Gipsies, so they said; on this side they were
looked upon as worthless wretches, best kept
at a distance. "It's a lucky thing for you they
never came on this side," said old John Dyce,
one morning, as he stretched his long, slim
form full length on the grass beside the old
oak stump where I sat. "They are very fond
of fair-haired children; every caravan has two
or three; they are so dark themselves they
must kidnap the light-haired youngsters."
Then he looked to see what impression his words
made. Having much red gold hair myself, I
felt instinctively that I would be marked for
kidnapping; this gave an added thrill to the
Gipsies, but I never feared them on this account. To be kidnapped would be an interesting adventure to a small boy who lacked the
courage to run away. But one bright morn-

A LARGE SKIDWAY; OVER 3000 LOGS

Photo by W. T. Clarke

ing a little barefoot boy, much sunburned and
enthusiastic, met me at the door as I was emerg-
ing from the old house to enjoy a day under
the grand old trees. "Herndon," he said,
"the Gipsies camped last night in the oak
grove below the eddy; they came across the
mountains from Nippenose Valley; they've got
some of the prettiest spotted ponies you ever
laid eyes on." The first part of this statement
thrilled me, and the second part set me into
action. In an instant I was scampering after
my barefooted companion down the road under
the restless oaks in the direction of the river,
a mile away. Then there was another run of
half a mile along the bank to the grove, where
in the distance I could discern the ramifica-
tions of the encampment. On the outskirts
were picketed many lean bay horses, the calico
ponies, a steer and two or three black and
white goats. Inside this bulwark of livestock
were the wagons, painted white with red and
blue trimmings, the tents and open fire-places.
We were a little shy about approaching near to
the outfit. We had never been so close to
Gipsies before in our lives. We did not know

how they would use us, although I was not
afraid because my hair was blonde. We sat on
the grass at a respectful distance, watching.
Everything was novel and interesting to our
boyish fancies, even the dull swishing of the
gaunt bay horses' tails to keep off the flies.
They may have been poor-looking horses, but
they seemed of peculiar moment to us because
they were Gipsy horses. The ponies were unusual looking—their colors abounded in the
West, but to us they were as rare as if brought
down from some far star. I patted one of the
black and white goats; I wanted to know what
a Gipsy goat felt like. The Gipsies themselves
seemed like an unapproachable crowd; they
kept close around their wagons and tents, and
my companion suggested if they were as bad
as old folks painted, they probably made no
move until night, and then started out to
forage. There were some Gipsy children in
the party. They appeared more lively than
their elders, but we looked in vain for the fair-
haired children supposed to be with every caravan. The children we saw were very dark, and
undersized. My companion again volunteered

the idea that the fair-haired children were
doubtless shut up in the wagons for fear their
parents would see and claim them.   There
were four Gipsy boys and one girl, about our
ages, who came out among the horses and ponies, and kept looking at us, as if they wanted to
become acquainted. Young though I was, the
little girl interested me more than the boys.
I noticed that she was not as dark as the boys,
but she was a brunette. Her skin was smooth
and white, and that perhaps made her eyes
and hair look darker than they really were.
But her brows and lashes were black. She
could see that I kept looking at 'her, and began
to stroke the mane of one of the ponies, as
much as to say, " You can stroke him too."   I
went over and began to admire the pony, which
was a stallion, and very showy. " What's his
name?" I made bold to inquire. " Prince, we
call him," said the Gipsy girl, stroking the
mane and foretop more vehemently than ever.
And thus the acquaintance began. My companion began talking with the Gipsy boys, and
then without notifying me slipped off through
the fields to get his dinner. Thus I was left

alone in the Gipsy camp. The Gipsy boys retreated off by themselves, and I continued my
conversation with the little girl. " My name's
Elsie Stanley; my father's chief of the party,"
was one of the interesting bits of information
I gleaned from her. I told her who I was, a
city boy spending summers in the mountains,
and it turned out my home in New York was
just across the river from where the Gipsy band
had wintered, Jersey City. The band intended
spending the next winter in that paradise of
Gipsies, Cincinnati. I confess if I liked the
looks of the spotted pony Prince, I liked those
of Elsie Stanley better. She was twelve years
old, just my age, and that made a bond between us. Though I had just twenty-five cents
in my pockets, I determined to ask the price of
the pony. Elsie said that he was for sale,
and offered to escort me to meet her father to
discuss the terms. We made our way through
the maze of horses, and eventually found Bill
Stanley sitting in the shade of his wagon,
mending a horse-collar. He smiled when he
saw me, and I felt that Gipsies were not only
very much like other people, but were good

natured as well. " I want forty dollars for that pony," he said; " He's just a little too light for our kind of work, but he'd make a fine saddler for some boy like you." " Well, sir," I replied, " I will ask my mother if I can have him, and let you know this evening." I hadn't the faintest idea she would buy me a strange, untried pony from a Gipsy, but I honestly intended to make an effort to convince her he was just what I wanted and perfectly safe. " We have a fine cowboy saddle and a genuine Mexican bridle that I'd throw in for ten dollars extra," continued the Gipsy leader, as he took me over to one of the other wagons, and dragged the outfit from under a pile of harness and tack for my inspection. Elsie was close at our heels all the time, and would constantly chime in and praise the pony, saddle and bridle. At first I thought she was a clever little saleslady, but later it occurred to me she was genuinely fond of Prince and wanted to see him get a good home. By the time I had seen all of Prince's trappings it was dinner time, and Mrs. Stanley, a large, strong featured woman, invited me to remain in camp and

partake of the meal. The cooking was good,
and everything tasted especially appetizing in
the open air. As we ate I kept telling every
one how much I admired the pony stallion.
I had never owned a stallion, and declared I
would have more pleasure with one than with
any other horse. After the meal Elsie and I
returned to the edge of the camp to take a final
look at Prince before I went out to broach the
subject at home. I kept lingering around the
pony; there was something I wanted to say.
At last I plucked up courage and asked the
little girl to come along when I went out to
the house. Among ordinary " cut and dried"
people she might have hesitated or run back
to beg permission. This Gipsy girl was more
self-reliant, as she promptly answered " yes."
When we got half-way out to the house we met
my mother taking her afternoon drive in the
surrey, driven by the old white-bearded family
coachman. She seemed rather surprised to
see me with a little strange girl, and I considered it an unpropitious time to discuss the
subject of buying a pony. After she had gone
by I told Elsie I wanted to wait until the drive

was over, and suggested meanwhile we walk
out the Gap in the direction of the five springs.
I stopped at the house for a moment to get a
tin cup, and as I came through the yard
plucked a bunch of blue-flags and gave them to
Elsie. We lingered quite a while at the springs,
drinking the pure waters which gurgled out
of the rocks, and listening to the bird-songs
and the breezes rustling the branches of the
old trees. Then we decided to continue our
walk further out the Gap. I showed her several more springs, the group of dense timber
on the edge of the mountain where the wild
pigeons used to nest, the path where the wild
turkeys came down from the mountain, the
tree on which a buzzard, the only one in the
township, roosted—and then I wanted to show
her "the three bridges" which crossed the
creek at intervals of nearly a mile apart, the
first one being a mile beyond the springs. By
the time we got to the "second bridge" we
were pretty well acquainted. We had discussed almost everything within the range of
our youthful experience, and they were serious
topics too, considering our ages. We both loved

nature, and often I would pause to call her
attention to the weird cries of the blue jays
perched high on dead pines, or the rat-a-tap-tap
of the red-headed woodpeckers. We sat for a
long time on the " second bridge." The creek
was especially swift at that point, and rushed,
and roared, and tumbled along like an ava-
lanche. On all sides the great, round cones of
the mountains shut us off from the rest of the
world. Every tree on the mountains was
clearly defined in the afternoon sun—high above
one of the summits a hawk was soaring, ma-
jestically, leisurely, drowsily. I put my arms
around Elsie, and she rested her pretty head
on my shoulder. The tumble and the whirl
and the swirl of the run sounded in our ears
like a lullaby. The last image of the waking
world I had was the hawk soaring, sweeping,
sailing. I do not know how long we dozed
in each other's arms, but we waked to hear a
banging and a thumping and a rattling around
the hill beyond the bridge. It was the rumble
of a loaded prop-timber wagon. Soon the
heavy truck hove into sight and " Gust" Wills,
the teamster, waved his blacksnake whip at

me, and leaned far over and whispered, making
sure that Elsie would hear, " Where'd you get
the girl?" We both laughed, and we watched
the creaking load until it was lost to sight.
Gradually its rumble grew less, and all was still
save for the lullaby of the run. Why we fell
asleep a second time I don't know, but we did,
and must have enjoyed it. This time when we
awoke, it was dark—the first thing I saw was
that constellation I used to call the "kite,"
which is said to resemble the Southern Cross.
Some " peepers" that had kept up their love-
making far into June were chorusing cheerily
in a nearby marshland. On the nearest hill
side ocasionally a whip-poor-will gave vent to
his soul-stirring notes. " Oh, Elsie," I said,
" this is the happiest night of my life; this is
just the kind of life I want to lead." " I enjoy
it myself," said Elsie. " I wish we would never
have to go back." Had I known that I would
never be able to lead the life I wanted to I
would have taken her at her word and wandered somewhere. We brushed off our clothes,
and started hand in hand, for the camp by
the river-side. The woods were dark and

melancholy, the mountains seemed to grow taller as they carved their outlines from the vastness of the night. Once we saw a high white stump covered with fox-fire—it glowed phosphorescent, like a ghost. We ran a quarter of a mile; when we stopped, breathless, we didn't know if we had been scared or had run because it was the thing folks were supposed to do upon meeting a ghost. We were just above the springs when we stopped running, and there I kissed Elsie for the last time. As I look back on it, it was like kissing a living symbol and a pretty one of the life I wanted to lead. When we passed the house where I lived all the lights were lit. I imagined they must be having company, but I learned later it was because the family was excited over my absence; they wanted the house to gleam out a lamp-lit beacon through the night. When we reached the railroad station I peered through the grated window at the round clock above the telegrapher's desk—it was half-past ten. I was surprised it was so late, never had time gone so fast in a life which had known no tedium. I said, " Elsie, it's half-past ten;

isn't it terrible; your family will be angry. I
hope they won't whip you." "Oh, that's not
late; I don't mind, I'll not be whipped. Gipsies never whip their children," said the little
girl reassuringly. On the edge of the camp,
braiding the tail of a big roan draft horse he
had swapped that afternoon, stood Bill Stanley. I can see him yet, his features standing
out bold and resolute in the glow from a
lantern on the grass. He greeted us uncon-
cernedly. "Have a good time together, you
two?" he said with a smile. "We did," said
Elsie emphatically, before I had a chance to
answer. "We were away out in the mountains and fell asleep twice." "I didn't have
a chance to find out if I can have the pony, but
I will know to-morrow," I faltered. "Oh,
that's all right; any time will do." The tail-
braiding was finished, and Stanley picked up
the lantern, and I shook hands with him and
with little Elsie, then we parted. I looked
back at my sweetheart disappearing in the
darkness. She seemed to be the life I wanted
to lead passing away from me. A short distance up the road I met the surrey and the

old white-bearded coachman. He recognized
me and pulled the horse to a sudden stop.
" The family is about wild over your disappearance; they thought you fell in the river,
or had been kidnapped. This is the third
time I've been to that Gipsy camp since dark.
They all said you hadn't been there since just
after dinner, but I wouldn't believe them. If
they hadn't told me where you were this time
I was going to get John Dyce, the constable,
after them." We drove the balance of the way
in silence, but at the X-roads I could see the
old mansion was still illuminated. I jumped
out at the gate, and raced up the boardwalk,
and in the front door. The family was in the
sitting room holding a sort of council, or so
it appeared in the lamplight. They appeared
so glad to see me returned safe and sound they
neglected to give me the scolding I may have
deserved. I went to bed thinking of how I
would go to the camp on the morrow, and
dreamed all night about Elsie and the life I
wanted to lead. I dreamed I had a little home
high up in the mountains, with a view of the
Susquehanna, and the rich farms, and of the

Alleghenies beyond, all surrounded by tall pine
trees, and ever-echoing with the tumbling of a
turbulent mountain rill. In the hollow close
by was a stable filled with spotted ponies, wild
eyed and restless, and rows of cow-boy saddles
and Mexican bridles hung on pegs upon the
walls. The woods were full of winding paths
and steep ascents, dark caverns, waterfalls, and
lonely depths. The cries of birds, the cracking
brush caused by deer and other animals could
be heard at my very door. When the stars
came out and I saw the "kite" in the south-
west, a catamount cried and hollered like a
banshee in the recesses of the forest. Elsie
was by my side always; I felt the charm of her
genial sympathy and love. I was free to come
and go as I wanted; I was a wanderer with a
definite purpose; I was leading the life I
wanted to lead. And when I woke next morning, oh, the difference, the reality of it all. The
rain was pouring down on the porch roof, and
the roads ran like young rivers. I was told I
couldn't go to the Gipsy camp, so I spent the
day drawing pencil-sketches of spotted pony
stallions. The next day was also rainy, and

I chafed at the bonds that kept me indoors.
The third day dawned as bright as the morning
when I visited the camp and met the winsome
Elsie. As early as I could, I started for the
ancient grove by the river-side. The river
road was rutted deep, as if a caravan had recently passed over it. My fears were aroused.
I quickened my pace and ran part of the way.
When I came to the rise from where I had first
seen the picketed bay horses and the spotted
ponies, all was deserted, empty, still. Only a
great circular space, bare of grass, told where
the camp had stood. The Gipsies had gone.
And with them apparently went the life I
wanted to lead. Heartbroken, I lingered
around the desolated spot, and then sadly went
home. Six years rolled around; they seemed
as one, they went so fast. One August afternoon while driving from Loganton with John
Dyce and old George Gast, I came upon Bill
Stanley and his Gipsy caravan. They had
stopped to taste the waters at the Sulphur
Spring. I climbed out of the buggy and went
over to the hefty chieftain, held out my hand
and said, " Don't you remember me? I am

the young man who wanted to buy that spotted
pony stallion when you camped over at the
river six years ago." Bill Stanley grasped my
hand, and smiled, but it was not the happy
smile of yore. " I surely do remember you;
those were good old days." I looked around
for Elsie, but in the medley of half-grown
children and young people, I saw no one who
resembled her. " Where's your daughter Elsie,
now?" I inquired. The big Gipsy gazed at me
inquiringly   and   then   answered   slowly.
" Elsie's been dead these past eighteen months.
She married one of the young lads in our
crowd; she had a lovely baby boy, but both
mother and child died three days afterwards.
We were very sorry to lose her; you know
what she was like; she was less than eighteen
years old." I expressed my regrets, but words
were futile to tell the grief that was really
mine. Her final passing to the " great perhaps" had taken the last chance of my ever
experiencing the life I wanted to lead. I
hadn't much to say to Bill Stanley after that.
Sometimes I find myself powerless to converse
—it is partly a mood without reason, but on

tnis occasion a sinking sense of sadness prevented my thoughts from correlating. I returned to the buggy where John Dyce and
George Gast were engaged in a talk about the
Spanish War with old Aaron Swartwout, who
had followed the caravan up from Loganton.
I didn't have much to say going across the
mountains. My two companions argued war,
politics, and religion until we reached the
river. We stopped at the old camp-meeting
grounds where Eliza Huntley took our tin-
types—it was a well posed group, but I looked
dejected and sad beside the beaming counten-
ances of the two mountaineers. As the picture was being made the thought was tortur-
ing my soul, " I will never experience the life
that I want to lead." And in the years that
have passed since then I have never been able
to lead that life, and now my thirtieth birthday is behind me. Sometimes I wander down
to what is left of the grove of old oaks
and walnuts by the river bank and watch
in vain for the Gipsy caravans trailing
along on the opposite shore. Old John
Dyce is no more, and I wish for his

genial presence stretched out beside me on the green turf. The old folks tell me that Gipsies are getting scarce, and those who do pass up the valley are not a happy lot and are no longer care-free. The world is getting more circumscribed, convention is penetrating further and further into nature's realm. Everything we do and say must be weighed lest it be disapproved by others. Even the wanderers and vagabonds have lost their zest for adventure, so say people who ought to know. And as these changes arise I feel that it becomes harder for me to even remember that there was once a time when I had an ideal of the life I wanted to lead. If the spirit of Elsie Stanley lingered among the old oaks and walnuts maybe she could show me the light, and the obstacles would fade away. But she is gone; she was the shroud of my gay, glad boyhood. She was the spiritual essence of my wanderings, of the life I wanted to lead.

XI.

THE HARPER

E were in the bar-room of the Indian Queen Hotel, after the Derrstown races. The low-ceilinged room was crowded clear to the green-shuttered door which led to the lobby, and there were three or four lines of country sports of various complexions in front of the bar. The air was thick with tobacco smoke, and above the roar of conversation could be heard the hammer of the heavy beer glasses and whiskey decanters. Sometimes through the din a few bars of a sweet, low-toned music was noticed; it came from the window-seat in the rear of the room, where sat an old-time harper. He would play a few bars when he thought he had a listener or two, but when they turned away to discuss the running race or the two-thousand-pound steer, he would stop, and drop his eyes ruefully. Everybody was happy after the races,

210

yet all were too keenly exuberant to care for
music.   He must have started playing and
ceased a dozen times before the handy man with
a pair of steps under his arm elbowed his way
to the centre of the room and lit the hanging
kerosene lamps.   That was a signal for a considerable exodus from the room.   It seemed to
mean that supper was being served.   Then the
porter came to the door and called out that the
'bus was ready to start for the six-ten train;
that made another exodus.   But those who remained were the most hilarious; bookmakers,
cattle - buyers, auctioneers, liverymen, retired
farmers, sportive business men, and drummers,
a motley crew, red of face, clean-shaven, jolly,
in fact what are called " typical Americans."
" Give us a tune, daddy," said one florid young
fellow in a checked suit, and as the old musician touched his fingers to the strings he tossed
a new dollar bill on the window-seat.   The
old man played conscientiously, but it would be
hard to identify or classify the piece.   It was
a medley of many old pieces, but it was harmonious, and not too sad to make any one
regret the investment of that dollar.   As the

playing continued fresh visitors entered the
bar and filled the gap left by the supper bri-
gade, and the west-bound travellers. " Everybody's feeling happy to-night," shouted the big
colored porter as he burst into the room after
returning from the station. Color lines were
forgotten, and a couple of white men slapped
him on the back and dragged him over to the
bar for drinks. The bartenders were both
small, short-armed men, and they were a weary
looking pair, besieged with customers. They
seemed to have hardly enough strength to get
a good " click" out of the cash register. I had
come in the bar-room several times, the atmosphere was so jovial and cheery, but I always noticed the sad-faced old harper on the
window-bench and the rather ornate design of
his instrument. There was apparently room
for two, so I went over and sat beside him,
slipping him half a dollar, and whispering to
him to go on with his fine music. Things
seemed to be coming his way; it took time for
folks to become aware of his presence, and his
spirits were reviving. Then a slim, long-
haired boy with a violin under his arm came

in, and stationing himself in a corner, began
violently playing the "Arkansas Traveller" dur
ing one of the old harper's pauses. That was
the old man's musical finale for the night:
fiddle music was what the crowd wanted, especially since he played such old favorites as
the " Log Cabin," " Leather Britches" and the
" Camptown Races." These tunes tickled
young and old alike; and some of the men
shuffled their feet to the measure of a dance.
I was surprised how mildly the old harper
accepted the fickleness of his audience, and
endeavored to engage him in conversation, to
learn the story of his life, which surely must
be interesting. " I've been playing this harp
through the Pennsylvania Mountains nearly
fifty years. I didn't go to the war on account
of it. I might have made a nice stake rafting
if I hadn't been so fond of it, but I'm bound
I'll stick to it to the end. I usually pick up
some sort of musician to accompany me at
Fair times, but I was disappointed to-night.
I never saw that young fiddler before, but there
is one instrument I love as dearly as my harp,
and that is a violin." From such a beginning,

he started on his life's story, warming up and
becoming more confidential as the evening advanced the general conviviality of the bar-room.
" I was born in the city of Camden, New Jersey, of good Quaker parentage, but I inherited
a love of change and adventure from my grandfather, who was captain of a sailing vessel
that plied between The Firth of Clyde and
Philadelphia. I left home, but instead of going to sea struck up country for the lumber
woods, and worked in a large camp on Mosquito Creek, in Clearfield County. Wolves
were a-plenty in those days. It seems I can
hear them yet fighting among themselves and
gnawing at old bones outside the camp at night.
We often heard a panther yelling, and one
night the big fellow came close to camp, and
so frightened the horses that some broke their
halters and stampeded in the stables. I came
down from Clearfield County on a timber raft
in the spring of '61. It was grand weather all
the way, a good, swift current of clear water,
soft, balmy air, and birds singing and trees
budding along the shores as we drifted by.
Mike Armstrong, our pilot, had a bad attack

of quinsy before we left Karthaus, and despite
the fine weather, kept growing worse. He laid
in his bunk in our shanty, and some days we
thought he would never come out of it. He
became so weak that the rest of us, we were all
very young lads, held a conference, and decided we had better tie up in some quiet eddy
and hunt a doctor. Somewhere in the vicinity
of McKee's Half Falls we saw a likely looking
place. There was a tavern, The Seven Stars,
handy, and the canal ran nearby; it ought to
be the right locality to obtain the aid we
needed. Mike was too far gone to object, so
we made fast and eagerly clambered on shore.
We went straight to the tavern, where we re-
freshed ourselves liberally before inquiring the
whereabouts of the doctor. The nearest one,
we were informed, lived at Port Trevorton, a
few miles away, and a couple of the boys hired
a buggy and went after him. Another
anchored for good in the tavern, while I decided to watch Mike and the raft. It was
too stuffy in the bunk-room, so I went up on
the tow-path and seated myself comfortably
under an old willow tree. The warm May at-

mosphere was fast bringing out the leaves,
which swayed gracefully in the gentle breezes.
The river ran blue and majestic, and in the
distance rose the craggy heights of Mahantango Mountain, the old "Camel Back."
It was an afternoon never to be forgotten.
The boys seemed a long time getting back
from Port Trevorton; I suspected the taverns
along the way were in a measure responsible,
but it seemed a shame to leave poor Mike
so long in misery. Several times I thought
I would walk out to the highway and see
if they were coming. Once I got up, and
was about to go, when I heard a man calling
to me from a little distance down the towpath.
I looked and could see he was standing on the
path opposite the front gate of a neat little
whitewashed cottage. He could see that I did
not hear him well, so he came up to where I
stood, and said that he had been calling me to
see if there was anything he could do for our
party. I told him we had a very sick man
on our raft, but we had sent to Port Trevorton
for the doctor. He said that he often supplied
raftsmen with fresh eggs, milk, and butter, and

sometimes they boarded with him for several days at a time. He was a talkative fellow, and finally invited me to come and bring the entire party over to supper, free of cost, if I could round up my comrades. He gave his name as Abel Shortridge. It was almost supper time when the two boys returned with the doctor. They had been imbibing pretty freely and it was almost a case of the doctor doing the escorting instead of the boys escorting the doctor. The boy who remained in the tavern came out about the same time, and when they were aboard the raft I extended the invitation. All exhibited a sudden repugnance for food, so I decided to go on alone as guest and representative of the rest. The doctor said he could pull Mike through in a day or two, which made me rest easily on that account. Abel Shortridge's home stood a hundred yards back from the canal, and the front yard was filled with good-sized cherry trees. Along the white-washed picket fence stood a tangle of dead sunflower and artichoke stalks from the year before. The path which led from the gate to the front door was lined on either side with

whitewashed clam-shells. A couple of large
conks in which you could hear the roar
of the sea if you held them to your ears, were
on the porch. Above the door was a carefully
carved wooden model of a three-masted
schooner, the " Nellie Casteel." Before entering I was convinced that my host-to-be had
been a sailor. Shortridge opened the door before I had a chance to knock, welcoming me
cordially. I apologized for the absence of the
others, but he winked in a manner which
showed that he understood. We went into
the parlor, for supper was not quite ready, and
I saw more nautical indications. There was
another and even better model of the " Nellie
Casteel" on the mantel-shelf, under a glass
case. There was a stuffed sea-gull and a respectable - looking violin on the centre-table.
Some tall tropical grasses, yellow with age,
stood in a corner. I showed considerable interest in these curios, and my host voluntarily
informed me that he had served for eighteen
years as able seaman on the " Nellie Casteel,"
which was a trading vessel sailing for South
American ports from the Delaware. ' I gave

it up,' he said, ' because my daughter was getting to be such a big girl, and I wanted to be
near her and my wife.' But how he came to
locate at McKee's Half Falls he omitted to
state. Pretty soon a bell was rung, like we
would hear at sea, which was the signal for
supper. We passed into the back room, where
the table was neatly set, and Mrs. Shortridge
and her daughter Parima, stood back of our
chairs to wait on us. I took a good look at
mother and daughter as I sat down.   Mrs.
Shortridge was a good-looking woman, but I
was captivated by Parima. She was quite a
little different and quite a little prettier than
any girl I had ever seen. I felt sure of this;
it was not impulse or inexperience that made
me think so. Young as I was I had known a
hundred girls, the last one always the prettiest,
but this one was prettier than all the others
combined. I was introduced by a sweeping
gesture from Shortridge, and the two women
seemed pleased to attend to my wants. Parima
was especialy attentive, and I talked to her as
much as I ate. I was also trying to discover
why it was she was so different from other

girls. She was an inch or two above the average height, slim, and golden-haired. Her
nose had a nice arch to it, but was a trifle
broad, and her lips were fuller than the average. The redness of her cheeks contrasted
with the whiteness of her skin. There was
something particularly pleasing about her
voice, and I concluded that this was the chief
point of difference. I concluded afterwards that
she was the first really refined woman I had
ever heard speak. My mother was well-bred, but
being a Quaker had very little to say, and I ran
away to the woods when I was too young to
grasp such distinctions. When supper was
over we all went out on the porch, and watched
the sunset and the shadows among the cherry
trees. At dusk Shortridge and his wife ex-
cused themselves, leaving Parima and me together. We had become good friends, and she
seemed to know a lot about rafts and raftsmen.
She asked me the time, and I found it to be
seven o'clock. 'That's the time I usually go
over and play a little music with old Daddy De
La Grange, down at the locks.' She went inside to get the violin, and I asked if I could

go with her, to which she assented. It was
an exquisite evening as we walked along the
towpath together. The robins were loath to
go to roost, but hopped ahead of us in merry
little companies chirping '*Cheerily, cheerily,
cheer up! cheer up! cheerily!*' Why is it their
note is so much clearer in the evening than in
the morning? Every ten feet, it seemed, rabbits would peer at us with their round black
eyes from out the tall young grass. The dandelions were as yellow as gold, as gold as the
young growth on the willows. The air was so
sweet and pure, the sort of air fit for Parima
to breathe. I could not have imagined her in
another place; the old home behind the cherry
trees by the canal was just the setting for her
rare, simple beauty. Old Daddy De La Grange
lived in a tiny log cabin set in the low ground
between canal and river. It must have been
eternally pestered by floods, and the great
flood of St. Patrick's Day, 1865, did carry it
away. The old man, who used to be captain
of a canal boat, was almost blind, but he still
strummed on a harp that his grandfather had
brought from France. Parima played the

violin with much feeling; she rendered " The
Queen of the May" and " Plaisir d'Amour"
particularly well. Old De La Grange accompanied her as best he could; he enjoyed it,
even though his attempts were hardly musical.
He fished out some music, brown with age.
They played it creditably. It was " Le Devin
du Village." When it became too dark Parima
lit a tall bronze lamp, and placed it on a chair
on the porch. I can see them yet playing by
the rich yellow lamp glow. The walk back was
particularly ideal, and I waxed sentimental.
' Parima,' I said, for I assumed that was about
the best name to call her, ' it makes me sad to
think that we must part; I never enjoyed an
evening so much, nor met any one who appealed
to me as much as you.' ' I feel the same,' she
answered. ' I don't know whether it was the
suddenness of your coming, the night, the
music or what, but I feel calm and peaceful
and happy as I never did before. You are the
first man I ever took with me when I played
for Daddy De La Grange; I will always think
of you and feel you are near when I hear the
music of that harp.' 'And I will always think

of you when I hear a violin.' 'It's a pity we aren't masters of our fate; to think that if the pilot is better, to-morrow morning will find me floating down the river, going further and further from you.' Parima answered with a woman's confidence, 'We will surely meet again. It cannot be we met to-night for nothing.' 'Fate is not making fools of us,' I said; 'there has not been anything flippant in our association. We have acted towards one another as if we had been close friends since earliest childhood.' Our hearts became too full to say much more, but I held her close, and kissed her deeply and lovingly, squarely and in the corners of her mouth before we parted in the yard beneath the cherry trees. Used as I was to hardships and rough associations, my better nature had won the victory to-night, and there were tears in my eyes as I went out the gate and hurried along the tow-path towards the eddy where the raft lay moored in the moonlight. The river was without a ripple, and on it was mirrored the craggy height of Mahantango Mountain. I wanted Mike to get well, yet I hated to leave Parima.

I was shocked at myself when I caught myself
secretly hoping that he would remain sick a
few days longer, so we could not get started.
But there were small hopes of that; all was
dark in the shanty; if he was worse the doctor
or a watcher would have been on hand. It was
hard to get to sleep; the spirit of Parima which
I had absorbed so freely, surrounded me, and
I could not sink into the elements of uncon-
sciousness. I was keenly awake and alive. I
got to sleep shortly before daybreak, but was
soon routed out, and joined the crew in casting
off our moorings. Mike was better, but too
weak to take much part. As we drifted out
into the deep water, and were opposite
Parima's home, I looked to see if she could
be standing in the yard under the cherry trees.
But she was not there; either she was sleeping
late or had household duties which kept her
inside. I watched the little cottage and its
trees until it was out of sight. Now I know it is
bad luck to watch anything out of sight, let
alone a cherished object. As the day progressed I could not join in the merry songs of
the raftsmen. The day was clear and we made

good headway, but there was an aching sadness in my heart. When we reached York we
split our raft into sections and went through
the canal to the Delaware, where we were
towed to Camden. I was within a quarter
mile of my old home, but as I was estranged
from my parents, made no effort to visit them.
There were times when I felt like seeking a
reconciliation just to tell my mother about
Parima. I had dreaded to make a confidante
of any of the boys on the raft; I imagined
them to be built on less sentimental lines; I
feared they would only laugh at me. But
human nature is pretty much the same; the
emotions that we imagine are ours solely, belong in common to the race. I took a position
in a large lumber yard on the Philadelphia side
of the river, but I was restless and unhappy
thinking about Parima. I had not arranged
to write, as I hardly knew my destination, and
that made me feel she was further away. I
could see her playing for old Daddy De La
Grange, and the aged man strumming as best
he could on the harp. I could see her clasped
in my arms, in the grove of cherry trees; I

felt the sensations which bit me like a knife as I kissed her squarely and in the corners of her beautiful mouth. Why was I sorting boards for a pittance while Parima was up there in the river country leading an idyllic existence. Then I thought that other rafts might tie up in the eddy and some other raftsman, young and impressionable like myself, might make her forget my solitary appearance in her life. I began to think I knew what my successful rival would look like; I pictured him taller and of a more commanding presence. I wasn't tall, but was broad and well-muscled, yet I instinctively felt that absence makes the heart grow fainter—with some. I consoled myself at times by thinking her affection for me was her first and most spontaneous love. It took me two months before I had gotten together enough money to pay my debts and have a purse large enough to quit my position and start for the river country. There is no more delicious sensation in the world than travelling to see your love in summertime, unless it is travelling to see her in the springtime. To save time I would go by train to Liverpool and

embark on Daddy Inch's ferry at the foot of
Mahantango Mountain for the west bank, and
walk up the lane to Parima's modest home by
the towpath. Never did I feel my senses so
acute as when I alighted from the train at
Liverpool Station. Before me glistened the
river in the afternoon sun, with the tall brick
warehouse, the hotels and iron works of the
town clearly apparent on the opposite shore.
Beyond the town were the graceful outlines
of the partly wooded, partly cultivated hills
of Perry County. Behind me loomed the
craggy height of Mahantango Mountain, the
old "Camel Back," bold, ragged, unscaleable,
its pine-crested summit nearly a thousand
feet above the stream. The oaks on its
lower levels were swaying in the summer
breeze; I could hear a blue jay calling somewhere in the wilderness. I stopped to take a
drink at the old well across the track from
the station; never had water tasted so sweet.
I went down the bank to where the ferry-boat
was tied up and which soon began its crossing
of the river. The water was low, and many
jagged rocks reared their heads out of the cur-

rent, slimy and black as sea lions. I felt a
sort of nervous apprehension as I toiled up the
dusty road from the slip to the main street.
Idlers were seated on the balcony-porch of the
Owens Hotel overlooking the river, dreaming upon the grand scenery of water and mountain and sipping their mead. Some were in
uniform, for it was war times. Contentment
was in their faces, but it was not in mine. I
walked along the street, under the cool shade of
the maple trees until the town resolved itself
from brick fronts to disjointed shanties, and
then I climbed down the bank and followed the
tow-path towards Parima's home. Only two
months had passed; everything must be as I
had left it. But nothing would dull my over-
consciousness, my sense of nervous apprehension. I passed old Daddy De La Grange's
cabin near the locks; it seemed strangely
quiet. Why did the old man keep the door
and windows closed this warm afternoon?
Further up the path I met some robins; they
seemed just as gay as they did the evening
I walked to Daddy De La Grange's with
Parima. And they were still singing their

even-song, '*cheerily, cheerily, cheer up, cheer
up, cheerily.*' As I neared Parima's dwelling
I heard the 'click, click, click, click' of an axe,
followed by the 'swish, swish' sound of a tree
falling through summer foliage. The noise
came from the front yard. Why were they
cutting down those fine old cherry trees?
Presently I noticed a diminutive Irishman
with bushy red whiskers and dressed in a
baggy soldier suit trimming the gnarled trunk
of the tree that had last fallen. He saluted
me in military fashion, and I 'returned the
greeting. 'How's it come Abel Shortridge's
cutting down his trees?' I called to him. 'He
doesn't live here any more; he left here under
mysterious circumstances nearly two months
ago. I'm home from the army on a furlough.
I've bought the place. I'm cleaning things up
a bit.' Resting his axe against a cherry log
he came over to where I stood by the gate. He
proceeded to tell me how Shortridge had come
into the locality a total stranger the year before, and arranged the purchase of the house
and thirty-five acres from the Widow Schreck-
engast. He had not paid the first installment,

but stripped the place of its fruit, and cut
three hundred ties in the grove on the hill. In
addition he had run up bills at all the local
stores, and borrowed money on all sides. When
his creditors threatened to close in on him, he
packed up his belongings and one night disappeared with his family in the direction of
the mountains. He was sure that it was in
the direction of the mountains, as a farmer
who lived back of Middleburg had told him he
saw two wagons loaded with household goods
passing his house at daybreak early in May.
Efforts had been made to locate him, but thus
far were unavailing. 'The Widow Schrecken-
gast is out her fruit crop, three hundred white
oak ties, and her earnest money.' 'While I,'
added the Irishman, proudly, 'paid her fifty
dollars cash on account the day I took over the
property.' But like his predecessor he was a
despoiler, for the cherry trees were falling to
suit his idea of possession. I was dum-
founded; my loss was so great I could not
speak. I could not rally myself with the
thought that I would surely find Parima. I
looked pale, and the Irishman presumed I was

fatigued, and invited me to remain to supper.
He was the sole support of an aged mother,
who was very unhappy over the thought that
he would have to return to the Army of Potomac in another week, as his 'sick leave' had
almost expired. I was persuaded to remain
over night, and I'm very glad I did so. Next
morning I helped the soldier cut up the cherry
trees, and made myself generally useful. After
dinner he asked me if I would like to 'come
down the tow-path a ways to attend the sale
of old Daddy De La Grange's goods.' 'Daddy
De La Grange dead?' I said in amazement. I
could hardly credit this other change which
had occurred in so short a time. 'He surely
is,' replied the soldier. 'He's been dead now
over a month.' We went to the sale, finding
a large crowd of people grouped about the old
cabin. The household furnishings and cooking utensils were practically given away. The
garden tools brought the best prices. The last
article to be sold was the French harp. Some
one bid fifty cents, and it hung there for several minutes until I raised it to one dollar. I
got the harp, the one tangible memento of my

evening's romance with Parima. Everybody
laughed when they saw me try to carry it away.
It stands five feet eight inches, my own height.
The auctioneer kindly found me the straps that
went with it in a cupboard over the fireplace,
so I was now equipped to go forth as a
travelling mountebank. As I lay hold of the
straps this idea crystallized itself in my brain,
' I'll use the harp to find Parima.' That's how
I became a harper, away back in August, 1861.
When I told the Irish soldier my intentions he
said, ' Cut the harp into kindling and come
back with me to the army; they have great
need of bright, stocky young chaps like you.'
I was firm to my purpose, and the next morning, when I saw a peddler's wagon draw up in
front of the house, made a bargain with the
Yankee to take me as far as Middleburg. There
I found a harvest dance in progress at the
hotel, and was pressed into service with three
other musicians to make a quartet. I never
played a harp before in my life, but I understood harmony, so I got through the night without being unduly criticized. Some said they
liked the harp music best of all. I can't see

how that could be, unless the spirit of old
Daddy De La Grange had followed me and
guided my fingers. After that night I was a
harper on faith, and practiced day and night.
I don't know what method I used, whether the
old man's or my own invention, but I took to
harp-playing as if by inspiration. When I
wasn't practising I was inquiring about for
news of the missing Shortridge family. I located the farmer who saw them pass his house
at daybreak; he lived on the road to Hartley
Hall. I went there, and spent several evenings in the tavern amusing the landlord with
my music. He said he had never heard anything like it before. From there I travelled
to New Berlin, as I heard of a strange family
coming into the neighborhood. It was a false
lead, and I followed it and others into the
valleys and back to the mountains again. I
was becoming proficient with my music. My
soul was in it, its melody was perforce sweet.
It was Fair time when I landed in Hunters-
burg, where I fell in with the musicians I had
met at Middleburg. We played every night in
the hotels, and the night after the Fair closed,

furnished music for a ball in the agricultural
building. I went from there to the fairs or
patriotic celebrations at Derrstown, Jersey
Shore, Hughesville, Youngmanstown and other
places, playing for thousands of people, sometimes in the open air. Many women heard me,
but there was no sign of Parima Shortridge
among them. Verily, she must be hidden in
some mountain fastness. I vowed I would
find her, and no labor was too severe to bring
me into some new locality where I had not
previously visited. Once on the Caledonia
Pike I heard of a young woman who answered
the description of Parima and who played a
violin. She lived in a remote farm-house, a
mile off the highroad. It was dusk when I
arrived outside the lonely, weather-beaten
house. The dogs barked hoarsely, the peepers
were beginning their choruses in the swamp.
I set down my harp, and struck on it, with all
the intensity of a soul that has met its complement, the first bars of ' Le Devin du Village.'
The door opened, and a flood of lamplight fell
upon me. I beheld several figures advancing

towards me. I shaded my eyes with my hand.
First there was an old man, then an old woman,
then a young woman—but she was not Parima.
' Does any one play the violin here?' I inquired,
hoping against hope that Parima, although not
at the door, might be an inmate of the household. ' Yes, I do. Why?' replied the young
woman who stood before me. She was not
Parima; she looked nothing like her. We
spent a pleasant evening, out in that desolate
farmhouse, she with violin, I with harp, while
outside the peepers chorused and the dogs
howled. But there was an emptiness in my
heart when I crawled into the bed in the cold
spare-room, and hid deep under the many-
colored quilts. That night more than ever I
consecrated my soul to the soul of Parima.
Year after year I have sought her, but in vain.
But I have been happier with her spirit in my
heart, than with the physical possession of
other women. I found my ideal in her; I have
never noticed another woman, because none
could attain her standard. I suppose I will
go on wandering to the end, working a little,

and dreaming much; dreaming visions so vast
and of such an expansive plane of happiness
that I have often said to myself that through
Parima I have touched the joys of the infinite."

XII.

IN THE BLOCKHOUSE COUNTRY

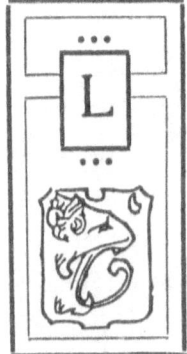 AND of beech, and maple, land of hemlock, pine and laurel. Land of streams, waterfalls and springs. Land where the wild pigeons, harassed on all sides, left last. The pigeon shot near Linden, in 1890, was a straggler from the Blockhouse Country. Land of beauty inexhaustible that even the woodsman's axe or the fire in the slashings cannot destroy. And above all, to me, a land of precious memories, where I felt emotion quickened in the blossoming-time of youth, that years have not quenched nor separation dulled. The deepest accents in my life were struck there, in the Blockhouse Country. It was on a sketching tour that I went there first, nearly twelve years ago. Though I was in the country for nearly a week, the only attempt I made was to reproduce the face of Sylvania, Sylvania Micheley. It was the finding of my

237

old sketch-book, while hunting for some newspaper clippings in one of the drawers of the
writing table in my study, and gazing on the
poorly reproduced features of Sylvania, that
led me to revisit the Blockhouse Country last
August, partly to live over again old memories,
partly to try and rediscover Sylvania. But why
was Sylvania such a potent factor in my life?
It was because she embodied my ideal of
beauty and loveliness. In the years since I
had seen her, many beautiful women crossed
my path, but none more beautiful than she.
And, strangely enough, when I admired a
beautiful woman, she always looked like Sylvania. Not that she was a common type; but
there are certain fundamental principles in
beauty, which all women must possess whom
we, supposedly civilized beings, call beautiful.
But to go back nearly twelve years; I had
long been fascinated by seeing on the maps of
Pennsylvania a village called Nauvoo. It
thrilled me because it was the same name as
that Mormon city in Illinois where the foundations were laid for a temple, said by a Reveal-
ing Angel to be the exact dimensions of the

Temple of King Solomon, but which was never built, because unsympathetic Gentiles drove the Mormons pell-mell across the river into Missouri. In like manner the name Nauvoo came to be the symbol of the dimensions of what would be to me true happiness, but never, like in the case of the Mormons, to get further than the building of the foundations. It was daybreak when I left the Riverside Hotel at English Town, and wended my way along the plank-road, with my thoughts centered on distant Nauvoo, which was to be my ultimate destination. On my back I carried a light knapsack, containing my paints and sketching materials. I very seldom bothered the colors, but sometimes tried to amuse my hospitable hosts in the lumber-camps by my work with the pencils. Never was a morning so crisp and clear as when I wandered up the plank-road. Little Pine Creek, and further on Blockhouse Run, were tumbling amber-colored and sun-jewelled, over the rocks, and singing a cheerful morning song. Bob whites, and an occasional robin. interpolated their tuneful solos into nature's concerto. And I felt as happy as the swaying

birches, the streams, the birds, the clear air,
or the cloudless sky. I had never known what
unhappiness or disappointment were. I had
never been sick a day; I was free to indulge
my sensitive wandering nature. Providence had
given me a keen appreciation of the glory of
the world, of the joy of living; I was able to
embrace happiness, and not have to regard it
as something always in the future. As I walked
I would sing snatches of the choruses of the
popular songs of the day, "At a Georgia Camp-
meeting," "Lou, Lou, How I Love My Lou,"
"Mammy's Little Alabama Coon," or "I've
Waited, Honey, Waited Long For You." I
was in no hurry; I wanted to draw a picture
or two, and when I got ready to stop for mid-
day dinner there were plenty of lumber camps
to accommodate me. For these reasons, I sat
down on the bridges across the creeks several
times, listening to the water's melodies, and
watching the yellow butterflies, or following
with my eyes the line of some tall, evergreen-
covered peak to its seemingly inaccessible pin-
nacle. On my way I passed several camps; I
could see the women in the kitchens; the chil-

A TYPICAL PENNSYLVANIA LUMBER CAMP

Photo by W. T. Clarke

dren were playing on the shanty steps, the pigs were wallowing in dilapidated corners of the corduroy road. On the hillsides the men were peeling bark; sometimes the wheeze of the cross-cut saws or the click of the axes stole to my ears through the forest silence. Some places the road ran through the forest; in others, through where it had been cut away, leaving nothing but the ruins of abandoned camps and stables, and the endless graveyard of hemlock stumps six feet high, an arboreal Pere Lachaise. Coming from one of these open stretches where the sun now shone hot, I entered a space where the tall white-hemlocks and beeches formed a canopy across the road. I was admiring the giant trees, when something made me look to the left, down in a little hollow, where a young girl was filling a tin milk-bucket at a spring. She glanced up at the same minute, to me standing in patent admiration on the corduroy road. Then she leaned down again, and filled her bucket. There was something so lithe, so fawn-like, so graceful in the line of her waist and hips as she stooped and rose, that I instinctively liked her before I had gotten a good

look at her face. When I saw her face, I
realized she was the most beautiful girl I had
ever seen. The bucket was heavy, and she was
slight, so she gladly consented to my carrying
it to the camp, the buildings of which were only
a hundred yards away. I kept looking at her
so hard, that I recall she asked me if I had
ever seen her before. I felt like saying, " Yes,
but not in this incarnation," for at that time
I thought I had found wisdom in Theosophy,
and was reading Col. Olcott's " Old Diary
Leaves." Now, I believe we have everything in
this one life; we must find or lose happiness
in the few brief years that are allotted to us.
But truly she was beautiful. It was a type of
beauty I had never seen before, but was destined to meet several times since. Maybe, I
have often thought, she left such an impression
on my retina that in seeing beautiful women
I have always first seen her. Every beautiful
woman resembles some famous painting and
she looked like Greuze's " Morning Prayer."
I asked her name, for she seemed natural and
genial, and she told me that it was Sylvania
Micheley. The last name meant little to me

then--now I know it is most distinguished, a
corruption of the French name of Michelet, a
house that has produced an historian, a phil-
osopher, a general and a poet. Sylvania, too,
was an odd name, but she was named for the
woods where she spent most of her life. Though
she was very slight, she could not be called
thin, and in her shoes, she told me, she stood
five feet six. Her light, or ash-brown hair was
inclined to be curly, and she wore it very full
at the sides, and in a net at her neck. Her
eyes were deep and grey, with black lashes and
brows; her complexion was pale. Her lips
were full, and when she smiled, which was
seldom, it showed that her little white teeth
were set rather far apart. Her mouth descended at the corners, an odd twist for a girl
of her age; there was something bitter, or sad
about it, something I could not understand.
I was fond of asking ages, and when I told her
I was eighteen the previous February, she said
that she would be the same age in the coming
December. Her nose, and I have been always
a great admirer of noses, was straight, and
Greek, but the nostrils were moulded round

rather than long. Her hands were very white,
but the nails were worn short from kitchen
work, and her hands ought to have been red for
the same reason, but weren't because her spirit
was too white. Such was Sylvania Micheley as
we walked along the moist corduroy road side
by side that clear August morning, under the
canopy of white-hemlocks and beeches. When
we reached the tall steps which led from the
road to the shanties which stood on the hillside, I asked her if I could remain for dinner.
She said that travellers often stopped there;
that they never turned any one away. Several
times I detected that she was eyeing me as
curiously as I had her; evidently I seemed like
a strange brand of young man. I accompanied
her to the door of the kitchen, where she introduced me to her mother, a woman of much
darker complexion and stronger build. I told
her where I had come from, and we happened
to have mutual friends at Waterville and English Town. This assured my welcome. I
talked with mother and daughter pleasantly,
until I saw they were getting too busy; then I
sat on the kitchen steps until dinner was ready,

and washed in the same tin basin with the
bark-peelers. They all gazed on me with curiosity; it was not me they were eyeing, it was
the knapsack I carried; what my trade, rather
than who was I, was the mystery. But the
boys were a good lot, the meal was jolly, and
the cooking good. After it was over Mrs.
Micheley introduced me to Jimmy Barto, the
jobber, who invited me to remain at camp as
long as I pleased. I asked him jokingly, if
he would have any work for me, but he looked
at my medium height and slight figure, and replied that barbering or kitchen-work would be
about the only things I could do. I must confess kitchen-work would have appealed to me
on this occasion, if I could work near Sylvania.
" No," I told him, " I'm taking a walking trip
through the mountains, and want to paint a
little picture of some pretty scenery." When
he left me, to follow the crew back to the
bark-slides, I found Sylvania sitting alone on
the kitchen-steps, which were now in the shade.
It was easy to become acquainted with her; I
wondered why at the time, for I was backward
with most girls. I know now; it was because,

like myself, she was serious-minded. There
was and always will be a barrier between me
and the frivolous. I have too much Quaker
blood to ever skim lightly over life's surface.
I talked to her of myself. That was a fault I
had when I was very young—now I like to
listen, for I learn much more, and can come
into deeper sympathy with people when I do.
But it was just as well that I talked about
myself on this occasion. I was a stranger, and
it gave her a better opportunity to form an
opinion of me, or my pretenses. But I was
not boastful; I had done nothing in life; but
I liked to talk of what I hoped to do. " Some
day I want to own the ' Gazette and Bulletin'
in Williamsport," was one of the things I told
her. Perhaps, if I had been less bubbling over
with my own hopes and desires, Sylvania would
have said more about herself on that first interview. She was quiet and sympathetic, and the
hours raced by, until Mrs. Micheley, fresh from
her afternoon nap, appeared in the doorway, to
tell Sylvania to go to the spring for another
pail of water. She beamed down on me in a
way which made me believe she approved of

me or else regarded me as harmless. In those very youthful days we regarded the parental smile or frown as the deciding factor in a romance. Sylvania and I went to the spring together. When we got to it we sat there ten minutes chatting before we filled the bucket. The time spent in her society was rapture. I could not get enough of it. Supper was even a jollier meal than dinner. A couple of the boys knew some of my friends in Jersey Shore. That strengthened my footing at the camp, for being so shy by nature, I must feel at home, else I could not tarry anywhere. After supper I waited in the lobby until Sylvania took her place on the kitchen‑steps; she made a pretty picture there, with her white hands clasping her knees, thoughtful and wistful, gazing at the setting sun whose crimson effulgence shone through a fringe of dead hemlocks on the opposite mountain top, as if Old Sol was peering through prison bars; for wasn't Old Sol to be shut up in darkness until the next dawn would release him? I suggested we go for a walk. That is the inevitable thing to do in country localities where parlors are un-

comfortable and conveyances slack, but it is a
very helpful thing, as it promotes closer acquaintance, and propinquity to love is God.
We took a long walk, along the road that led
in the direction of Davison's Tavern at the foot
of the Packsaddle, towards Buttonwood, towards Nauvoo. Of course, I told her of Nauvoo,
the still-born Mormon metropolis, and how I
wondered if this little hamlet in the hills might
possess a single similar attribute. And then
it became dusk, and it became dark. Angels
of love which during the day follow behind us,
in the darkness march on in front. In the
forest depths they barred my way; I stopped
walking and told Sylvania how much I loved
her. That was the happiest moment of my
life. Sylvania did not say much, but she made
no effort to turn back. After a while we came
to a slashing, and saw the new moon for the
first time that night. Ever since I have always associated the first phase of the new moon
with the night that I declared my love to
Sylvania. There was no hurry to go back to
camp; her mother was a heavy sleeper, she
said, and this was the first happy night she had

spent in two years. I asked her why, but she
would give no further information. But other
than on this subject she would talk frankly,
was sincere and interested. I carried a watch
in those days, but I would not look at it; I
wanted to feel "out of space, out of time" on
that rarest of nights. When we finally said
good-night, the moon was gone, and the air was
cold. She might have gotten indoors and into
bed without rousing her mother had it not
been for the little watchdog, a weird-looking
mongrel which, chained to his barrel, set up a
raucous barking, as we ascended the tall steps
to the kitchen. As she closed the door I could
hear a voice, choking and half asleep, saying,
"Sylvania, is that you? Where have you been?
Is it morning?" This worried me, as I was
afraid the mother would henceforward view
me with disfavor. I remained on the porch
of the lobby all night. I did not want to
rouse the boys, and make them think I had
been "skylarking" with Sylvania, and when I
met them by the wash-basin at dawn they con-
gratulated me on being an early riser. At
breakfast Sylvania looked natural enough, and

her mother gracious, hence I had given myself
unnecessary concern. That day, and that
night, and the next and the next, I spent with
Sylvania, at least when she was not occupied
with her household duties. I thought I knew
her pretty well by the fourth night, and the
new moon kept nodding to me to "go ahead,"
giving me fresh courage. In our walk we
neared Pat Daly's camp, a half-mile up the
road. We could hear a chorus of woodsmen
singing, "Mammy's Little Alabama Coon" and
"My Hannah Lady"; Sylvania shuddered.
"Don't let's go any further," she said, so we
turned off and followed a trail-road which led
down to the creek. On the opposite bank was
a skid-way of hemlock logs, which looked, in
the moonlight, all the world like some huge
mausoleum of my hopes. In story-books lovers
during the course of a stroll in the woods often
sit down on stumps, but such would be impossible in many parts of the bark-woods
nearly twelve years ago. The stumps were
six feet high, and chopped up to points, better
suited as perches for jays and kingfishers than
for human beings. But we must sit down, so

I got a couple of rounds of freshly peeled bark, placed it under an old birch and there we sat. and threshed out our love-story. I had told Sylvania many times that I loved her, since the stroll on my first night at the camp. The second night she had told me that she felt for me something that she had never experienced for any other man; in short, she must love me. By the third night she said she was sure she loved me, and to-night, why couldn't I tell her out and out that there was only one thing for us to do, and that was get married, as soon as I could arrange means to properly support her. In those days I had only finished my Sophomore year at college. Well, she was in my arms, and one can easily imagine how it feels to hold the *most beautiful woman in the world* in one's arms, and have her perfectly content. Sensations like this *ought* to last forever, instead of generally occurring but once, and never coming again—anyhow, with that particular *most beautiful woman*. I asked her if she would marry me, and said I could surely make her happy. She hesitated a moment, and then answered, " I know, Herndon, dear, you

could make me happy, but I would never marry
you." It was then and there that the mammoth pile of hemlock logs across the creek began to look more than ever like a mausoleum.
I asked her how it would be possible to feel
that I could make her happy, and yet not want
to marry me. It seemed like a paradox. " It
is because I love you more than I could any
other man that I would not marry you," was
her reply to this. An even greater paradox.
But I did not lose heart, but kept on questioning. Why should I lose heart when she rested
so willingly in my arms? I thought at first it
was because I was a city youth and she a mountain girl that she feared she would not be able
to accustom herself to the changed surroundings. But that was not tenable, as she was
refined, she was elegant, she was young and
adaptable. The simple manly way would have
been to accept her decision, and spend the balance of the evening discussing general subjects
—and next morning departed the camp. But
here was a paradox; Sylvania declared she
loved me; she acted as if she did, yet would
not marry me. Lovers were the original ene-

mies of mystery. They want to fight their
battles by the light of day, even if they do
most of their wooing in the dark. Sylvania's
nature was genial and frank. She could not
be like some women, and become taciturn and
stubborn when pressed for a reason. And
finally, when the young moon, fearing that
perhaps he was becoming "third party,"
abruptly dipped out of sight behind the mountain, Sylvania told me her story. "Two years
ago this month," she began, "Mother was running a camp for Mr. Barto at Hunter's Lake,
about a mile from the summer resort. None
of us liked it much, because the boarders were
always coming over and watching us and taking snap-shots of the boys as they peeled the
bark. They seemed to think there was something wonderful about the sight of a lumbering operation, but we didn't. The party who
owned the timberland had a beautiful summer
cottage on the shore of the lake. Why he
wanted the timber cut we couldn't understand,
as he was said to be a wealthy business man in
Williamsport. One afternoon a young fellow
from his home town—I'll tell you his name, but

keep it dark—the son of one of his cousin's,
came up on a bicycle. It was counted a remarkable trip, as the roads were rough and the
distance thirty miles. He was a good-looking
boy, and looked fine in his tweed cycling costume. The next morning the land-owner
brought him over to call, and he admired me
just as you did, and we soon became good
friends. He was my first love, I thought, and
it seemed very romantic to have a well-dressed,
handsome city boy paying attentions to me.
Even then I was proud, and never could care
for an ordinary man. I encouraged him, and
he took advantage of it. His proposal of marriage came in due season, and I accepted him.
He said he was young, a college student, and
must get the consent of his parents, who were
wealthy and aristocratic, before the engage-
ment was announced. But he said we would
surely be married some time. I believed him,
and loved him more every time I saw him. He
had a fine voice, and one night when the moon
was shining brightly took me for a row on
the lake and sang those same songs we heard
at Daly's camp down the road. I was par-

ticularly captivated with him when he sang,
and the moon, which is a deceiver, nodded to
me that it was all right. I was in his arms,
and he took advantage of me, and I, silly, love-
sick, trusting fool, yielded to him in my happiness. He was with me every night and we
were very happy together until early in September, when he left abruptly for Williamsport. He was to write me, but I never heard
a word. I wrote to him, but it did no good.
I became anxious and feared he was sick, so
one afternoon when I met the land-owner on the
road, I asked him about the young fellow.
Evidently he had been watching our love-affair,
or my manner evidenced too much concern, for
he turned sharply and said, ' See here, Miss
Micheley, I am surprised you don't know how
things stand; you must quit putting any store
in that boy; he's got lots of girls wherever he
goes, and they mean nothing to him after once
he leaves them.' That was enough; I saw I
had been deceived. I wandered, dazed, far
into the woods, and lay beside a log weeping
for hours. But I was always proud, and I
bathed my eyes in the lake, and braced up and

went home and helped get supper as if nothing
had happened. Mother noticed my red eyes,
but thought I was merely grieving over the
separation from my lover. After supper I
wrote him what I had heard, and made one
last appeal to his sense of honor and manhood.
I think it was a strong letter, even though I
was only sixteen when I wrote it. I waited for
a reply and got none. Yet I felt that he would
some day come to his senses and return. At
Christmas time, when we were busy packing
up our things to move our camps from Hunter's
Lake into the Blockhouse Country, mother
handed me a large square envelope, when I
came in to get dinner. I opened it; I stared
at it in amazement; my blood stood still; it
was the engraved announcement of the young
fellow's marriage to some girl at Carlisle,
where he attended school. I learned afterwards he had been engaged to her the entire
time he was going with me. But he had ruined
me; I will never be the same again. If I
married you, the shadow of that duplicitous
boy would always be between us. You could
not get it out of your mind that he was my

first love and that I had been too much in
love and weak and, perhaps, loved him still.
I know your nature, sensitive, introspective,
and imaginative. Sooner or later his shadow
would have obscured our love. Even if you
never felt that way, others would tell you about
me, with the same result. We all must marry,
I don't deny that, but when I come to do it, it
will be to a person of a coarser sort, who will
confuse my past in a cloud of his own indiscre-
tions. I could not have married you and kept
the truth from you; I love you too much."
Here Sylvania buried her curly head in my
breast and sobbed pitifully. "I will marry
you anyhow, Sylvania," I said, "You have been
frank and honest about your past; I'm sure
that shadow would have no lodgment in our
home. I love you too much to ever deepen
those lines of sadness in the corners of your
mouth." And I kissed the drooping, wistful
corners of her mouth. "My aim will be to
make you happy, and to forget." "No, no,"
sobbed Sylvania, "It can never be; there is a
physical barrier to our happiness; I will always love you, but I can never be your wife; I

love you too much." There were birds chirping in the tree-tops; another day would soon
begin. Reluctantly we wended our way back
to the camps, Sylvania leaning heavily on my
arm. As we neared the buildings the watchdog remained silent. " It is good-bye, but not
for always," I said when I left her at the top of
the tall steps. " We may meet and love again,"
said Sylvania. I kissed her long and deeply
on her tear-dimmed eyes; I squeezed her white
hands before we parted. As she shut the door
I could hear a muffled voice inside, the voice of
her mother, " Where have you been, Sylvania?
Is it morning?" Sadly I slipped into the
bunk-room and secured my knap-sack without
waking anybody and started out along the
corduroy road. In the grey half-light before
dawn I must have seemed a spectre to the mongrel watchdogs chained to their barrels at the
camps I passed, for they eyed me savagely, their
hair raised on edge, but not one barked. I was
too deep in sorrow to be human. At daylight
I was in front of Davison's Tavern, at the foot
of the Packsaddle. I did not want any breakfast. I did not care to push on to Nauvoo. I

wanted to get out of the Blockhouse Country,
land of indestructible beauty and sadness. I
climbed the steep hill in the face of the rising
sun, and as I wandered along the broad plateau
in the beechwoods before descending into the
Gray's Run region, the wood-robins jauntily
displaying their pied breasts, like pigmy sporting men with gay vests, were beginning their
carolling, like tiny silver bells, the requiem of
my happiness. I had never been unhappy before, and this unhappiness coming so soon after
and so closely allied to my great elation in
knowing Sylvania made me feel that sorrow
is only the hither side of joy. And Sylvania,
at this minute, she was probably at the spring
filling the water bucket—in the Blockhouse
Country.

XIII.

SHADOWS

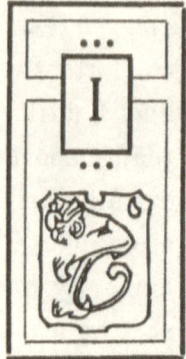I DID not see her the first time I passed through the car. The red-cap porter who had charge of my traps went on ahead and deposited them in the Elmira car, so I hurried after him to bring him back. When we returned to the Lock Haven car all the seats by the windows were taken and I had to crowd in beside an old lady whose suitcase was so large that there was hardly room for her feet. I looked through the window as best I could; it was an overcast day; on the hill I could see the Insane Asylum with its Grecian columns, and in the distance the First Mountain appeared scarcely darker than the mist. Then I began to look at my fellow travellers. I always liked to "size them up," before the train started, giving them names, occupations, and missions, and if I could guess at what stations they would get off. The car

was so crowded by the time for starting, that
several men with loaded market baskets—it
was Saturday afternoon—were standing in
the aisle. As I scanned each face, old ladies in
black, be-spectacled and bonneted, aged war
veterans, with bronze Grand Army buttons in
their coat lapels, horse-traders, travelling men,
country sports, workmen, young mothers,
babies, young girls and boys, I noticed the well-
dressed figure of a woman in the middle-
twenties wearing a modified peach-basket hat,
who sat by the window on one of the seats
across the aisle, but near the front of the car.
Beside her sat a very fat woman. I would
have extended my vision from her, had it not
been that her pale brown or ash-colored hair
was so decidedly curly; crispy like spun sugar.
Where had I seen hair like that before? Yes,
I knew two or three women that had it, but
they couldn't be here, travelling on an afternoon local from Harrisburg. And then something told me " it must be Sylvania from the
Blockhouse Country." I looked more carefully; she was very well gotten up. She had
a black dotted veil thrown over her hat, which

was of the latest pattern. In her ears were
long black jet earrings, also up to date. She
wore a dark blue suit, jauntily and daintily
cut. " She has Sylvania's spun-sugar hair, and
poise of the head and neck, but by this time
Sylvania would be twenty-eight, and broken
by work, while this woman doesn't look twenty-
two and bears the stamp of a life of leisure,
yes luxury." But I was determined to investigate. I reached into my overcoat pocket,
took out my tin drinking cup, and sauntered
up the aisle to the water-cooler. I had a drink
of the grimy water, and started back to my
seat. I looked hard at the well-groomed
beauty; she eyed me intently, but neither of
us spoke. I passed on, and took my seat, but
I felt most uneasy. At Dauphin the stout
woman got out, and seized with a fresh de-
termination, I walked to the vacant seat, and
spoke to the fair lady by the window. " Isn't
this Miss Sylvania Micheley?" I inquired. Instantly she smiled, but what a sad smile it was;
time had touched her not at all except that she
was even paler and it had deepened the downward curves in the corners of her mouth.

" Yes, I used to be Sylvania Micheley, now I'm
Mrs. Noah Creamer; you're Herndon Levering,
of course." That was who I am, so I sat down
in the vacant seat, and felt so much at home,
that I also moved my overcoat and suitcase.
" You certainly look well, Sylvania; you haven't
changed a bit, though it will be twelve years
next August when we last met. You have been
well-treated, no doubt, but I don't like to see
those lines of sadness in the corners of your
mouth." "Oh, Herndon," she said, " haven't you
forgotten those lines? I never noticed them before you called my attention to them; but I
always thought of you every time I saw them
in the looking-glass." " Never mind," I said,
" they add, rather than detract, from your
looks; they do to any one who likes a serious
expression as I do, and you are just as young-
looking and pretty and nice as ever." " Thank
you so very much, Herndon. I love kind
words. I think you look just the same as you
did, now that I've had a good look at you,
except that you've taken on weight, and are
doing, what's a strange thing for you, trying
to be fashionable by growing a mustache. I

was sure it was you, but I hated to speak. On this occasion I felt it was ' up to you'." " It is peculiar I never heard of you directly or indirectly in all these years," I continued. " I frequently did think of you, and last summer took a walking tour through the Blockhouse Country, moved by some perverse desire, to try and locate you. There isn't a camp left from the mouth of Blockhouse to its head; all the timber is gone and nobody knew where the old jobbers and crews had gone. They would be as hard to trace as the trees they cut and the bark they peeled." " Well, I've heard of you once in a while," said Sylvania; " I've read about your books and your trips, and sometimes, years ago, wondered why you never dropped me a line—the old postmaster at Buttonwood could have found me." " That's too bad," I said; " I felt you didn't want to hear from me; our parting was so peculiar it seemed best we kept our distance." "And yet," broke in Sylvania, " your last words were, ' It's good-bye, but not for always.' " "And yours were," said I, quickly, ' We may meet and love again.' My words were a prophecy, that is

now fulfilled; I hope yours will be the same."
There was a pause; we both said nothing for
several minutes but sat watching the crowds
filing out of the car at Millersburg. Sylvania
recommenced the conversation. "You went
into the newspaper business, as you said you
would, but you never got the 'Gazette and
Bulletin,' that prophecy was in the right
church but the wrong pew!" I had to laugh
at this. From now on the talk became more
personal, but being older I said little about
myself. I was anxious to learn what had been
the soul's progress of Sylvania since we parted
nearly twelve years ago. Gradually I learned
what I wanted; despite her valiant efforts to
right the early wrong in her life, her sincere
aims to procure happiness for herself and husband, she was far from happy. Hence the
lines in the corners of her mouth had grown
deeper. For two years after we had parted in
the Blockhouse Country very little had transpired with her. Many men had admired her,
but she had felt no inclination towards any of
them. She had often thought of me, but never
once regretted her decision not to marry me.

Three years after she had met me, when she
was in her twenty-first year, her mother had
charge of the shanties in one of the camps on
Gray's Run, a lumber region which had just
been opened. One of the jobbers was a young
fellow, who had recently inherited a small fortune. He wasn't good looking, nor was he
well-educated or intelligent; he was the
" coarser sort" of man for whom she had been
looking. He fancied her the first time he saw
her—every man did that; he had been enough
in the cities to know a good-looking girl when
he saw one, and here was one prettier than he
had ever seen even in a show. "As far as the
' coarser sort' part went he was surely my
ideal," continued Sylvania. "All that he had
done in his life up to the time he met me was
to have been expelled from a couple of board-
ing schools, been drunk on a number of occasions, and inherited some money at the death
of his father. He was attempting to carry on
the old gentleman's lumber business, but making an awful mess of things. He used to ride
around through the woods on horseback, on an
expensive cow-boy saddle, imagining himself a
Napoleon of the bark business." From this

Sylvania went on to say, with a tinge of bitterness ill repressed, how he had made love to her,
and she, thinking it best to marry and get a
home for her mother as well as herself, consented. But first she told him of how she had
been deceived in her early youth by a suave,
well-dressed bicyclist from Williamsport, who
had deserted her and married another girl.
She also told him how she had thought best
not to marry a reputable young man (meaning
me) two years later because of her past. Up
to this point she had been frank with him, but
she concealed the fact that she was accepting
the young jobber because she thought him
coarse enough never to " throw up" the story
of her early dishonor; he had sinned against
women himself many times and his wife's fail-
ings would be overlooked in his burden of in-
famy. But this was flimsy philosophy; the
coarse man is the very one who remembers
these things. He has nothing else to think
about. Twelve years ago I was too inexperienced to reason this out, but now I knew it to
be a fact. I knew the rest of the story, just
as if I had heard it before, but out of sincere
interest I listened until she recited it. All

went well the first year of the marriage, the
young husband was proud of his exceptionally
beautiful wife. He took her to Philadelphia,
Atlantic City, and even St. Augustine. Relatives in his home town and in Wilkes-Barre
and Harrisburg entertained in their honor.
Sylvania took kindly to society folks, and her
good looks made her sought after as a guest
at parties, church fairs, and gatherings of all
kinds. Really she was beginning to feel happy,
for the first time in five years, since the days
of her early mishap. But the novelty of a
pretty wife began to wear off with the husband
after the first year's round of gaiety. It first
evidenced itself in petty criticisms of her appearance and manners after they came home
from parties. A little later it came out in the
form of jealousy, she danced too many times
with this man, or walked too long on the
piazzas with that one. At heart serious-minded
she didn't care a whit for society, she only tried
to be popular to please her husband, so she
declined to attend any more functions. This
made the husband furious, his friends would
say his wife was " queer," he couldn't stand for

that.   During these excitements he resumed
his old drinking habits, and when in his cups
became abusive. First he had criticized her
appearance, then he swore at her for going out
too much and staying in too often. It looked
as if his moral character was on the " down-
go," especially as his business was in a critical
state, and creditors would have carried off
everything had not his mother helped him on
divers occasions. " Finally the climax came,
the one that I thought would occur if I married you, but which I am now certain would
have descended on me no matter whom I had
married. I was to suffer for my indiscretion,
there was no escape for it on this earth. I was
cornered by inexorable retribution; physical
sin demands a physical punishment." Thus
did Sylvania reach the critical part of her history. It appeared that one day she had gone
to the main street to do some shopping, and was
on her way home carrying a couple of bundles,
when out of a hardware store emerged the
dapper figure of a young man. Their eyes met,
it was the dashing bicyclist who had been
her undoing six years before. If she could

do it over again she would have quickly looked
straight ahead, and gone her way, but she was
flustered, and when he bowed she did likewise.
His manners were so easy and ingratiating that
she forgot the past while he plied her with
pleasant questions and praised her appearance.
Before she knew what she was doing she
handed him her bundles and he started to escort her to her home. When within half a
square of the old mansard roofed residence the
thought flashed through her mind that her husband knew the young fellow by name and by
sight, and if he laid eyes on him the worst
might happen. But she did not have courage
to tell the youth that her husband was aware
of her old-time relations with him, and with
face blanched and tongue thick she let him
accompany her to the gate. As she was swinging the iron gate open she saw her husband
coming around the side of the house. He had
been working in the flower-beds in the yard,
was coatless and hatless, and dirty; the well-
dressed young escort probably took him for
the hired man. For some reason he wanted to
linger and talk about the past, but Sylvania

could see by her husband's expression that
trouble was imminent, so she turned from him
abruptly and ran up the concrete walk to the
house. The infuriated husband was after her,
and once inside slammed the door with such a
savage bang that it shattered the colored
glasses in the toplight. He grabbed her by the
throat with the fury of a demon, before she
had a chance to explain things, and was faint-
ing when he released her. He called her every
vile name he could conjure up, accusing her of
secret meetings with her old lover, and threat-
ening to throw her out of doors. But later he
relented, not because he was sorry, but he said
he did not want his friends to know he was
married to an " erring wife." From that time
on her life was torture, and her nervous system
collapsed under the strain, and she was in
doctors' hands for weeks. When she got a
little better, the coarse husband permitted her
to go on a visit to one of his married sisters
who lived in Harrisburg. She did not want to
go overly much, but it was a relief to get away
from the tyrant. Even after her illness she
could not induce him to believe that her meet-

ing with the handsome youth was only an accident; he was accusatory and insulting up to
the moment of her departure on the trip. The
sister treated her well, and she was now feeling considerably better, though she dreaded the
thought of going back to the house which had
ceased to be a home. Her voice was choked
with grief, just as it was the night I left her
in the Blockhouse Country, nearly twelve years
ago. She pulled down her veil so that her
fellow travellers could not see her tears. I expressed my sympathy, and the desire to help
her if I could, for it seemed a shame to see one
so young and so beautiful in such a despondent
state.   " The excellent resolves of youth deserved a better reward," I told her. As I said
this, the brakeman was calling out " Selinsgrove Junction, change for Selinsgrove," and
Sylvania began getting together her traps as
she was to leave me at Sunbury. " You'll have
a chance to see my husband; he's arranged to
meet me at the station; but don't wave to me
or he'll think there were more sinister episodes
in my past. I have often thought you would
have been considerate to me; even with your

sensitive nature you could have forgotten the
past effectively.   One only grows wise with
years.   It's too late now, but think of me often,
and wish me well.   It will do me good.   I need
your sympathy, I need your love, even at a
distance.   I see no hope ahead, if I got a
divorce where would I go?   I would be alone
and lost, for my mother died three years ago."
I clasped her gloved hand, for the train was
now crossing Shamokin Creek, and whispered
to her, " It's good-bye, but not for always; we
will surely meet and love again."   " I know we
will; you are my only hope," said Sylvania, as
she picked up her satchel and started towards
the door.   There was a crowd in the aisle so she
had to stand a couple of minutes after the train
had stopped.   She looked straight ahead as if
she knew no one on board.   I crossed the
aisle and gazed through the car-window,
and on the platform selected as the husband
a man who was eagerly watching for some
one.   I would have known him in a thousand, only in a thousand there would surely
be several hundred such individuals; he
was no rare type.   Tall and angular, clean-

shaven, about thirty-five years old, he wore a
flashy brown suit, tan shoes, and had a brown
felt hat pulled over his eyes. He wore glasses,
had a muddy complexion from smoking too
much—in his hand was the inevitable cigarette
—his nose was broad and hooked, his lips were
thick, and chin receding. While studying this
ill-favored being, Sylvania had descended from
the car, and he ran forward and kissed her
ostentatiously. Then he grabbed her satchel,
and stuck the cigarette in his crooked teeth.
I watched the pair as they walked along the
platform to where a big red automobile was
waiting. The husband's mother was evidently
very generous. As she got in I fancied her
eyes met mine, and I repeated to myself like a
litany, " We will surely meet and love again."
All the rest of the journey was a blank to me—
I could not tell you where the sun set, or where
the afterglow shone ruddiest on the river. All
I could think of was Sylvania, Sylvania whom
I had known and loved in the Blockhouse
Country and whom I had met once more.

XIV.

WHEN GHOSTS WALK

EVERAL weeks after parting from Sylvania, in the Block-house Country, I was wandering aimlessly along the boardwalk at Atlantic City, looking in the shop windows. In the window of a jewelry and novelty store I saw a small silver box with the initial *S.* on it. It was such a curious little box, and the twist of the initial so unusual that I went inside and priced it. To price anything in an Atlantic City shop is equivalent to buying it, so eager and alert are the attendants to make sales. I had to buy the trinket, and I was not sorry, as my thoughts were so full of Sylvania, that anything bearing her initial, or anything remotely pertaining to her, interested me to a marked degree. The next question was, what to do with the box; it might come in handy for postage stamps, or even cuff links, but it should have a more mystic purpose, a purpose more intimately connected with Sylvania. That night as I was admiring it for the last time before turning off the electric light, I felt that the box should contain a lock of Sylvania's hair. Why had I omitted asking her for a lock the night we parted? It was rank stupidity on my part—nothing more. In my pocket I carried a small knife which had a pair of scissors in it; I could easily have snipped off a lock, with her permission, of course, of her ash blonde hair, hair that resembled spun-sugar more than tresses. But we had parted, probably never to meet again, at least not for years. I had let this golden opportunity slip by. Now that I had a silver box in which the lock could have been kept I felt the lack most keenly. If I couldn't put Sylvania's hair in it, the purpose for which the bauble was clearly intended by its maker, nothing else should go in it, no stamps, nor coins, nor cuff links, not even the hair of any other girl, fair or dark. The box must remain empty unless it fulfilled its especial mission in the world of life inanimate. For years I kept the box on my bureau, empty and useless, but al-

ways looking new. Freshly engaged servants
would speedily notice and polish it. Surely it
had a long dynasty of good friends. Sometimes I took it with me on trips; more than
once it crossed the continent and the Atlantic
Ocean. I had a feeling that some day I might
meet Sylvania again, would snip the lock, and
quickly put it in the receptacle which had
awaited it so long. With every succeeding
year the chance of seeing Sylvania seemed to
grow less. I had travelled repeatedly through
the section of country she must frequent, often
asked about her, but there was a conspiracy
of silence. Several times I relegated the box
to closets and desk-drawers as a relic of a
too by-gone age, but the freshly engaged servants would periodically resurrect it and install
it in state on my bureau. By these acts I felt it
deserved its right to exhibition, so molested
it no more. I had seen it so much that it
meant nothing to me when I looked at it; no
old nor sad memories were evoked by its presence. It had become a fixture like the bureau
on which it rested. But I had gotten out of
the habit of taking it on trips. It might stay

on my bureau at home as much as it pleased, but I would have none of it on my journeyings. Then one afternoon I met Sylvania on the train travelling up the Susquehanna Valley, and a rush of memories, sentimental, grave, and reproachful, engulfed me like a spring flood in a marshland.   When she left the train at Sunbury I felt for her much the same adoration as I had when I left her in the Blockhouse Country nearly twelve years before. As the train bore me on through the gathering darkness my thoughts were alone of her. Nothing else in life mattered, it seemed. I had eyes and thoughts only for that slender figure, that round, still babyish face, that mass of ash blonde hair more like spun-sugar than tresses. When the train stopped at Loyalsock and I tried to gaze out at the steel-colored, swiftly running river, the thought flashed through me, " Why didn't I get a lock of Sylvania's hair?" After twelve years another chance had come, but I had forgotten. I know she would have let me have it as a keepsake. It might have looked strange to be seen cutting a lock of hair off a young woman in a crowded car, but

if I was to have the lock I could have stood
the cynosure of the multitude without a
quaver. " Oh, why hadn't I gotten that lock
of hair?" I might not see her again in twelve
years, maybe never. I had possibly missed
my last chance. I turned in my seat in nervous indignation. I blamed myself inwardly
and outwardly, but it was too late. When I
reached my destination I was not in as happy a
mood as I might have been. But I put on a
brave exterior. I had gotten along fairly well
for twelve years without having seen Sylvania
or reaped the benefits of possessing a lock of
her hair. I could doubtless get along just as
well for the next twelve. If men can lose by
death beloved and dutiful wives and yet survive and often marry again, why couldn't I
pass over an unimportant episode with some
one I knew at best but superficially. But what
the acquaintance lacked in years it made up in
intensity. But what of that? Hot fires burn
out just as surely as do slow ones. When the
time came to retire I went into the old, high-
ceilinged room and lit the lamp. I loved to
smell the odor of the oil-suffused wick, the old-

fashioned smell of the room, that aroma of old
books, old pictures, old furniture. When I began to unpack the suitcase, I found, to my
surprise, the servant had put the silver box in
it. I put it on the bureau. The window was
half open, and the rival love-songs of the
peepers floated in, buoyant, invigorating. With
them came the bouquet that the pine woods
give off at night, and no other time. There is
a night world and a day world. There are
some nights replete with night lights, night
scents, night sounds, night life, that I prefer
to any day. I always prefer the night in a
haunted room. In this room I had seen many
ghosts. After I put out the light I could hear
a train of coal cars plugging away up the
valley. I could imagine I saw the headlight
mingling with the filmy smoke in the night, the
red glare from the fire-box, the vast, heavy,
sullen "battleships" following complain-
ingly behind. It was too early in the season
to hear the first whip-poor-will. April twenty-
seventh has been the fixed date annually for
its opening concert in this locality these many
years. It was even a little early for the trill-

ing frog-songs. The coal train chugged, chugged, chugged; fainter and fainter it became. Sleep claimed me and I was glad to go. My dreams took up where I had left Sylvania. We were still travelling together, up the valley, in the gathering darkness. I was complaining that the train travelled too fast. Even in the dream I had the terror of a parting. My life had known too many of these. Sylvania was saying that I should have a memento of her to remember her by when we would be no longer together. She suggested, mind you it was she who suggested it, in this dream that I should cut off a lock of her crisp, spun-sugar hair. I drew out my knife and opened the scissors. I began to cut—her hair seemed as stiff as wire. My scissors were bending with the strain. Why couldn't I cut off that hair? I made a final valiant effort; the hair did not cut, but I was awake, alone. I could hear the train of " battleships" no longer; all was silent in the dark world outside. The room was inky black; I couldn't even make out the lines of the giant walnut wardrobe in one corner or the black marble fireplace opposite the bed. With my

right hand I reached out convulsively, and
grasped—something, smooth, soft, like spun-
sugar. I rubbed it between my fingers;
it couldn't be spun-sugar, it was a lock of
hair. "I am still dreaming, and wide
awake; what a psychological phenomenon!"
Still holding the lock of hair, or whatever
it was, I sat up in bed. I was surely
awake, but what was in my hand. I got
out of bed, and found the bureau. My left
hand touched something cold; it was the silver
box. In one hand I held a lock of hair, in the
other the silver box, and my thoughts were of
Sylvania. I groped further with my left hand,
and found some matches. I struck a match
and held the lock of hair, or whatever it was,
up to the light. It was a lock of hair. Before
the match burned out I could see that it was
ash-gold in color, and curly and crispy like
spun-sugar. It was Sylvania's hair. How did
I get it to-night? By what prank of fate had
it come into my room? Perhaps she had cut
it off intending to give it to some one—who?—
and it had gotten into my coat pocket, and
fallen from it on the bed. Perhaps Sylvania

had been searching for the missing lock all
evening. Determined to make sure, I lit a
candle, and held the little bunch of hair before
the calm, soft, affectionate light. Candle-
light never lies; it is cozy, and betrays no confidences. If I knew anything at all about it,
the hair I held in my hand was Sylvania's; it
couldn't be any one's else. By fair means or
foul it had come into my possession; I would
cherish and defend it come what may. I looked
around the ghostly old room to make sure I
was still awake. There was the rackety four-
poster with quilts in disarray which I had just
quitted, the ponderous walnut wardrobe in the
corner, the pictures on the walls in their circular frames, the round tables laden with
musty books, the heavy walnut chairs, the
black-marble fireplace with the busts of Byron
and Tom Moore on either side of the antique
gilt clock on the mantel-shelf. In the mirror
of the bureau I could see myself, the same face
with dishevelled, curly hair I knew so well.
In my hand I held a bunch of tresses, tresses in
texture like spun-sugar. I took up the little
silver box with the letter *S.* on the lid, and

opened it. From it came an odor, the smell of the ancient forests in the Blockhouse Country. I carefully laid the lock of hair in it, and closed it again. After a wait of nearly twelve years the little box had come to its own. Everything is possible to him who will wait, and watch. Now when I travel I always take the little box with me. When I am home I give strict orders that no one will touch it, and that means no one must open it. It would make me happy but for the fear that some day the lock of spun-sugar hair will disappear as mysteriously as it came. I have just run over to the bureau and looked before finishing this story. It is still there. The story is not in vain. I hope it will remain inviolate unti' Sylvania shall cross my path again, and I compare it with her hair, and beg an explanation.

XV

THE CLOSED HOUSE

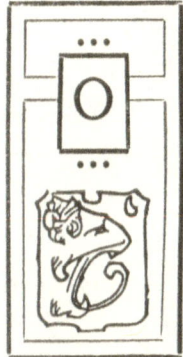

N the back street at Straubstown, on the lane next to the moun- tain, half hidden by wide- branching sugar maples stands a neatly painted white house. As all the houses on this street are frequently painted, in fact all the houses in the town reek with fresh paint, this neatly finished cottage would attract slight attention were it not that the shutters are always closed. When the painters come around every other year to give the house a new coat of white and the shutters a new coat of blue, the orders are that the shutters must be painted on the house and with- out opening them. The house is also noticeable from the numbers of little wooden birdhouses on the trees. These are always repainted when the house is done over. They are inhabited by a swarm of robins, bluebirds, and martens, who make the air sweet by their singing. Several

285

elderly ladies occupy the cottage, so the village
gossips say, but the one who owns it is never
seen outside the confines of her own room.
Grief over the death of her husband in the
Civil War is the cause ascribed by her relatives
and loyal friends for her complete retirement
from the world. This is a beautiful idea, and
places a halo of saintly devotion around the
old lady whom no one has seen in nearly fifty
years. But there are other people in the town
who say that an unfortunate love affair taking
place two years after the death of the soldier
husband is the real reason why she became a
recluse. One old man, who keeps the graveyard in order, is very fond of telling the story
to strangers. He can see the closed house from
where he works among the graves and monu-
ments. After he has pointed out the graves of
Indian fighters and revolutionary soldiers, or
of the woman who was buried just outside the
cemetery fence in 1864 because she was said to
be a witch, he will indicate with his sickle, the
closed house. After the visitor has observed it
for a minute he invariably says, " What do you
think of that house yonder?" If you give him

the slightest encouragement by saying, " Isn't
it queer-looking!" he will relate the story with
as much precision of detail as a guide on a
battlefield. The story generally runs like this:
I say " generally runs like this" because the old
man has told it in my hearing four or five
times, with amazingly little variation. " You
see that neatly painted house down the street?
The lady who lives there has never been out
of doors in forty-eight years, and the shutters,
except to have new slats put on occasionally,
haven't been opened in that time. People
around here like to say that she went into retirement because she lost her husband, who
was a gallant young officer, in the Civil War.
The young fellow was killed in 1862, and I can
take oath on it that the shutters were open for
over two years after that, until Christmas Eve,
1864. It isn't that our townspeople have
flexible memories, but there are very few alive
to-day who were old enough to understand
much as far back as '62. Those that were
know in their hearts what I say is true, but
they don't like to spread a scandal, so wink at
the ' dead husband' story. When she was mar

ried in October, 1860, this lady was accounted
the belle of the village. She was also the
wealthiest girl, as she had inherited three for-
tunes from bachelor uncles who died, and was
the heiress of her parents, who were both in-
dependently rich. The young man she married
was a college graduate, a promising law student, and also heir to considerable property. It
was uniting the two oldest and most influential
families in town, representatives of the old
Scotch-Irish Presbyterian autocracy. The
general run of people were pleased, but there
was considerable envy aroused. I remember
it well, as many thought the couple too well
blessed. They had good looks, money, family,
friends. Some of those who envied lacked all
four qualities. One old woman, who had talked
a lot before the wedding, was standing outside
the church after the ceremony, and ran up and
wished them bad luck all their lives. The
town constable put his hand over her mouth
before she had gotten the words fully out, and
many thought the happy couple did not hear it
at all. At least so most everybody hoped. The
wedding took place on a rainy day, a bad omen

generally admitted by educated and unedu
cated alike. During the wedding trip which
was taken in an elaborate carriage drawn by
two coal black horses, and driven by a colored
coachman in livery, the bride's father had the
cottage renovated, refurnished, and repainted.
He planted those maple trees in the front yard
and along the sidewalk, that Chinese sumach
by the kitchen door and those two honey-
locusts along the garden fence. He also set out
a Norway spruce; it grew higher than the
house, but was blown down on the fortieth
anniversary of the husband's death. They say
it almost shocked the lady to death; she wasn't
used to such loud noises. Young as he was,
the bridegroom took an active part in politics
and would have been nominated for the Legis-
lature if he hadn't gone to the war. In 1861,
before the outcome of the war was generally
conceded, he showed his patriotism by enlist-
ing. His father could have gotten him a commission at Harrisburg, but he preferred going
as a common private. But his appearance
was so much above the ordinary, that he was
soon singled out for a lieutenancy, and by the

beginning of 1862, he was a captain of artillery
on the Peninsula. He was highly commended
on several occasions, though he didn't seem to
have done much fighting. But the town was
proud of him. He held the highest rank of any
soldier who had gone to the front from this
locality, so there was talk of presenting him
with a sword when he came home on a furlough.
A subscription was being taken up when news
came of his untimely death, caused by the
bursting of a cannon during a practice drill.
Report had it, he had been blown to pieces. I
guess it was true, for they never opened the
coffin. We had to take for granted his remains
were in it. The burgess sent somebody to
Philadelphia in a hurry and a handsome sword
was bought. This was draped with crepe and
flowers and laid on the coffin. After the interment it was given to the widow. The widow
certainly showed a terrible amount of grief.
The old woman who had wished them bad luck
when they came out of the church after the
wedding was on hand in the same place at the
funeral. She tried to whisper to every one
how she had predicted the disaster. She be

came so boisterous that the same town constable had to lead her around to the back of the church and keep her there until after the services. Her ugly talk created more comment in the village than the ostentatious funeral. Every one said she was a witch and was a disgrace to the town. A month after the funeral the old woman died, and in the natural course of events would have been buried in this graveyard. The parents of the dead soldier and of his widow, although of a different denomination, had enough influence to block this. When it was rumored she was to be buried after night in the Potter's Field at the Poor Farm, some of the working class of people got together, and induced the old German who owned the cow-pasture by the cemetery to permit her burial there, just across the graveyard fence. Now the cow-pasture is pretty well built up and it won't be long before somebody's cellar will occupy the spot where this so-called witch's bones repose. Poor old creature, I wonder if she was in any way responsible for the ill-luck that followed the couple she cursed! The soldier's widow went on living very quietly in

her neat cottage. I saw her many times working with her flower-beds, or sitting knitting on
the back porch. People, even those who once
envied, pitied her now. She seemed so single-
minded, so devoted to her husband's memory.
She had an iron settee put near his grave in
the Presbyterian burial-ground and often sat
there on Sunday afternoons. It was a touch-
ing sight. But grief alone was not to be the
limit of her ill-fortune. One night in October,
1864, a carriage stopped in front of the cottage.
A strongly built man, with a closely-cropped
beard turning grey, got out. The colored
driver handed him a heavy portmanteau, and
drove away. Owing to the mud on the carriage, it had evidently come a long distance,
we surmised it to be a livery rig from another
county. The stranger, so the story goes, introduced himself to the widow, and said he had
been chaplain of the regiment to which her late
husband belonged. He had been the last person to speak to him before he had been blown
to atoms by a bursting cannon. He had admired the dead officer, and wanted to express
to the widow the esteem in which he had been

held by his companions in arms. All this
pleased her, especially as she had reached a
point when she was not insensible to masculine
charms. Those who saw the stranger said he
was not bad looking, and while he could look
one in the eye, he had a downcast look. This
was ascribed to the noble melancholy which
overspread his rare soul. He was such an interesting gentleman that he was invited to remain over night, and that led to his being urged
to stay a few days longer. Then he apparently
fell ill, and was in a critical state for days.
The fair young widow nursed him and the old
doctor, while declaring he couldn't make out
the nature of the disease from which the man
suffered, said he had never witnessed such devotion. It was the week before Christmas before the patient was able to be about the house.
He had had many sympathizers, among people
who never saw him, as he had his fond nurse
give instructions he was to see no one but the
doctor. His identity was the subject of considerable speculation, but of a favorable
nature, until a young soldier returned who
had served in the alleged chaplain's regiment.

' Your old chaplain's in town; he's sick at the
widow's cottage on Freedom Street.' The
young private was much surprised. ' We have
no old chaplain; the one we have now is the
same one we've always had.' To make sure he
wrote to a friend, who replied that the chaplain was there and had been on duty daily. He
couldn't be sick at Straubstown and on duty on
the Peninsula at the same time. It was not
a case of bi-location. The real chaplain was a
tall blonde and the one sick in Straubstown
was a stockily built brunette. The story of
the mysterious invalid got to the ears of the
Federal authorities and detectives were sent
to investigate. It was probably the first and
last time the detectives ever visited Straubstown. On the morning before Christmas the
widow sent out a dozen little notes written in
the copper-plate handwriting so popular in
those days, announcing to her intimate friends
that she was going to marry the estimable army
chaplain, and inviting them to come to the
house that evening to meet him. Her relatives, more particularly, and her friends were
shocked, but as she was twenty-five years old

they considered her old enough to suit herself. About a dozen persons dropped in that evening to meet the 'intended.' Some called out of regard for the bride-to-be, the rest out of cold curiosity. The young widow, dressed in white, looked very happy. The stranger was clerical enough in appearance to suit anyone. He had shaved off his mustache, and wore only a grayish beard. He looked all the world like a Methodist hierarch, although he claimed to be a Congregationalist. He could tell many stories of his work among sick and dying soldiers. He even told how President Lincoln once complimented him for his kind deeds. As he talked his fiancee gazed at him in speechless admiration. Cakes, candies, fruit, and coffee were passed around later in the evening. The future bride played the organ while the churchly-looking intended sang patriotic airs and hymns. In the midst of this song festival there was a loud pounding on the side door. The stranger stopped singing, and his face, always waxy pale, grew even whiter. The young widow jumped up from the bench and ran to the door, opening it. Before the company

stood six stalwart men, calm, slow of speech,
determined. Their leader stepped forward,
and in the presence of the roomful of guests
placed the stranger under arrest. The bride-
to-be swooned over a sofa, while some of the
men tried to induce the visitors to tell who
they were and on what grounds they made the
arrest. One guest, a former district attorney
of the county, had more influence than the rest,
so one of them told him the facts. The in-
truders were deputy U. S. marshals and detectives. The pretending army chaplain was
none other than Ludwig, the notorious mountain outlaw, wanted on a couple of dozen
charges ranging from murder and counter-
feiting, down to chicken stealing. With his
side-partner Consor, he had terrorized the Central Pennsylvania mountains for twenty years.
In October they had been brought to bay in
the Seven Mountains by a posse and Consor
was killed. Ludwig with his proverbial luck
had made his escape, but it was thought that
he, too, had been shot, and crawled into his
lair and died. As nothing had been heard of
him for nearly two months, he was counted as

dead, until the presence of a mysterious
stranger in Straubstown answering his description had been reported. He had sometimes worn a beard in the past, so was easily
recognized under his ministerial disguise. He
was hurried to Pittsburg and ultimately
hanged. The young widow, shorn of her hopes,
and humiliated before friends and the town,
took brain fever and came near dying. The
same doctor attended her who had looked after
the 'sick preacher,' but in this instance was
never in doubt as to the diagnosis. When she
was so low, all the shutters were ordered
closed. After she got better she directed that
they be left closed. This was done, and her
voluntary captivity began. Her parents tried
their best to get her to go out for a walk, but
they could do nothing with her. She vowed
she would never show her face again outside;
she who had been so proud, but had been so
mocked by Fate. The old woman who wished
her ill was dead; those who envied her were
now genuinely sorry; there were many who
loved her; she had no one to fear in all
Straubstown. But indoors she remained,

growing waxy-white, silent, severe, resembling so her servants state, the strange man she once agreed to marry. But they also say that her soldier husband's sword hangs over the mantel-shelf."

XVI.

THE GIANT HORSE - SHOE

 HILE traveling down on the Beech Creek Railway, on Number Thirty-six one windy March evening, at dusk, after the train left Peale, the conductor called my attention to the wonderful horse-shoe in the Black Moshannon, which flows three hundred feet below the tracks. I told him that I had always marvelled at and admired this great natural curiosity ever since my first ride on his line, on a sight-seeing tour as a school-boy fifteen years ago. Its perfect accuracy of dimensions stamped it as approaching the divine, rather than the natural. Being a stream in horse-shoe form it far exceeded in interest the " horse-shoe curve" on the main line of the Pennsylvania Railroad, or the one on the Tyrone and Clearfield division, where a carload of circus performers went to their death about seventeen years ago. Even the

little tips at the points of the horse-shoe are
carefully worked out in this horse-shoe of
Black Moshannon. And at dusk, as the train
flew by, the stream had assumed the hue of
silver, and it looked like a shoe from some
celestial steed imbedded in dark, brown, desolate earth. Beyond were the solemn brown
hills, some few still summit-fringed with pitch
pines, but all looking lonely, sad, oppressive.
The grey sky had a few lingering streaks of
silver in it; all was cold and wintry even
though the blue birds and robins had been
singing in the bare trees for a week past. It
was the proper hour to view the horse-shoe, and
judge its place in the scheme of nature. The
conductor and I were admiring it, when a
strange-looking, swarthy-complexioned individual, big and fleshy, leaned over and touched me
on the shoulder. I looked around, and he
apologized for disturbing me, but asked if I
cared to hear the legend of the giant horse-
shoe, which appeared to interest me so much.
I told him I would be delighted to hear it, as I
had long puzzled over its origin, so he began
his narrative. " You would hardly believe it,"

he said, " but that horse-shoe, according to the
Indians, is almost as old as man himself. Long
ages before there was any thought of creating
this world, there were two great spirits, brothers, self-existent, waiting, watching, and planning. Each felt that to perpetuate his existence he must create something, and make his
nature live on in varied forms. One of the
spirits, whom the Indians came to revere as
Gitchie-Manito, or the Creator, solved the question and willed the ball of this earth into being.
His infinite wisdom and skill that evolved such
a mighty orb out of chaos, puzzled and alarmed
his fellow-spirit Chit-ta-mic-co, the great ser-
pent, or evil one; but all he could bring into
light were a few stars, which fell through space
into the eternal void. The globe of our earth,
as it hung in space, balanced by celestial har-
monies, seemed so beautiful and complete, that
Gitchie - Manito sought to further enjoy the
pleasure of having created it by giving physical
form to his spiritual existence. Therefore, in
short order, a race of beings appeared which
were the physical complement to their Maker.
This further aroused the grief and envy of the

unsuccessful Chit-ta-mic-co.   Though he was
probably as great spiritually as Gitchie-Manito,
he seemed to lack his creative powers.   He had
failed dismally to will into being a world, but
he determined to create beings that would be
as beautiful as himself, compeers of the
physical manifestations of the identity of
Gitchie-Manito.   But   his   attempts   were
hideous failures.   Instead of seeing his spiritual image before him, he could only will into
existence the creatures which we now call
animals, birds, fishes and reptiles.   The best
he was able to do was to make apes of different
kinds, horrid gibbering travesties on the divine
attributes of man.   But Chit-ta-mic-co being a
beautiful spirit himself, was pained to see the
hideous horde that he had loosed upon the
earth.   And if he felt a loathing, the beings
who were created by Gitchie - Manito felt it
more so.   It was hard to reconcile them to their
animal companions.   They   tried   to   destroy
them whenever they could, regarding them in
their dumb, untutored way as caricatures of a
Grand Idea.   Some few kinds of beasts were
subjugated and put at cruel tasks, but the

majority were marked for slaughter whenever seen. This was contrary to the precepts of Gitchie-Manito, who sought to soften the hatred which welled up in the hearts of his creations for those of the unsuccessful God-Spirit Chit-ta-mic-co. One night Gitchie-Manito, being worn out with his labors and trials, slept. While he rested evil thoughts were brewing in the mind of Chit-ta-mic-co. He determined to undo all that Gitchie-Manito had evolved. He willed a flood, and lo, the banks of all the silver riband-like rivers that irrigated the world of his rival, overflowed their banks and threatened to annihilate every living thing. But the spirit and wisdom of Gitchie-Manito had poured freely into many of his beings, and out of gratitude to their Beginner were determined on self-preservation. They built rafts and floats, and many climbed aboard amid the rising waters and were saved. In recognition of the known desire of Gitchie-Manito they assisted aboard many of the animals and birds which were the handiwork of Chit-ta-mic-co. Some were too unwieldy and heavy, and these were pushed back into the frothing depths to perish.

When Gitchie - Manito awoke he saw the attempted ruin of his Great Thought. Looking
down with love on his world, and his creatures
and the surviving productions of Chit-ta-mic-co,
the waters receded and peace reigned on earth.
Then another thought crossed his celestial in-
tellect. He spoke to Chit-ta-mic-co and asked
if he felt sorry for what he had done, saying
that in return he cherished no rancor. ' Yes'
he replied, ' so sorry that I wish I could depart
to the uttermost bounds of space, and in the
gloom and despond eke out my repentance.'
Then Gitchie - Manito willed into existence a
giant creation, in form like a cross between a
dragon and a horse. ' Ride this, Brother, to
the furthest ends of all known things, if it is
your will, and begin your career anew.' The
animal was shod with steel so he could tread
without pain the fiery depths of seething underworlds through which he must travel, and the
thrice-defeated master spirit mounted him, and
away they flew into distances incalculable to the
mind of man. But once arrived at the uttermost end of things, Chit-ta-mic-co began re-
pining. He was foolish to have acknowledged

LOADING LOGS

Photo by W. T. Clarke

failure and gone off so meekly, especially
mounted on a steed of another's making. But
the all-seeing eye of Gitchie-Manito was generally upon him and he dreaded to cross blades
with him again. The world of Gitchie-Manito
was prospering—man was making the most of
his opportunities, and a spirit of tolerance still
existed extending even to many of the creations
of the absent Chit-ta-mic-co. Every one was
happy, even happier than before the deluge.
The loving-kindness of Gitchie-Manito loomed
large in his physical counterparts. From afar
he viewed them with a love parental. They
were a part of himself, yet each was so individual, such a separate entity. And one
bright day as he watched the comings and
goings of his children, like a child watches the
activities of an ant-hill, the Great Spirit slept.
Chit-ta-mic-co had long waited for this opportunity. He rose from the depths of his
gloomy retreat, beyond the underworlds, and
mounted his mammoth charger. He would
ride steel-shod over Gitchie-Manito's earth, and
completely wreck the Earthly Paradise. The
giant horse, though of Gitchie-Manito's creat-

ing, became rebellious and entered into Chit-
ta-mic-co's scheme. On they came, silent but
ominous, until their giant shadow hung like a
titanic storm-cloud above the earth. Just as
this huge steed sunk one giant hoof into the
soft brown earth, right in the track of one of
Gitchie-Manito's riband-like water-courses, the
slumbering Great Spirit awoke. With a look
that was calm but withering in its intensity he
stared at his unsuccessful Brother, now his
enemy. Chit-ta-mic-co quailed and quavered,
but the eyes of Gitchie-Manito were on him and
fly he must. He looked at the giant steed so
intently and with such an expression of disappointment that it took fright, and before
Chit-ta-mic-co could unhorse himself he was
carried off on a journey that would know no
finish, an endless galloping around the uttermost bounds of space. But the giant steed had
left a hoof-print deeply outlined in the soft
earth, and the riband-like watercourse flowed
through the depression, and took it as its own.
The world is going on much as it did in the
days of Gitchie-Manito's beginnings; the seeds

of unrest and evil sowed by Chit-ta-mic-co still exist, and man has not as yet wholly exterminated the animals, birds and reptiles of his creating. But Indian wise men, who claim to have been close to the great heart of Gitchie-Manito, say that some day he will call Chit-ta-mic-co to him, and forgive him, and on that day all sin and unhappiness will leave the earth. The world is surely growing better now. That makes us feel that some day, as suddenly as sunshine can pour forth after a storm, we will find ourselves living under changed conditions, where there will be room for nothing else but joy. Until then man is an unhappy wanderer, and insecure in life and destiny. Wouldn't it be wonderful if this change came to pass during our own generation?" It was dark outside and the gaslights threw weird shadows across our faces, when the stranger finished his narrative. The train, half an hour late, was rattling along on its rocky bed, and nearing Beech Creek Station. When it stopped there, he threw his great black cloak about him, bidding me a cheery " good-night," and descended into the night.   After he had gone the conductor asked me who was my strange friend, but I had never seen him before.   And he was no more strange than the legend he told me.

XVII.

TWO CRAZY MEN

E were walking one evening at sundown in the cut in the direction of M G Box when my companion tactfully drew my attention to the top of the steep bank, where stood gazing down on us, two strange specimens of humanity. Bushy of beard and pitifully shabby they were posed motionless, with hands in pockets, with expressions that betokened a lack of reasoning faculties. "Those are the two crazy men you have heard me speak about so much," she said. I returned their gaze as we passed along, and wondered what could have put two brothers, apparently sturdy and leading composed lives, out of their minds. "Would you like to hear the story of those two unfortunates?" asked my companion, after we were comfortably settled in the cozy box. I said that I would, and while the telegraph instruments were clicking away and the

309

river splashing below us and in the distant darkness, heavy freights plugging up the hill chugged to the tune of " ten-too-many, ten-too-many, ten-too-many," I was told the story of the two crazy men. " In the early eighties old Saul McCracken died, leaving his lumber business and a snug fortune to his two sons, Ebenezer and Ezekiel. Instead of moving into Andersonburg and buying fast horses and spending money, they determined to continue operating their father's timber lands, which lay on the big flats beyond the cut. They seemed satisfied with the old house, and kept it just as it was during their parent's life-time. They were industrious and shrewd, and the rise in the price of lumber soon brought them in a larger income than the poor old gentleman ever dreamed of in his lifetime. The Mc Crackens were good-looking young men, and wore, according to the style of thirty years ago, black beards that reached to their waists. Of these they were very proud. They had no other vanities. In a shanty by a large spring a mile back on the flat lived Samuel Atter, whom the McCrackens called their " right hand

man." He was boss in the woods, blacksmith,
wheelwright, road-builder, horse-buyer and performed a dozen other jobs for his doting em-
ployers. Samuel had a wife and a number of
children, but all were married and living in
various places, except one daughter, Christine.
This unmarried daughter was counted a beauty,
and being the youngest was greatly indulged by
her parents. The McCracken brothers watched
her grow up, and often jokingly told her father
that when she was old enough they would find
her a rich husband. The little girl used to
listen to these remarks, and they made a deep
impression on her childish mind. A wealthy
husband seemed to be the thing she was intended for, and when on winter evenings
around the stove her father and mother, together with some of the loggers and skidders,
discussed the wealth of the McCrackens, she
made up her mind that she ought to marry
one of the rich men who lived practically at
her door. She had a lot of intuition, and to
get one of these rich men she determined to be
nice to both. She was ready to bring out
chairs for them when they came to talk busi-

ness to her father, and would stand at a respectful distance, leaning against one of the
uprights of the porch, eyeing them intently as
they gave their orders and stroked their long
black beards. Often she would appear at the
McCracken home, and volunteer to do housework or cooking. Her services were gladly
accepted, and she had clear sailing, as the two
bachelors would never employ a housekeeper.
It was a relief to have some one put their
desks and bookcases to rights, and cook their
ham and eggs. Sometimes she would overhear
them say they wanted some trifle at the store,
or expected a letter, and no matter how muddy
the roads, she would run to the village, nearly
a mile distant, and carry out their errands.
Several times they offered to make her presents
of money. Christine always refused. She
wanted the money badly enough, but she
wished most to pretend she was disinterested.
She was playing for bigger stakes. Despite
her interest in the McCrackens, she had time
to cultivate a more or less sordid romance
with a young English miner at Glen Yarrick.
She was so sly that her parents never realized

how much time she was spending with the McCrackens, and the rich brothers could not see how she would have time to be meeting a lover. 'Christine's a good girl,' they would say to one another, in their rare lapses into conversation. 'She never bothers with the boys; she's what you call a sensible girl.' She was, if sensible means consistent interest in one's own advancement. When Christine was nearly twenty, and was nearly worn out with waiting, Ebenezer McCracken began courting her. He was forty at the time, but looked older, as his black beard was beginning to be streaked with grey. It was a rude, homely courtship, but it was brief, once it got started, and in three months after the first words of love were said a heavy carryall, containing the McCracken brothers, Samuel Atter, his wife, Christine, and a driver, ploughed its way through the slushy roads to the county seat, where a license was taken out. That afternoon, at the Presbyterian parsonage, Christine Atter, 20, became the wife of Ebenezer McCracken, 40. There was no wedding trip. The festivities were slight. The same

carryall load plus Rev. McNamee, the Presbyterian clergyman, returned to the McCracken
home, where a supper was served, partaken of
by the wedding party, some of Christine's married brothers and sisters, and a few of the
neighbors. The newly married couple took up
their abode in the old homestead, where they
came after the ceremony, and Ezekiel elected
to also remain there. A German woman was
engaged to do the rough work — Christine's
strength was not to be overtaxed. As far as
the neighborhood knew, Christine did no
other work than to cultivate a bed of
carnations. But Christine's artfulness was
still in the expanding stage. She was
continually asking her husband for twenty-
dollar gold - pieces; she was collecting them
she said. These she hid in a tin-bucket under
some rocks back of the spring house. Ebenezer
was bountiful towards her; he always gave
her twice as many gold-pieces as she asked for.
She told him that Ezekiel was close, and might
disapprove of all this liberality; it would be
best not to tell him. Ebenezer felt rather
ashamed himself that he was giving so much

gold to his child-wife, so he was only too glad to keep it from his brother. While this was going on Christine was clandestinely meeting Ezekiel in the woods and telling him that she loved him ever so much better than Ebenezer; she was so sorry he had not asked her to marry him. Ezekiel was touched at this exposition of his charms, and gave her a twenty-dollar gold-piece every time he heard it. Naturally he did not tell what he was doing to brother Ebenezer. Christine put the money she was getting from Ezekiel in a bucket under some rocks back of the spring house, in the same place where she put her ill-gotten gains from Ebenezer. One evening Ebenezer had forgotten to give an order to his factotum, Samuel Atter, and started through the woods by a short cut to that worthy's shanty. In the depths of the hemlock tangles he came upon Christine and Ezekiel. He could scarcely believe his eyes. They were not ghosts; they were the real persons. But it seemed inconceivable to look upon the staid Ezekiel with his arms around Christine, and kissing her on the mouth. He walked up so quietly that they

did not know of his presence, until he slapped
Ezekiel on the back heavily, shouting, "Robbers; you have robbed me of my happiness."
The guilty pair took the discovery very un-
concernedly. Christine made no attempt at
explanations at all. Ezekiel struck a defiant
attitude, and told his brother that Christine
had found out that she loved him better than
her lawful spouse; it was a great tragedy, but
true love could not be repressed. Ebenezer
burst into tears; he loved Christine and
Ezekiel; it was hard to hate them after learn-
ing the awful truth. Ezekiel kept saying that
'Providence hath ordained that Christine and
I should love one another,' and other high-
flown sentiments too much on the jellyfish
order to perpetuate in this story. When he
had justified himself to his own satisfaction,
the trio returned to the McCracken homestead
Indian file, with Christine between. Night
was coming on, and as they entered the house
Christine suggested that Ebenezer and Ezekiel
adjourn to the library and talk the matter over
while she helped the German woman get supper. It was to be a serious talk, and both

brothers waxed eloquent before the 'Rock Oak' stove. The German woman knocked on the door at half-past six; it was then half an hour after the regular supper hour, but the brothers shouted out angrily, 'Let us be alone.' She knocked again at half-past seven, when they called to her they would come out when they were good and ready, and not a minute sooner. The German woman knew their violent tempers, and concluded to let them alone. At midnight they emerged from their retreat; the problem had been solved. Ebenezer would allow Christine to get a divorce, and she would marry her soul-match, Ezekiel. The estate would be divided, and the newly-mated pair depart for the West. When they emerged, with faces twisted to resemble martyrs, they saw the German woman dozing, her head on the dining-room table. The lamp was nearly burned out. The supper was unpalatably cold. 'Christine, Christine,' both brothers called in close harmony. Christine did not answer, but the German woman awoke. 'Where's Christine?' the brothers chorused. 'Dot I can't say,' replied the German woman lethargically. 'She vas out back of der spring house shust ven you'ins began your conferinks, but she neffer come back.' The brothers looked at one another. Their interview, lasting six hours, had turned from tragedy to farce. They were soon on the trail, although they wanted to make themselves believe that Christine had merely gone to her parents' house while her husband and his brother settled the momentous question. Lanterns were lit, and the brothers, in Indian file and supperless, started along the forest path to the home of Samuel Atter. They found the house in darkness; it took half an hour to rouse the inmates. Christine wasn't there, and her family said they hadn't seen her. The brothers then declared she must have been lost or met with foul play in the woods. They tried to organize a search party, but the Atter household refused to join it. 'Christine will turn up in the morning,' said old Atter, as he shut the kitchen door in the faces of his benefactors. The brothers were too crestfallen to attempt a search by themselves, and returned to their home, and spent the night, taciturn and mopey.

around the stove in their library. In the morning they summoned up courage to go on a search, but they only got as far as the Atter residence. Old Atter came out shaking his head. 'Too, too bad, gentlemen; I hear some bad news about my girl. The boys over to the mines at Glen Yarrick saw Ethelbert Derham, that English miner, and Christine get on the night passenger train bound East. They had some heavy bundles with them, and they seemed excited. There's no doubt of it, as a dozen saw them, who knew them both well.' A shudder went through the sturdy frames of Ebenezer and Ezekiel McCracken. Their naturally pale faces assumed the greenness of death. Members of the Atter family say they would have fallen had not persons supported them. When they recovered their equilibrium both brothers broke down and wept like children. Then arm-in-arm they made off with staggering steps in the direction of their mansion. They must have talked money matters on the way back, for the next week they advertised a sale of their farm stock, and closed down the lumber operations. The German

woman was discharged, as was the hired man,
and they began to do all their own work. The
neighbors surmised that each had impoverished
himself with gifts to the artful Christine. After
the fact became known that the McCrackens
were no longer wealthy, Samuel Atter openly
approved of his daughter's elopement with the
English miner. However, she never came back,
but her parents got letters from her, somewhere
in the coal fields of Kentucky, where Ethelbert
Derham blossomed out as an operator on a
large scale. Gradually the McCrackens kept
more and more to themselves. Naturally un-
sociable, their lack of money made them more
shunned than ever. They made no effort to
seek people, and the public left them severely
alone. Those who saw them said they were
losing their minds. But they never got violent,
and the neighbors were so indifferent that they
never sought to have them incarcerated in an
asylum. And so they go about, like poor,
singed moths, friendless and helpless. They
are pointed out to strangers as ' the two crazy
men.' No one ever gives them a kind word
or a helping hand. They have never had an

open sympathizer for their heart wounds. They still work over the missing Christine's carnation bed. They bestow on it a world of loving care. It is the memento of happy days which they imagined were real."

XVII.

THE SECTION HOUSE ON THE HILL

EDNA GALBRAITH had not seen Clyde Bowler for fully two years before her marriage to Elmer Bantz. The parting between the young couple had been stormy, as she had intercepted a letter he had written making an appointment to meet another girl. As this was about the hundredth time she had accused him, and generally correctly, of unfaithfulness, it seemed time to break off an affair that had ceased to be a romance. But Edna had not done it without many misgivings. Again and again she was on the point of writing him to come back and all would be forgiven, but her self-respect rebelled. Edna was the prettiest waitress in the Waters House, the toast of a legion of travelling men, while Clyde was connected with the construction company putting in the new county bridge across the river. He had lived at the hotel for

six months. during which time his interest in
Edna had gone on, ever since the first night
at supper when she had brought in his ice
water and butter, and asked him for his order.
Some of the other girls to whom she confided
her troubles said they believed he wanted to
break with her before leaving; that was why
his conduct with other women had become so
audacious.   But this only aroused Edna's
anger; she didn't speak to the girls who said
this for three days. " She still loves him,"
they whispered among themselves. The fact
remained that Clyde left the day after the
quarrel, looking not at all unhappy.   Edna
looked very pale when she served his last meal
in silence, without even a word of the chaff
that had usually gone on between them. She
dropped forks and spoons several times, and
altogether made a very forlorn appearance.
Edna was a tall, striking-looking, graceful girl,
a regular grenadier of a girl; had she lived in
a great city, she would have become a noted
cloak model. Many travelling men told her
this, but her thin lips smiled incredulously.
Her hair was jetty black, and worn parted in

the middle and fluffed at the sides. She had black eyes, rather small perhaps, but redeemed by arched black eyebrows and long black lashes. While her complexion was naturally pale, there was sometimes a faint flush in the cheeks. Her arched nose turned up just a trifle at the end, which meant that she could never look old. She rarely smiled, and when she did it was a smile of incredulity like when travelling men would say she ought to go to Philadelphia and become a noted cloak model. An actor told her that she had the features of Louise Homer and the expression and figure of Ethel Barrymore, whatever that might mean. Why she fancied Clyde Bowler out of a dining-room full of more or less attractive men was a mystery to her friends. He was a short man, squat, and bow-legged, with arms unnaturally long. He had rather full brown eyes, that were never at rest. You could not catch his eye for "a fraction of a second," using one of Edna's favorite terms. His dark brown hair was inclined to wave; it was probably the best looking thing to him. In disposition he was flippant, and pert; he liked to tease, was cruel,

selfish and ofttimes sullen. Edna sometimes
thought it was these frequent alterations of
mood that made her like him. He was not
generally polite or generally impolite, like most
of the men she served. Sometimes he would
tease her and keep laughing during the meal;
on other occasions he would be glum and never
say a word. He never paid her a compliment
in the six months he lived at the hotel;
he never gave her a present, he never mentioned marriage. And yet she loved him
to distraction. He seemed to wield a strange
hypnotic influence over her. The other
waitresses professed to be afraid of him; the
other regular guests disliked him. Edna said
the other waitresses and guests were jealous.
There was no cause for this, as he certainly did
not act like a lover; if there were any advances,
they were all made by Edna. Though she professed to be happy, the six months' love affair
with Clyde almost broke her down nervously.
He delighted in making her jealous, to " take
her down" when others were present, to brow-
beat and insult her. He liked to show his
power over her as a blacksnake does before
swallowing a robin. Edna was in reality un-

happy when she was with him, and unhappier
when she was away from him. He would sometimes sit through supper without saying a
word, look at his watch and jump up quickly
saying, " I'll be late for my date," and hurry
from the dining-room. Edna would be heart-
broken; she always imagined he was going to
meet another girl. Invariably next day some
one would tell her of seeing Clyde out driving
or at a picture show with a girl. Of course
he never took *her* driving, or to shows; he
merely kept her as his subjugated plaything.
Edna was probably a weak girl, but more probably very much infatuated. Often the manager
of the hotel scolded her for inattention to other
guests; she was looking at or thinking about
Clyde all the time. She hated other men.
Sometimes they would ask her to correspond
with them; she would flounce out of the room
and say to the other girls, " The idea of that
fresh fellow wanting me to write him." Other
men's smiles were to her insults. After Clyde
left the other guests breathed easily. Edna
was so ravishingly lovely that they tolerated
her incivilities; another girl would have been

" reported" a score of times. Edna had other troubles besides her love affair. Her mother was dead. She boarded with an aunt by marriage, who was disagreeable and secretly disliked her. Her father also boarded there when he was in town. He drove a team in the woods; his visits to Youngmanstown were principally when he lost his job, or felt an irresistible desire for a spree. He had been a good-looking man in his day, but was now a battered bulk of his former self. The aunt occasionally took in other boarders, and the week before Edna's break with Clyde had rented a room to Elmer Bantz, the new section boss. Elmer was a clean-cut young fellow, with brown hair and blue eyes, tall, lithe and powerful. If he had been born nearer civilization than in the wilds of the Seven Mountains, and had gotten an education, he might have some day filled an important position on the railroad. As it was, he had the " prize" section, and was highly esteemed by his superiors. Despite her break with Clyde, Edna had utterly ignored the young man's presence in the house. She contrived to go nearly a week

without being introduced, as they ate at different hours, although they often ran into one
another on the stairs and in the yard. Their
rooms adjoined, but a thin partition of lath
and plaster separated their beds when they
slept. When they were presented, Edna gave
him a curt bow, which cut the young fellow to
the quick. But there were long months ahead,
and eventually a friendship sprung up between
them. It wasn't tempestuous or exciting, but
Edna admitted that Elmer was kind and she
respected him. But still he belonged to that
class of men whom women call " unattractive,"
and if he made a proposal of marriage, would
have to wait for an answer. Many of the
so-called " attractive men" do not propose at
all; they take for granted they are accepted
from the start. Elmer, like many of his type,
was generous, seeking by gifts to make up for
the lack of that intangible " charm" which
women look for in men. He took Edna to
shows, and for drives, and gave her candy,
fruit, and even pieces of inexpensive jewelry.
He proposed marriage, but was not given any
encouragement. Still he was in love for the

first time in his life, although he was past twenty-eight, and he could not realize such a thing as defeat. It was probably a year after he had first mentioned the subject that Edna accepted him. It came suddenly. He had taken her to the Grangers' Picnic at Centre Hall, and they had a delightful day together. Elmer was at his best; the good that was in him seemed magnified that day to such an extent that he barely missed being attractive. Edna never looked so pretty—her eyes were their blackest and snappiest, her complexion the whitest, her nose haughtiest and most clean-cut. It was one of those crisp September days with northwest winds, days of accomplishment and progress. The breezes were impregnated with the life-giving qualities of the pine-covered mountains. On the special train which ran down the valley that evening Elmer and Edna lay back in their seat, a trifle dusty and foot-sore, but in more complete harmony than they had ever been before. Had Edna been able to feel in *rapport* with the young section boss previous to this, his entreaties would have received favorable answer.

It must have been the northwest winds, or the
golden hour that did it. The train was passing
through the stretch of original forest, inky
black with its tangle of pine, hemlock and
rhododendron, that lies between Zerby and
Coburn, when Elmer looked around and whispered his love story to Edna. The sun was
hidden by the forest depths; it was like an
arboreal tunnel, a labyrinth for lovers. Time
and place were working in unison with the
calm in the girl's soul. She wanted something
definite in her career. She accepted him.
And for a few hours thereafter probably loved
him sincerely. Those few hours of genuine
affection to a man who had never stopped long
enough to find out what it was to be loved
were enough to store Elmer with happiness to
last for the balance of his days. He was not
to know much more. Edna was seen with him
constantly after that, but she never acted quite
as nicely again as she did that evening coming
back from the Granger's Picnic. She had secured her "something definite" in life; it
wasn't exactly her ideal, consequently she
couldn't be expected to treat it as such. But

she was dutiful. She never noticed another
man, was even more indifferent to the travelling men than in the days when Clyde Bowler
boarded at the Waters House. One morning
when she came to work she found a letter addressed to her stuck up on the sink in the
pantry. It was in a small, screwed, feminine
hand. She didn't recognize it at first, nor the
post-mark, Akron, Ohio. Many travelling men
learned her name and wrote her letters or
cards; this might be from one of these. Before
she opened it, however, she scrutinized the
handwriting; it was from Clyde Bowler. What
could he be writing about? She tore it open;
it was only a short note. He never wrote
much, though he got letters sometimes of forty
pages from girls whose hearts he had broken.
In this letter he said he had heard that Edna
was to get married; he was sorry to hear this,
as he imagined that despite their little difference in the past, she still cared for him alone.
He hoped she would write to him occasionally,
even if she did get married; he would come
to see her if he ever got to Youngmanstown.
Edna did not know whether to be pleased or

hurt. The former lover seemed to be displaying a proprietary interest in her which she
resented; yet it was Clyde, the only Clyde.
She should have thrown the letter in the stove,
but instead hid it in her dress. She served
breakfast in a state of daze. She spilt a cup
of hot cocoa in a Baptist clergyman's lap,
scalding his thighs, which resulted in a calling-
down from the head-waitress when the dining-
room doors were shut. Returning home she
put the letter in her bureau-drawer under some
petticoats. It worried her to have it there.
Her conscience urged her to burn it, but perverse elements in her stayed her hand. She
compromised, she thought, with conscience
when she took the letter out of her own bureau
and put it in a drawer of a bureau in a vacant
room, sometimes let to boarders. That evening when Elmer came home he brought a young
man with him. This youth was to take charge
of his section after his marriage, as he, Elmer,
was promised the section below town, which
carried with it the new section house on the
hill. Elmer was showing him around the
house, so he might have a choice of rooms when

they happened into the one where Edna had
secreted her unwholesome letter. Mechanically
he pulled open the drawers of the empty bureau. He saw the letter addressed to his sweetheart. His first thought was that it was from
one of her girl friends or relatives, so did not
glance at it a second time. The handwriting
being feminine, he was deceived. When his
friend, after selecting a room, which happened
to be his old room, had gone, Elmer began
thinking about the letter. What was it doing
upstairs in the drawer of that bureau in that
empty room? He tried to fight his doubts,
but failed. He ran up the stairs, his heart
beating, hoping against hope that his fears
were unjust. He opened it. " Dearest Edna,"
it began. He read the letter with mingled
disgust and anger. " Lovingly yours, Clyde,"
it ended. Some other man had a hold on a
corner of his fiancee's heart—he was not to
have it all. He put it back in the drawer, and
tottered downstairs. At first he decided to
demand an explanation from Edna when she
returned. He was naturally peaceable and
reticent, and Edna being the one woman in the

world for him, and being fearful of losing her, he remained silent. She noticed that he was more than usually quiet and undemonstrative, and asked him the reason. He told her that one of his men had been killed by the west-bound passenger train the week before; it grieved him whenever he thought of the widow and five little ones left behind. He continued to love, yet it wasn't the love of old. Duty was largely its context, pride its other component. Edna was a girl who thrived on love. If Elmer had told her of his discovery, there might have been a few sharp words, ending by the girl's tearful apologies, for at this stage she meant no harm. She could not help but see that Elmer was more distant, and instead of questioning him, retaliated by being more reserved herself. By the time of the wedding, they acted towards one another as if they had been married ten years. Elmer had good friends, and easily obtained the passes and permission to take a wedding trip. Harris-burg—to see the new State Capitol—was the first point of interest visited; then Philadel-phia, then Atlantic City. The bridegroom was liberal and thoughtful on the trip; he saw that she missed nothing; he made her many little gifts. But loverlike qualities were more absent than ever; finding that letter had shrivelled his passion like tobacco in a drying room. Not being completely happy, Edna came home with very little to tell about. We only notice things when we are happy, or when some one is with us who makes us happy. On trips when we see things we admire we know what person we care for most; that is the person we always wish was along to help enjoy what seems wonderful to us. The young couple moved into the section house, which had been comfortably furnished. Elmer's mother and sisters, and Edna's aunt and father, as well as several of her cousins were on hand to greet them. The supervisor, a kindly, simple man, sent them a Billiken with a card attached wishing them good luck. This was put on the dresser in the dining-room. Every one seemed happier than the bridal pair; but nothing was noticed. The section house stood on a hill above the tracks. It was a two-story and a half affair, of conventional design, and painted

the conventional drab. It had a garden connected with it, and there were several sickly
maple saplings growing in the front yard. A
flight of wooden steps ran down the hill to the
highway, and the tracks. In the distance, beyond the fertile stretches of White Deer Hole
Valley, rose the camel-backed ranges of pine-
crested Cochnehaw Mountains. But Edna was
industrious and set out to make the best of
conditions. Love, a very necessary occupant
of every home of married people, was missing;
it would take a lot of very hard work to forget
its absence. If she had been willing to have
children that might have redeemed the union.
But she wanted no children. When Elmer
came home from work he was assured of a
tolerably cordial greeting. He was thankful
for one thing; Edna, though undemonstrative,
was no complainer. It was another case of
" the heart knoweth its own bitterness" on both
sides. As she got her household duties regulated, Edna came to have more time to herself.
She often walked to town, three-quarters of a
mile away, where she made purchases, or called
to see her aunt and other relatives. Once or

LAST RAFT IN WEST BRANCH, 1912

Photo by Fred Miller, Karthaus, Pa.

twice she dropped in at the hotel, to speak to
her old comrades in the dining-room. Elmer
could see her from where he superintended his
men on the tracks, as she walked to and from
town; he wondered why she went so frequently.
Once or twice when the morning sun beat down
on his head ferociously, he would think of that
letter, and wonder where it was *now*. In the
excitement of getting married, he had neglected to look in that empty bureau before
leaving the house. One Sunday they went to
spend the day with Edna's aunt, and Elmer
slipped upstairs and into the unoccupied room.
He pulled open the drawer with feverish haste.
The letter was gone. He was wild with an-
guish, and could only restrain himself from
shouting out his grief by the thought that the
room had been cleaned subsequently and the
letter probably thrown out. He was not aware
that when women once treasure an object, they
preserve it to the end. After this incident
Elmer was more reserved, more dubious than
ever. One morning he saw a short, broad-
shouldered, long-armed man marching along
the highway in the direction of his home. The

weather was hot, and he had removed his derby
hat, coat and vest. Even then he would stop
every hundred yards or so and mop his brow.
" He must be an agent of some kind; what
else would send a dressy chap like that out
here on such a day?" remarked the boss, to
one of his men. He was seen going in the
house, as near as Elmer could figure it out,
at about ten o'clock. It was half-past one
when they saw him wending his way down the
road in the direction of Derrstown. Evidently
he was an agent moving on towards the next
town; but why did he stay so long in that one
house? " Must have some new-fangled sewing machine," said one of the hands, jocosely.
It was the longest afternoon for Elmer that he
had ever put in. When he got home, he re
solved he would not ask Edna about her caller;
he'd wait to see what she had to say. But he
couldn't contain himself; he was scarcely inside the door when he asked her who she'd been
entertaining so long. She hesitated a half
minute, as if trying to think up a falsehood,
but couldn't, and faltered, " Why, it was only
Clyde Bowler, an old friend of mine; he used

to board at the hotel; he's been in Ohio for
two years." She need not have been so ex-
plicit; Elmer knew enough when he heard the
first name. He compressed his lips; he would
not speak his thoughts. Had his wife been
corresponding with that old lover, or what
brought him to their home? This and other
sinister misgivings were choked still-born in
his throat. The evening passed on prosaically
as many others had; husband and wife retired
together. Edna slept, but Elmer tossed and
rolled, while his burning soul consumed itself.
Days passed; Edna occasionally went to town,
but no signs were seen of the gorilla-like little
stranger. Elmer belonged to several lodges
in Youngmanstown, which took him to meetings sometimes three nights a week. He
usually left home immediately after supper,
and would not return until midnight. In his
absence Edna read cheap novels, and then went
to bed. At least that had been her custom.
But subsequent to the initial visit of Clyde
Bowler, she began receiving visits from him on
nights when Elmer was away. He had left his
position in Ohio, and temporarily was doing

nothing. He boarded with friends at Derrstown, and slept most of the time, except when
being entertained by Edna. She gave him a
schedule of nights when her husband was generally absent, but to make sure she would set
a lighted lamp in the kitchen window as a
signal that " the coast was clear." Clyde,
secreted in a grove of white oaks, would hurry
across the common when the signal was flashed
to him. At first he pretended to come in the
guise of an old friend and advisor. Edna, of
course, confided her loneliness, her unhappiness, the disappointments of her married life.
From friend and advisor Clyde assumed the
role of consoler, at which he was adept. On
the third visit the misguided young wife confessed her undying love for him; he had her in
his power again; he was her proprietor.
Wildly infatuated, she would have done anything to see him often; she began inventing
excuses to send her husband to town at night.
There were not any near neighbors, but there
was a house or two near the oak wood where
Clyde hid himself. The occupants noticed a
man running across the common at night, and

into the back door of Elmer Bantz's home, like
some hyena hunting carrion. If they were be-
lated, they often met this man, with a cap
drawn over his eyes, tramping along the road
towards Derrstown close to midnight. Clyde
" loved" Edna less now than he did three years
before when he boarded at the Waters House.
He was older and more hardened. He only
went to see her for the sport of turning her
from her husband, and for the pleasure of having another man's lawful wife madly enamored
with him. He wouldn't marry her if the husband found out; oh, no, not he. He would
have the joke on both wife and husband then.
These were samples of his thoughts as he
tramped the midnight roads to Derrstown.
One black October night while Elmer was helping to clean up after a freight wreck, Edna
and Clyde were together in an ecstasy of one-
sided love. The girl was stroking his hair and
eyebrows, and kissing him, and calling him
extravagant " pet" names, when there came
loud knocks at the kitchen door. They were determined, dismal knocks. Edna hated to go
to the door; she was so happy making love to

her betrayer. The knocking continued, she
must go. "Stay here, darling one," she whispered, giving him a final kiss, "and if it's
trouble I'll turn the knob of the sitting-room
door, and you can slip out the front door."
She had kicked off her Oxfords, and slipped to
the door in her stocking feet. She opened the
door, and peered out anxiously. Two tall men,
very pale, and with eyes quivering, stood before
her. She recognized them as a couple of
Elmer's section hands. When they saw her
they took off their hats, and came into the
kitchen without saying a word. Edna turned
up the lamp which sat on the window sill. The
men stroked their hats, their vests, their mus-
taches; their silence was oppressive, ominous.
At length one of them said bluntly, "Mrs.
Bantz, I'm terribly sorry to tell you that your
husband's been hurt to-night." Then the other
man said, "He was hit by a special containing
some officials as he was coming across the
tracks from the tool-house." "They're going
to take him to the hospital at Derrstown, but
the doctors are afraid he can't recover." Edna
was sitting in a heavy kitchen chair speechless,

petrified. She jumped up screaming, " My
Heavens, my Heavens, he's dead, he's dead."
Then she turned and ran into the front
room, turning the key after her. Clyde
was lolling, partly asleep, on the Davenport
where she had left him. When she came in he
gazed at her half smilingly with his restless,
shifty eyes. " Elmer's dead; Elmer's dead;
give me your help and sympathy," said Edna
in a half whisper. " You must never leave me
now." The little man got up from the Davenport and stretched his long, gorilla-like arms.
" Give you help and sympathy; never leave
you; what's that? Who do you think you are?
You're a fool if you think you'll get it from
me. I'm no charity organization. You can't
make a mark out of me." Edna gazed at him
in amazement. He found his hat and coolly
went out the front door, disappearing into the
night. Edna fell, face downwards, on the
Davenport in a faint, her black skirts tumbled
about her in charming disarray. The two
stolid section hands waiting in the kitchen let
ten minutes on the loud-ticking clock go by.
Then they called through the door, but there

was no response.   Putting their weight against
the flimsy woodwork it gave way.   The lamp
had almost burned out, but they could see
Edna lying senseless on the sofa. " Run, quick,
Bill, and get some cold water," said one of
the men.

XIX.

AN ETERNAL FEUD

 RECALL very well when I read the simple paragraph in the *Democrat* stating that Patrick Niles, a woodsman, had been badly crushed by a falling log, while working on Mosquito Creek, and had been taken to the Williamsport Hospital. The following day when I met John Dyce while walking to McElhattan Springs, he opened his pocket-book and took out the clipping about this accident to Patrick Niles. He asked me if I had seen it, to which I replied " yes," adding that I hoped the poor fellow would recover. The old hunter shook his head, and said that " he feared it was all over with him, as he was the third in a link of remarkable coincidences." I probably owe more of my respect for the supernatural to John Dyce than any one else, as he took such a human view of it that it was never uncanny. Of Highlander and

Scotch-Irish ancestry, he was well fitted to
chronicle the mysteries of the mountains. We
proceeded to the Springs, where we sat on a
bench, and the story was told as follows: " In
the early years of the Nineteenth Century the
Niles family occupied a respectable homestead
in County Derry, Ireland. The head of the
family was Patrick Niles, a sturdy, old-fashioned Presbyterian. His ancestors were
among Cromwell's importations into the Emer-
ald Isle, and how his parents came to give him
the name of Patrick, when they hated everything Irish, is more than I can say. There is
a beautiful fishing stream in Derry called the
Swatragh. Among the first Scotch-Irish to
settle in Pennsylvania came from along its
banks, and they named the pretty stream in
Lancaster County, which now goes by the name
of Swatara, after it. The Niles homestead was
on a hill at the edge of a meadow, not far from
where a lane forded the Swatragh; the place
was known as Niles' Ford. Patrick Niles
often went to market and to fairs, and one
evening, just before sundown, his family saw
him standing on the opposite side of the ford.

He was a temperate man, so they could not
imagine why he would tarry so long, and not
cross on the footbridge which spanned the
stream directly below the house. He stood so
rigid and motionless that they feared that he
was ill, so one of his sons, a boy named Isaac,
called to him. There was no answer, so he
ran down the hill and along the stream in the
direction of his father. As he drew near, the
figure smiled and then seemed to diminish and
grow smaller, and when he reached the spot
where he had stood, no signs of him were to be
seen. Thoroughly alarmed, the boy looked back
in the direction of the homestead; he could
see his mother and sisters running about the
yard in a state of the wildest excitement. Evidently they, too, had seen the figure fade out
of sight. Isaac surveyed the ground carefully,
but couldn't find a footprint to prove that his
father had actually been there. He returned
to the house, where his family stated that they
had been watching from the yard, and had seen
the entire phenomenon. They confirmed his
view of it, that when he had approached, the
figure's face lit up with a smile, then gradually

faded out of sight. 'Father will think we've all gone crazy when we tell him this after he gets home,' said the youngest daughter, Mary. 'I'm afraid we'll never see him again alive,' said the mother, who knew a few of the old-time *tokens*. Patrick Niles did not return that night. The boys went to the adjoining villages the next morning, but there was no one who remembered having seen him. That afternoon two constables came to the homestead to tell the sorrowful news that the dead body of Niles had been found back of a stone wall, with several stab-wounds in the abdomen. A large quantity of money was found in his pockets; he had not been murdered by robbers. From the looks of the body, the unfortunate man had evidently been killed late the afternoon previously. In other words, about the time when his shade or double had appeared to his family on the opposite side of the ford. There were no signs of a scuffle on the road; he had evidently been stabbed quickly before he could defend himself, and his body hidden out of sight. No trace of the culprit was ever found, although the case attracted great attention at the time. Patrick Niles did not leave his family in very good circumstances, so the wife decided to emigrate to the United States with her five children. Besides, the horrible details of their father's death made them want to get away as far as possible from the old scenes. They settled for a time in Philadelphia, but city life was not congenial to any of them. They heard of a tract of timber land that was susceptable of cultivation on the Sinnemahoning, and all moved into the wilderness. It was not long before they became influential residents. Isaac grew to manhood, a fine, athletic-looking fellow, and married a daughter of one of the old-time settlers in the Sinnemahoning country. He became interested in lumbering and rafting, and accumulated quite a snug little competence. He was one of the first men I met when I took to following the river, and he invited me to stop at his home. At that time he had taken up a large tract of original pine on Mosquito Creek, and every spring sent a fleet of rafts to Marietta. He was one of the pioneers of rafting, and made money out of it before it was overdone. The great disappointment of his life was that he had no children. He made a great deal of all the young people, and when he met me on Mosquito Creek getting out a raft of spars, he couldn't do enough for me. He had an adopted daughter, Daisy Plunkett, a pretty red-haired girl, who was greatly admired by all the young woodsmen, but she didn't seem inclined to marry any of them. She was in love with a young half-breed Indian, it was said. We never saw him, but it was reported that she used to meet him somewhere in the mountains. I used to wonder why, if she was so much in love with him, that she didn't elope. When I got to know the half-breeds better I understood all right. While they were agreeable and some of them good-looking, they wouldn't work, and would rather sleep in a 'lean to' in the woods than in a house. I recall once that Niles asked me if I had ever seen Daisy talking to a half-breed, but I had never been that fortunate. I only tell this to show that while outwardly he was a genial enough man, at heart he was of a suspicious nature, not altogether happy in his home life. His wife was

devoted to him, but between them was always
the barrier of childlessness. His home on
Mosquito Creek was solid-looking and comfortable. It was built on a hill overlooking
a meadow and a ford. Locally it was known
as 'Niles' Ford.' Evidently old memories of
Ireland were clinging to him; he wanted a spot
that reminded him of his happy childhood.
That was stronger than the desire to blot out
the associations of his father's death. But
the landscape surrounding his new home must
have been vastly different from that in the old
country. Mosquito Creek was hemmed in by
tall mountains, culminating in the Knobs,
which were so high and massive that they
seemed to be pillars holding up the clouds.
Much original timber was standing; the mountains looked blue-black at all seasons of the
year. Three hundred and sixty million feet
of timber were floated out of this creek, to say
nothing of what was sawed in mills on the
ground. Isaac Niles transacted considerable
business with parties in Sinnemahoning, and
it was nothing for him to walk there and back
across the mountains in one day. Like his

father, he was a temperate man, and while absent attended strictly to business. It was late
one beautiful summer afternoon when Niles had
gone on one of his trips, that his wife and Daisy
went out on the front steps to wait for him.
They looked across the ford and to their dismay
saw him standing there, rigid and motionless.
The rich-colored rays of the sun were shining
in his face, but he seemed utterly regardless of
everything. Both women called to him, but
he did not answer. Knowing his temperate
habits, they were sure he could not have been
drinking; he must be ill. 'Go and see what's
the matter with father,' said Mrs. Niles, nervously, so the girl ran down the steps and the
hill, not stopping until she reached the ford,
opposite to where he stood. When she drew
near she could see him smile, which was all the
more unusual, as he smiled seldom despite his
kindly nature. Then he began to diminish and
grow smaller, until he vanished completely.
The girl was so overcome with fright that she
could not move for several moments after he
had gone. She looked around, and could see
her mother sitting on the steps, with her head

buried in her apron, evidently weeping. Daisy
hurried back to her, and the woman confirmed
what she had seen. A figure, certainly it was
that of Isaac Niles, was standing on the opposite
side of the ford. When the girl had approached, it had smiled at her, and then faded
out of sight. 'We'll have quite a joke on
father when he comes home to-night,' said the
girl in an honest effort to revive her mother's
spirits. 'We'll never see him again alive,' said
the woman, trying to dry her tears. True
enough, the sun set in all its crimson glory,
dusk softened into darkness, the crickets and
the frogs took up their singing lessons, the
lamplight gleamed from out the kitchen windows, but Isaac Niles did not return. Although it was June, and a clear night, the
wolves howled piteously on the ridge back of
the manse, keeping the cattle and sheep awake
and making them rattle their bells in a mourn-
ful dirge. The next morning Daisy saddled
one of the horses and rode boldly across the
mountains to Sinnemahoning. Every one said
that Isaac Niles had not been seen there in over
a week. She recounted the story of his disap-

pearance, and several of his friends started out to hunt him. That evening, just before sunset, two of these men, looking tired and careworn, came into the Niles kitchen. Daisy had returned a few minutes before, and was helping her mother prepare a little supper. They told the grief-stricken women how they had found the dead body of Isaac Niles, with a bullet wound in his abdomen, lying behind a pile of spars, on the mountain several miles above Sinnemahoning. His watch and money were in his pockets; the motive of the crime was not robbery. They judged he had been murdered the evening before. Daisy's grief was pitiable to behold, for despite a desire to regulate her affairs of the heart, Niles had treated her well. Mrs. Niles took the news rather coolly. 'I had expected this all along after seeing his ghost last evening.' Then she told them what had happened, Daisy corroborating her, and also the story of the death of her husband's father, Patrick Niles. As in the case of his father, the murderer of Isaac Niles was never discovered. For a time suspicion rested on the half-breed who had been attentive to Daisy.

But he was able to prove a complete alibi, as he was in Lock Haven at the time. Daisy never married him. Isaac Niles had no one else who had aught against him, so it was declared after the most rigid investigation. It will always be a mystery, except that he was evidently murdered by a representative of the slayers of his father, a survival of some eternal feud. If the ghosts of Patrick and Isaac Niles could have spoken, they would have cleared up everything, but they only had strength enough to appear; they could not deliver their messages. This Patrick Niles who just met with an accident on Mosquito Creek is, I am sure, no relation to the others; he belongs to a different breed; but some unkind force, which lay in wait for his namesakes, has made him pay a similar penalty. Probably, if the facts were known, he has been badly crushed about the abdomen by some falling tree, felled unexpectedly on him by his Nemesis." I looked at John Dyce's serious, thoughtful face, as he finished the narrative. "What do all these things mean?" I asked, "is there a *Control* in Nature that we can only see at times?"

XX

DRIVING OUT OF ROCKY

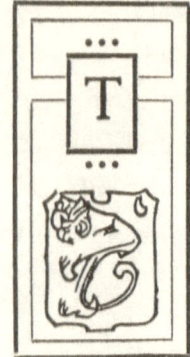

HREE small frame houses stood along Rocky Run, near where it empties into Pine Creek. Two of them were occupied by old soldiers and one by a soldier's widow. The old veterans and the widow had sons, all in their early twenties, who worked as log-drivers and bark-peelers. The three boys were lifelong friends, as their parents had been, and their similar occupations made the bond closer. One of the boys, Fred Rhoads, had a sweetheart, Celandine Peterson, but the other two were as yet heart free. Fred was the widow's son, and he could not very well get married "until he got ahead a little," as he would have two dependent upon him. Celandine lived about half a mile up the Run, in a little ravine that opened into the main hollow. Her father was a Norwegian, her mother German, and she inherited the good looks of both

356

races. She was rather tall, with hair like
purest gold, and high color that came and went
with her varying moods. She had rather small
eyes, " cat's eyes" jealous girls called them—
eyes that were more green than blue or grey,
but filled with expression. They were eyes
that foretold an eventful career. Fred
Rhoads was a tall, dark chap, brave and light-
hearted, typical of his class. The other two
boys, Ben Herman and Austin Miller, were of
fair complexion, but strong and sturdy. Rocky
Run was one of the last tributaries to Pine
Creek opened up by the lumbermen. For years
it had been cruised over by experts, who pronounced it too dangerous to drive. Lumber
railways of the cog-wheel engine and fourteen
per cent. grade type, had not as yet come into
vogue, and a territory that did not have a
stream capable of running logs had to lie fal-
low. But the demand for lumber, especially
for large bodies of standing timber, was becoming more active; regions once overlooked
were being operated. A large tanning and
lumber company purchased the timber which
stood for five miles along the headwaters of

Rocky, and despite its jagged rocks, it must
be "run." The first drive was quite a local
event. Farmers from the Pine Creek Valley
brought their families in wagons to see the fun.
Any one could see logs floating in a smooth
current, but it was something more to see logs
bounding and leaping over the rocks and foam
of Rocky. "Rocky can never be driven," had
been the shibboleth of the old-timers, but modern skill and ingenuity was overcoming all this.
But the first drive ended in a casualty, and not
a frolic. When the yellowish hemlock logs came
within sight of Pine Creek, rubbed full of
bristles from contact with the rocks, the drivers
said that one of the boys, a big Swede, had
fallen in and been drowned somewhere along
the drive. "Too bad," every one agreed. "But
what do them Swedes know about driving?"
was the way the native audience dismissed
the subject. But nevertheless a drive with
the remnants of a big Swede somewhere
underneath had lost most of its zest as
a spectacle. "They'll be more careful in
another year," said the Methodist preacher,
trying his best to smooth matters over.

Celandine Peterson was at the bank with
her mother and little sister, and waved
to Fred Rhoads and his chums when they came
by after the tumult. They didn't smile much,
and Fred stopped and told her about the accident, three miles up stream. " You remember
big Gus Helgerson, that tow-headed fellow that
boarded at Blackwell's? He was the victim."
Celandine turned away; she had seen enough
of the first drive out of Rocky to suit her that
day. The big Swede's body was never recovered; it was probably ground small enough to
feed the mountain trout before reaching Pine
Creek. When the drive had gotten to Williamsport in safety, every one began feeling
elated again. The logs from Rocky had reached
market, the permanency of the local industry
was assured, there was enough timber standing
on the run and its tributaries to last fifteen
years yet. The boys wouldn't have to go away
to work; it would be bark in summer, driving
in spring and fall, skidding and road-building
in winter. Men, boys and teams would always
be in demand. Fred Rhoads and his chums
were among the first to strike out for the bark-

woods after the drive. They wanted no holiday; besides, Hoytville was too far away to go
for a jubilation. The weather was still cold,
and Celandine was still kept busy "firing up"
the stoves when time came to bid goodbye to
her lover. She promised to visit him in camp
—it would be lots of fun to come up there with
her sister and a couple of their girl friends the
first fine Sunday. But before even the first
Sunday had rolled around Fred appeared; she
thought him a ghost, she was so unprepared to
see him. "They must have a woman to run
Carter's Camp—that Irish woman went on a
huff, and they can't do anything with her;
won't your mother and you take the job?" The
German woman hesitated, as all German
women must. She consulted with her Norwegian husband, who was still more undecided.
Fred had come determined to move the Peter-
sons to Carter's Camp. He wanted to please
his boss; he wanted Celandine to be near him
—always. Five miles wasn't much to inter-
vene; some lovers are separated by a thousand
miles, but five miles to a busy man is more
than a thousand to a globe-trotter. Celandine

was finally named as arbitrator, and decided
instantly that they must go. Minnie, the
younger sister, was equally anxious; she liked
one of the bark-peelers; she didn't even know
his name, but she liked him, and wanted to see
him again. They looked like a party of nomads
when they started up the run. The old bay
horse was drawing the express wagon loaded
with Mrs. Peterson's favorite and indispensable
stove, her favorite utensils, some rocking
chairs, bedding, and clothing. The Norwegian
husband held the lines, walking along beside
the wagon. Mrs. Peterson and Minnie walked
single file behind, and bringing up the rear, at
a very respectful distance, were Fred and
Celandine. They were holding hands already,
and some times he would slip his arm around
her waist and give her a squeeze. It was an
elysium they were headed for—a summer together far in the wilderness, with not a jarring
element. What desolated country they were
passing through! It would have made a good
illustration for some work on Judea. Last
year's operations had left a honeycomb of hemlock stumps everywhere, anon, and everywhere.

The hardwoods were still standing, but the fire had been through them two weeks before, and scorched brown the silvery trunks of the beeches, and shrivelled the tender spring foliage. But the springs babbled gayly, the jays chattered, the hemlock-warblers and the wood-robins burst impetuously into song, while the peepers piped vociferously, forgetting it was sunny afternoon and not yet dusk. The fire-weed had begun to sprout already. The approach to camp was heralded by the tinkling of the cow-bell; no mountain ravine is complete without a cow-bell tinkling far in the distance.

The camp was a rambling affair of loose, un-planed hemlock boards, built on oak posts, a foot or so above ground. Opposite were the stables; they must be handy. The summer passed in one glorious spell of delight. Fred and Celandine and Minnie and all the rest thought work was play. It was October before Clem Carter would let Mrs. Peterson and her household depart for their home. The good woman was getting restless; another week and she would have gone huffy like her Irish predecessor. Carter saw this, and wisely let her go.

He was thinking of another year. The parting between Celandine and Fred was affecting, but like most affecting partings, wasn't for long. In another week he had quit, and was making nightly visits to the Peterson home. His two chums quit soon after, and always walked with him on Sundays as far as the girl's home; then they turned back, knowing that three or four's a crowd. Early in February the three boys returned to the woods to help get ready for the drive. It was to be twice as big as the one last year; four million feet were coming down. The Sunday before the big event Fred was with his sweetheart. He had a big heart, consequently there was room for melancholy in it. He spoke about the drive last year, when Gus Helgerson lost his life. " If anything like that happened to me, I don't want you to mind; there's lots in the world much better than me. Take Ben Herman, for instance; he's worth two of me." Celandine didn't like such gloomy talk, especially as it was a sunshiny afternoon, and sunshiny afternoons in early April are always appreciated. Celandine dreamed about dark water that night; she didn't like the

dream, but said nothing. Driving day came
around. There was even a bigger crowd around
the confluence than the year before. There was
a new Methodist preacher; he had never seen
a drive before, and was eternally asking if
there were really four million logs coming.
When they hove in sight it looked as if there
were twice that number, but the logs bobbed
so in the rocky bed that each one counted four.
The drivers wore a far more serious mien than
they had when the big Swede had gone under.
" Gee, it was hard," they said, " to tell that
pretty Peterson girl that Fred Rhoads fell
in just the same place as Gus Helgerson, and
we'll never see him again." Celandine walked
home stunned, but she was as brave as only a
mountain girl could be. Ben Herman and
Austin Miller quit the drive and spent the
evening with her. Ben was particularly
sympathetic and devoted. Probably poor
Fred's presentiment had been strong enough
to make him confide in Ben as well as Celandine. Bark-peeling time was soon at hand
again. Clem Carter came personally and
coaxed Mrs. Peterson to come back to camp,

but she refused. Celandine did not urge her;
that was the reason. She could not go back
to the scenes where she had been so happy with
Fred last summer. Ben came regularly to see
her, tramping the five miles joyfully. Once he
asked her if he could take his friend's place.
All Celandine would say was, " Poor Fred said
you were twice the man he was." All through
the fall and winter Ben was attentive; he was
in dead earnest. He wanted to ease Celandine's
lonely heart; he really loved the girl. " No
one could help it," Austin Miller would say.
She had half consented to marry him some
time, when he had to go up the stream to help
with the drive. He went away light-hearted,
so different from poor Fred. Five million feet
were to make the journey to Williamsport.
Every one for miles around, even Fred's
widowed mother who was struggling along on
her pension money, Ben's parents, and Austin's parents, the Methodist preacher, who had
been sent back again by the Conference, were
on hand to see the drive go by. " Bad luck
seems to follow us," said one big, brawny
driver. " That poor Ben Herman, who was

going to get married soon, got hit in the head by a log as it bounced over a rock, was stunned and went to the bottom." Celandine walked bravely home that afternoon. She had survived one buffeting by Fate; she could stand another. Austin Miller dropped out of the drive and was on hand to comfort her that night. Her frightful double loss made her ·cling to him, as the symbol of what had been, and what might have been. He did not go to work all that summer. He felt it a duty to try and brighten her pathway. · No girl ever tried more to look and act pleasant than she. Austin often had admired her beauty; it was chastened and more beautiful now, since sorrow had touched it so deeply. *She* was twice the girl she was before. Austin loved her dearly, and one day in October asked her to marry him. " I cannot marry you now; I am afraid; every man who has had my heart has met with an untimely end; to bestow it on you would be to kill you." Austin was not dismayed; he kept on with his attentions, which were plentifully encouraged. In the spring he told her he wanted to take part in the drive.

" I'll surely be careful, after all that happened
to my friends." " I can't prevent you, Austin;
you know what's best," said Celandine sadly,
" but do be careful." The fact that Fred and
Ben had lost their lives in the drives out of
Rocky made Austin feel that the percentage
of chance would favor his escape. Besides,
he had been idle since April all on account of
his desire to be near Celandine; he must be
getting busy again. In his heart he said to
himself, " If she'd said she'd marry me I'd
never have done this." Celandine loved him
as much as a heart-broken girl could, but she
feared to tell him. Over five million feet were
the quota that year. The same big crowd was
on hand at the mouth of Rocky, except that
Fred's mother was dead and Ben's parents too
grief-stricken to witness another drive. Aus·
tin's father and mother were anxious to see
the sight; their boy had come down safely
with three drives; he could surely make the
fourth all right. It was a grand clear day
when the logs started. Austin, full of life and
vim, was always in the thick of the fray. Not
a log must stay behind. Sometimes a couple

of the boys would attack a single log with their cant-hooks so that there would be no danger of a delay or jam. Clifford Betts was swinging his cant-hook at a stubborn pine log spotted with patches of bark like a leopard, that seemed out of place in this hemlock concourse, and accidentally hit Austin on the head. He lost his balance and dropped into the seething current. The heavy pine log started, and struck his head as he rose to the surface. Other logs repeated this, and he was killed before the eyes of his "buddies." "This stream's spooked," said the drivers as they neared the throng of people. "Another boy's been lost; that fine-looking fellow, Austin Miller." A little further up the run Celandine Peterson was walking out the ravine to her humble home, sobs shaking her slender frame, while hot tears were reddening her soulful eyes and smooth, full lips. It was all over with her; even the man to whom she had never told the story of her love was gone; the word love would never cross her lips again now. She sat in a kitchen chair all that night, rigid, and with mouth compressed. She fought grief to a standstill and conquered it. She

would not go crazy or become a nervous wreck.
The next morning she was helping about the
house, erect, calm, but sad-eyed. Her parents,
fatalists and of nebulous religious belief, pitied
her the more because they had no consolation
to offer. The Methodist preacher called, but
he found in her a braver woman than he bar-
gained. She did not need wheedling nor pray-
ers. That was the last drive out of Rocky.
That very summer a railway was built clear to
the three springs that formed the headwaters,
and a big sawmill erected where Clem Carter's
camp had stood. There is a modest graveyard
on a hill overlooking a patch of dead water
on Pine Creek. It is shaded by a weeping
willow and several choke-cherry trees. In one
of the corners are three small white-pine
boards, stuck in the earth like headstones.
There are no names on them, no marks to tell
their story. In front of them and around them
grow a profusion of spring and summer flowers, yellow, purple, crimson; jonquils, iris,
poppies, that seem to be always blooming.
Often in the late afternoons the slim figure of
a blonde woman, still young, comes and sits

on the grass beside them. She brings fresh
flowers, and occasionally buries her head
among the blossoms. She is telling the story
of how the world is going, the story of her own
love, to these empty graves, of how she could
have made three friends supremely happy, yet
cannot be happy herself.

XXI.

A ROCK OF AGES

MONG the many accomplishments of Pipsisseway, the great King of the Susquehanah Indians, was his fondness for art. As an art patron he encouraged many young designers and filled his broad domain with examples of their work. Nature had outdone herself in making his kingdom, with its lofty mountain ranges, vast forests, lakes, waterfalls, rivers, and streams. Pipsisseway felt that while art could never excel Nature's handicraft, it might exist side by side with it, and develop an aesthetic sense among his subjects. Accordingly he set an army of artists at work. Colossal statues, like the famed "giantess of McElhattan" which was uncovered in the bed of McElhattan Run after the flood of 1865; huge faces cut out of projecting rocks like the "stone faces" near Selinsgrove, near Bloomsburg, near Halifax and on

Spruce Creek; and decorations like those on the " Picture Rocks" in Lycoming County, were completed under his supervision. It has come down to us that there were one hundred " stone faces" completed during his reign, which lasted but twelve years. To-day but four or five, notably those near Halifax and Bloomsburg, exist in a recognizable condition. The first white settlers, on beholding these marvellous works, were content to say, " Nature did it," and inquire no further. Scientists descended from these settlers accepted the old theories, and passed them on to the general public. If any one questioned, and suggested that they might have been done by Indians, the men of science would point to their irregular proportions as proof of their conclusions. But they should have considered that time, and the attendant disintegration of the rocks, which were in the most part soft, could have made an eye smaller on one side than on another; an ear missing altogether, or a nostril pushed out of shape. Pipsisseway's sculptors made the huge " stone faces" in the Pennsylvania mountains, but as Homer and Shakespeare are called myths, they

rest in oblivion in good company. Pipsisseway
contended that a stone face peering from a
rocky cliff gave " personality" to the landscape.
Modern landscape architects feel similarly
when they erect a summer-house or tower on a
conspicuous height. These stone faces were
carved to represent distinguished ancestors of
the great monarch, and one or two were por-
traits of Pipsisseway himself, or his brothers,
or some of the leading chieftains in his victory
over the Kishoquoquilas at the Indian Steps.
The " stone face" in Spruce Creek Valley is
said to be Pipsisseway, typifying that his race
were forever on the watch as the rulers of the
disputed territory. In addition to these colossal statues, smaller pieces of delicate design
were executed. Sculpture for a time lessened
interest in the pottery works at the royal encampment, located on the present site of
Wayne Township, Clinton County, which had
reached a state of great perfection. Everything must be hewn out of stone; it showed
more skill than if moulded by the hands. Pipsisseway's favorite sculptor was a young Indian named Wiconisko. There is a beautiful

stream of that name in Dauphin County, but
he was probably named after it, and not the
stream after him. Indians of ordinary birth
were often named from the places where they
were born. At the time of the great victory
over the Kishoquoquilas, Wiconisko was about
twenty years of age, but most precocious in
his artistic talents. Like many artists, he was
of lowly birth, the son of a shad-fisherman, and
his early education was even more limited than
that of the average Indian of his time. Some
of his little statues carved out of common limestone were brought to Pipsisseway's attention.
The great King admired them, and ordered that
the youth be brought before him at once. When
he appeared, he found him to be handsome and
intelligent, his genius overshadowing his lack
of education. He was given a retired spot by
the river bank, near the royal camp-grounds,
to carry on his artistic endeavors, and a dozen
servants to assist him. Pipsisseway was full
of ideas, and nearly every day came in person
to the sylvan studio or sent word about some
new figure or group that he wanted chiseled.
So many of Wiconisko's dainty statuettes were

grouped about the royal lodge-house that Pipsisseway's young Queen, Meadow Sweet, expressed a desire to meet the young sculptor and
see him at work. " He must be inspired by
the Gods," she said; "no one has ever lived
who could perform such wonders in stone."
One bright afternoon the king and queen, accompanied by their personal suite, surprised
the young sculptor in the midst of his labors.
He was overcome by the sight of the two rulers
of the realm, and fell down on the earth in
grateful obeisance. He was commanded to
rise, and treated with the kindliest consideration by his royal visitors. Wiconisko was
only a few years older than Queen Meadow
Sweet, so the nearness in their ages made her
take an added interest in his productions.
King and Queen were so much pleased with
what they saw that they tarried until the sun
had sunk almost to the summit of the Quinn's
Run Mountain. When they departed the
Queen smiled genially at Wiconisko. After
that the young sculptor's lot was more secure
than ever. He was sent to the Spruce Creek
Valley to carve out the colossal head of the

conquering Pipsisseway; he superintended the
decorations of the " Picture Rocks," and other
important commissions. The other sculptors
and artists would have become jealous, and
murdered the young fellow, but that by common consent they considered him too much
their superior to conflict with them. Nature
had indeed been kind with Wiconisko. He was
young, he was singularly handsome, he possessed immortal genius. Though he was not
tall, his features were unusually well-cut and
proportioned, and his slight figure lithe and
active. Many Indian maidens of high degree
fancied him, but he seemed to be entirely oblivious of the female sex. " He is in love with
his work," they would exclaim in their despair.
One Indian maid is said to have drowned herself in the eddy near his workshop. He never
shed a tear when her bedraggled body was
rescued and brought to him. " He will never
marry," the Indian soothsayers told the
love-sick girls who besieged them. In the
midst of his greatest triumphs his generous
patron Pipsisseway breathed his last. This
was a great blow to the entire artistic coterie,

as they rightly imagined that the " golden age"
of Susquehanah art would come to an end.
Meadow Sweet announced that all her late
King's favorite ideas and policies would be
carried out; that art should be properly encouraged; but the artists had their fears nevertheless. One of her first visits after the poig-
nant period of her grief had passed was to
Wiconisko's workshop. Attired all in white,
according to the Susquehanah custom of
mourning, and with a veil of filmy material over
her face, she bespoke grief in its most spiritual
and refined form. Wiconisko could not suppress his delight at seeing her, and tried to
make her stay as pleasant as the circumstances
would permit. She explained to him that she
wanted him to erect a colossal, full-length
statue of Pipsisseway in warrior's regalia on
the summit of the highest mountain in the vicinity of the encampment. " I think that is the
mountain the sun sets back of," replied the
sculptor. "A statue there would attract attention on every side, especially when illuminated
by the rich colors of the declining orb." Meadow
Sweet acquiesced; it was clear that this was

not only the highest but the most noticeable
mountain in the region of the camp. Work
was to commence as soon as a monolith of
sufficient size and suitable material could be
obtained. Although the statue was never
built, the mountain became known as " Mount
Pipsisseway" until the first settlers changed it
to the " Hog Back Mountain" or " Quinn's Run
Mountain." But its fairest, dearest name is
" The Mountain that the sun sets back of."
For once in his career Wiconisko could not
muster enough energy to set out to find the
monolith. A week of inertia passed; daily reports were brought to Meadow Sweet that he
had not started, and she grieved considerably.
" Why," she reasoned to herself, " can't he begin this work, after all the kindnesses that
Pipsisseway bestowed upon him?" Several
times she thought she would visit the workshop to find out the true reason of his slowness,
but prudence forbid. Wiconisko, in his heart,
was as sorry as Meadow Sweet that he could
not bring himself to begin the journey, but he
was forced to admit to himself that he loved
the widowed Queen, and could not carve a

figure of her late husband. He had fallen
in love with her the afternoon when she first
visited his workshop in company with Pipsisseway, but it had remained a smouldering spark
until the great monarch's death. With that
event, and the visit of the beautiful widow to
the studio, it had burst into intense flame, more
fiery and furious than the sunsets back of Hog
Back Mountain. If he would die for it, he
could not start away and leave her; he would
not glorify her late husband with a colossal
statue, even though he had been his best friend
and patron. It might be, he reasoned with his
over-excited imagination, that Meadow Sweet
cared for him; if he was sure of that, she
could understand his disinclination to go
ahead with his commission. He must tell her
of his love, come what may. She had smiled
at him when she visited the workshop with her
husband; she had come to see him on her first
public appearance after Pipsisseway's demise.
She might care for him; why not? He was
young, good-looking, a genius—he was only her
inferior in birth, but what was that? Along
these purposeless lines the love-sick sculptor

argued with himself, and against himself. At
length he summoned up courage to visit his
royal patroness. The lodge-house which she
occupied was carefully guarded, to ensure
privacy, but the august guardsmen fell back
when they saw the young sulptor approaching.
This gave him renewed courage—his instinct
told him he would be welcomed. The royal
hand-maidens ushered him into the presence
of his beloved and withdrew. The Queen was
seated on a dais, on a mass of fawn-skins, clad
all in white, with the filmy veil falling over her
face. Through it, the mobile, *spirituelle* features were barely discernible. Wiconisko
bowed low, and the Queen with a friendly gesture bade him to be seated. This was an un-
precendented honor, and further aggrandized
his courage. Meadow Sweet began the conversation, as was the custom, expressing regret
that he had not found it convenient to go in
search of a monolith from which to carve the
statue of the departed monarch, Pipsisseway.
" He thought so much of you, Wiconisko," said
the Queen, impressively. With these words
the sculptor's courage almost entirely deserted

him; it would have been better for him had
it all gone. He could not commence his carefully prepared speech, but sat silently, facing
the Queen. After a few minutes he regained his
composure and spoke his heart directly. " Oh,
fairest Queen," he began, " I did not begin that
statue of our lamented monarch because—because I loved you—I loved you the first time I
saw you when you came to the studio with your
husband and smiled on me." Meadow Sweet's
dark eyes fairly blazed through the veil; but
she controlled herself admirably. " You; *you*
have been in love with me since that afternoon
I came to your studio with Pipsisseway?" she
demanded. " I have," replied the sculptor,
trembling like a leaf, for he knew that his
dream was shattered. " Then I am utterly disappointed in you," said the Queen; " if I
smiled on you, I don't recall it; I have a habit,
I fear, of showing too much approval, but it is
never personal. You can withdraw from my
presence at once, and I will give you until
dawn to-morrow to leave the regal encampment." Wiconisko rose to his feet, and backed
out of the royal presence, shivering like a

whipped dog. With bowed head he passed between the double line of sentinels, a very different being from what he had been twenty
minutes before. A few minutes can transform
a man completely. Life had found its meaning to Wiconisko when he first saw Meadow
Sweet; now through her its meaning had been
lost. He was like a person who had approached
a locked door and discovered that he had lost
the key. When he reached his workshop his
eyes rested upon a small block of dark ganister.
Seizing it, he reached for his chisels, and began carving a statuette to divert his grief.
He never worked so dextrously nor so fast.
Within an hour he had turned the block into a
seated figure of Queen Meadow Sweet, complete even to the veil covering her exquisitely
lovely face. It was surely his masterpiece,
for it was carved out of love, not out of stone.
When it was finished he eyed it critically,
smiling a cynical smile of satisfied vanity. If
he could not have Meadow Sweet in the flesh,
his powers enabled him to reproduce her in
stone. He tucked the statuette under his arm,
and picked up a couple of implements for grub-

bing and digging which rested against an old
oak nearby. Thus equipped, he started out a
path which led to the higher ground back of
the encampment. At the edge of this rise he
stopped, and reverently laid down the statuette. He began digging and picking and soon
nad a respectable sized excavation. Hunting
around until he found a number of flat stones,
he walled, floored, and roofed the cavity. On
top he threw the dirt on thick, and covered it
with sods. He had left an opening large
enough for a human being to crawl through.
After some search he discovered a stone large
enough to block this entrance, and placing the
statuette under his arm, and dragging the tools
after him he pulled himself into the pit. Once
inside he drew the flat rock against the opening, a voluntary prisoner. He lit a pine torch
and stuck it in a crevice in the rocks, and it
burned until the oxygen was exhausted.
Wiconisko placed himself in a sitting posture,
putting the statuette before him where his eyes
could feast upon it. Then he took out his
scalping knife and severed the arteries in his
wrists. Life flickered out about the same time

as the pine torch ; death and the statuette were
together in grim gloom and silence. Two centuries and a quarter had to pass before an un-
looked-for judgment day transpired. Adam
Steck, one of the hardy pioneers of Wayne
Township, was ploughing in his recently
cleared " back lot." There was a slight mound
at the far end that might have been caused by
a depressed boulder or the burrowings of some
animal. Heading his team of oxen in the direction of the barrow, he drove the plough-
share through the centre of it. There was a
rumbling and a crumbling, and the plough
sank out of sight up to the tips of the wooden
handles. Stopping the ungainly oxen, he
dragged the plough out on the bank, and began investigating. Lifting the flat stones and
sods away, he came upon a skeleton in a sitting
posture in an excellent state of preservation.
In front of it was a small stone statue of a
female, on a pedestal, with a veil over her face,
dextrously carved and exquisitely beautiful.
There were also the remnants of a couple of
Indian implements in the barrow. The tools
interested him, as did the statuette, but the

A PENNSYLVANIA MOUNTAIN SUN SET

Photo by W. T. Clarke

ugly skeleton filled him with disgust. Quickly
covering the cavity with earth and stones, he
reburied all that was left of Wiconisko, to
await a further day of judgment. Adam Steck
quit ploughing for that afternoon. He took
the implements and the little figure to his
home along the river bank, where his family
viewed them with open-mouthed curiosity.
The hired boys told the story at the post-office
that night, and soon all Wayne was aware of
the " find." Many came to see the curios, and
old legends of the Indian encampment which
stood on the site of Wayne Township were re-
vived. " Some one ought to have that figure
who could appreciate it," said Adam one day.
A distinguished visitor from Jersey Shore took
him at his word, and asked for it on condition
that later he present it to the Museum at Lancaster. And that institution became the resting place for a time of the effigy of Meadow
Sweet, true wife and loyal widow of Pipsisseway, the great war chief of the Susquehanahs.
Eternity is long; the greater part of it
Wiconisko must spend far from any sign or
token of the woman he had no right to love.

XXII.

SHE KNEW THE POET

LONG Penn's Creek, between Zerby and Coburn, is still standing a splendid forest of original timber, white pine and white hemlock principally. The highway from Spring Mills to Coburn runs on the north side of the creek, and affords the traveller an excellent view of the giant timber. There is one point where there are several small clearings, and log-houses, one of them inhabited by David Frantz, the old-time wolf-hunter of the Seven Mountains. A short distance below this a road branches off from the main thoroughfare, and crosses by a narrow span the turbulent waters of the creek. At the cross-roads stands a sign-board with the finger pointing to the mountain. On its neatly painted white surface is the single word, " Povalley." This, translated into modern phraseology, means that the road leads to Poe Valley. But

the spelling " Poe" is also incorrect, as the
valley was probably named for Daniel Poh, a
Pennsylvania-German frontiersman, who took
up considerable land in this locality. If you
cross the bridge and follow the mountain road,
especially in latter-June, a rare treat lies in
store. The mammoth evergreen trees completely arch the road, while huge rhododendrons (*rhodendendron maximum*), some of
them nearly forty feet high and blooming
luxuriantly, perfume the way with their wax-
like blossoms. Along the road-sides tufts of
Pennsylvania tea are getting ready to open
forth their feathery white flowers, beloved of
the bees. Every half mile pure, gurgling springs
are met with, their trickling overplus keeping
the road always damp, even in the dryest
spells. The jungle is so dark that the crickets
make music all day. Fourteen years ago, when
the writer first crossed into " Povalley," the
scenery was even wilder and more primeval.
Last summer the bark-peelers began devastat-
ing the mountain top, turning its color from
moss green to a grizzly brown. The heavy
bark-wagons and log-sleds have since then worn

great deep ruts into the hitherto smooth, loamy
road. But it is a wilderness nevertheless, as
near to the primeval as the Eastern States afford. Life and scenery are pretty much as
they were sixty years ago in this remote corner.
Wild life is still abundant—a stray panther
or two are said to wander about their old
haunts; now and then a "mountain nightin-
gale," a black wolf barks at the icy moon;
wildcats (*lynx rufus*) and catamounts (*lynx
canadensis*) are fairly abundant. I will never
forget a sight witnessed when crossing from
Poe Valley one lowery summer afternoon.
There had been a storm, and the horses waded
fetlock deep in slush. We had come into a
vast open country where all the timber, ex-
cepting oak saplings and a few mature yellow
pines, had been removed. Out of a thicket
flew two superb golden eagles so near to us that
the whirring of their wings frightened the
horses on which we rode. The majestic birds
shot upwards with the velocity of biplanes,
until almost reaching the level of the storm
clouds. Then they began soaring, covering
tremendous circles in their flight. Masters of

the high air, they surveyed the paltry earth below to their satisfaction, and disappeared from
sight in the storm clouds. I imagined them
circling triumphantly above the storm. It
was the most magnificent picture I have ever
seen in nature. Where the road begins its
descent into Poe Valley, the first glimpse of a
stately old brick mansion, half-hidden behind
apple trees, situated almost at the foot of the
mountain, is obtained. It attracts attention
immediately because of its tall chimneys and
" hip" or New England roof. There isn't another roof like it on a dwelling in all the valleys. I was not surprised when my companion,
who knew the valleys well, told me that it had
been built by a Massachusetts man named
Haskins. The New Englander had not lived
much longer than to complete it, and after his
death it passed into the hands of a family
named Walters, who owned it for three
generations. My friend had gone to school
at New Berlin with one of the boys of the family some years before, so we decided to stop
there before continuing our trip into the valley.
Besides, my friend wanted me to meet the

old lady, Mrs. Helena Halit, an aunt of the
Walters boys, who once knew the renowned
poet, Edgar Allan Poe. What was more, the
famous writer when a young man had made a
trip from Philadelphia to the valley bearing
his name, in the vain search for a heritage, as
he believed himself to be a grand-nephew of
the frontiersman, Daniel Poh or Poe. It was
during this trip that he met Helena Walters,
afterwards Mrs. Halit, and had formed a romantic attachment for her. The prospect of
meeting a sweetheart of the impressionable
poet, whose writings at that time—I was a
Freshman at college—were making a profound
impression on me, made me want to tarry all
the more at the old mansion back of the apple
trees. We tied our old horse Frank to the
rusty, warped iron fence, and entered the yard,
overgrown with untrimmed apple trees and
boxwoods. We had barely gotten to the corner of the house when Ben Walters, the young
man we were looking for, appeared, greeting us
warmly. He escorted us to a side porch,
shaded by an old virgilia tree, gave us rocking
chairs and brought out some home-made ice

cream for our refreshment. At first the conversation related to old school days at New
Berlin, and then my companion pointedly
asked young Walters if his aunt, who had
known Edgar Allan Poe, was at home. " She
certainly is; she's sitting on the porch on the
other side of the house. She's nearly always
at home; sometimes she *will* take a notion to
visit friends at Coburn or Hartley Hall. Her
travelling days are coming to an end, I am
sorry to say; all her old friends are dying, and
she's not as active as she was; she's now past
seventy-eight." Before being presented to the
interesting lady, I asked the young man to tell
me the story, as best he could, of Poe's love-
episode in this secluded valley. From what he
told me it seemed that several Poes had died
old bachelors, leaving hundreds of acres of
timber and farming land to be divided among
more or less remote relatives. Edgar Allan
Poe, who was somewhere between twenty-seven
and twenty-nine years old—his birthday was
a movable feast—was at this period on the
staff of a Philadelphia newspaper. He heard
of his wealthy namesakes, and upon informa-

tion that the late Daniel Poe was his great
uncle he started out to seek his inheritance.
In Philadelphia jealous literary colleagues
gave it out that " poor Poe had gone off on
another of his sprees." In reality, this and
many other trips were taken to improve his
material condition, and not to indulge any
taste for liquor. By canal, stage and on foot
he reached Poe Valley, and put up for the night
at the Walters mansion. The family had come
from Berks County the year before, and everything about the place looked new and attractive. Helena Walters was then a girl of eighteen years, very slim, straight, and blonde, the
very ideal of the susceptible poet. He became
very much enamored of her the moment he saw
her, and she seemed to take an interest in the
young stranger. It was not an interest that
sprang from the heart, as she was already
secretly bethrothed to Abram Halit, the son
of a prosperous farmer living on the opposite
side of the valley. She had no especial pre-
dilection for literature, but her nature was
sympathetic and naive, which appealed immensely to the poet. Tired as he must have

been after a fifteen-mile tramp from Hartley
Hall, he sat with her until midnight on the
porch where the old lady has since spent so
many hours. The old folks had gone to bed
on the promise that Helena would soon follow,
but she wanted to stay up and listen to the
young man's marvellous tales of the big world.
In some ways he was "different." He was a
most engaging talker, and even the full moon
stopped to listen poised on the tree-tops, she
said, so pleasing were his little bits of worldly
wisdom. That night he must have gone to bed
happy, one of the few nights of such a nature
in his stormy career. The next day he pretended to be looking up information concerning the inheritance, but he did not get very
far away from the Walters mansion. That
evening he expected to spend blissfully with
Helena, but a complication arose by the appearance of her fiance, Abram Halit. The poet
tried to converse, but his brain was chilled by
the presence of the third party, and he went
upstairs at nine o'clock. The next morning
when the family went to make his bed they
found all the slats broken; he had tossed about

all night in sleepless misery. During the morning he pursued his inquiries concerning family matters, but after dinner asked Helena to go for a walk with him. They started up the mountain road—among the rhododendrons— that was about the only way they could go, and he confided to her, so she said, that he loved her, and wanted her to come away with him into the big world. Whether his biographies state that he had a wife does not matter here— the dates are uncertain; he might not have been married at this time. Fortunately for the future peace and happiness of Helena, she did not see any extraordinary reasons why she should abandon the stalwart Abram Halit for the small, slight, ardent, blue-eyed youth by her side. " I cannot see why I should love you more than my fiance," she said; " I am perfectly satisfied with his love; he is all that I require." " But I am different," replied the young writer. " I am a poet." But the word poet did not convey as much meaning to Helena as if he had said that he was a horseman, an axeman, or a wolf-killer. " I have always loved Abram," she persisted; " I could

never love another." " I am your chance to
move out into the big world, where you deserve
to shine as the wife of a poet," said the young
man, in final entreaty. But Helena, woman-
like, was obdurate. The young poet looked at
her sadly, and took from his pocket a slender
volume. It was called " Tamerlane and Other
Poems." He handed it to her saying, " That
is what I am; I can say no more." She took
the book, glancing through its pages hastily,
but there was no air of understanding in her
manner. It was not her destiny to go or
shine. The poet held out his hand to say
good-bye. " I will go now; I will not return
for my valise. I have lost all I came to the
valley to find; but I will never, never forget
you; my spirit will often return and be with
you." Helena looked at him blankly; she had
never heard such talk from man before; it
really was a good idea he was going away, he
was *odd*. Too surprised to urge him to at
least remain long enough to secure his baggage,
she allowed him to leave her on the mountain
road, and disappear from view among the ever-
greens and laurels. Nearly a year passed and

she was making her final preparations to marry
Abram Halit. A small package came to her
by post; might it be a wedding gift? She
opened it; it contained a curiously carved silver locket, and woven inside was a lock of ash-
brown hair. It will be recalled that when Poe,
at the age of eighteen, enlisted in the U. S.
Army as a private soldier, he was described
as having "brown hair, blue eyes, fair complexion." Helena viewed the missive with as-
tonishment; she very naturally showed it to
her lover. They both laughed a little about it;
then it was laid away in the dresser, where it
remained for fifty years. On the date appointed Helena Walters was married to Abram
Halit, and the union proved a happy one. Several years afterwards the post brought the
contented wife another small volume. It was
called "Tales of the Arabesque and Grotesque."
She remembered she had lost the other book
he gave her when they parted. She laid this
one on the parlor table unread, and as the
donor sent no address, it was never even acknowledged. Seven years after the parting on
the mountain road, an envelope came by mail,

addressed in a hand as fine as copperplate.
Helena opened it; and found a piece of poetry
written in the same exquisite hand; it was
called " The Raven." She read the first stanza;
it seemed very ponderous and tiresome. She
laid it wearily between the pages of " Tales of
the Arabesque and Grotesque," to slumber for
half a century. A few years after this Abram
Halit died, and once, while poring over the
" Family Monitor" she read the brief announcement of the " Death of the poet, Edgar A. Poe,
author of The Raven." That was the name of
the piece he had sent her, she recollected. Years
passed when she never thought of her strange
early love except on days when she dusted the
copy of " Tales of the Arabesque and Grotesque," which lay on the marble-topped parlor
table. Poe's spirit must only have visited the
valley on cleaning days! Her brothers, younger
than she, married and reared families; some of
the boys and girls went to academies and col-
leges, where they accumulated much culture.
Wherever they went they heard of Edgar Allan
Poe. That seemed a very familiar name; it
was first of all the name of the valley where

they lived; but it was also the name of the
author of the dingy little book which lay unread on the parlor table. What was the connection? Aunt Helena would know. She told
them willingly, and they were amazed. A
chapter in the life of America's greatest poet
had happened in their own home. It had just
missed sliding into oblivion unrecorded. They
talked so much of Poe, and what their teachers
thought of him, that the old lady began to take
herself more seriously than formerly. School
friends of the young people wanted to meet her
because she knew the poet. I had expressed
the same desire for the same reason. We
opened the door leading to the porch where
she sat rather quickly, so I had a good chance
to study her face before she noticed us. Despite her advanced years her skin was almost
free from wrinkles; there was a defiant curve
to her aquiline nose, a far-away light in her
pale blue eyes; a certain archness to her some-
what shrunken lips; all traces of " the glory
that was Greece, of the grandeur that was
Rome." In her day she could readily have
been loved by any poet; but she could never

mentally reciprocate. I told her how glad I
was to meet some one who had known my
favorite poet, who was America's greatest
literary genius. She smiled with approval, not
at the words I said, but at the reverential tones
of my voice. I complimented her on her excellent appearance, and turned sadly away.
Hers had been a beautiful mask, with skeleton
steel within. Last July a year, I was tempted
by the familiar signboard pointing to " Povalley," and let old Arab take me there. It was a
delicious ride at sundown under the giant ever-
greens, past rhododendron tangles, and gushing
springs. Myriad crickets were chorusing
shrilly. On the summit where I had seen the
eagles pierce the storm clouds, vast stretches
of mountain twilight calmed my senses. Where
the road turns down from the plateau I saw
the tall chimneys and the " New England" roof
of the Walters mansion—alas, now deserted.
Most of the ancient apple trees were dead from
the scale; some one had maliciously cut down
the virgilia tree; the trunk and skeleton
branches half-hidden in the tall grass resembled a prostrate elephant in one of Col.

Roosevelt's hunting pictures; the boxwoods were sere and broken, the iron fence all fallen, the yard deep with viper's bugloss, daisies and poke-weeds. Silent and empty the old house had its charm; once a fair occupant had touched infinity there, but in the darkness had mistaken the rustle of an angel's wing.

XXIII.

BATTALION DAYS

HE DAY was raw and overcast, typical of late March. Rain, cold and sleety, came by spells. The dull grey river was high, well up to the level of the banks, and dotted with "white-caps" from the sharp winds. The red birches and willows along shore swayed and shivered; nature was in a state of unrest in the last hours of her winter-long sleep. The old brick house above the ferry loomed tall and forbidding, with closed blinds and bolted storm doors. On the road that led from the house to the stable stood a bedraggled-looking hearse, and several "cabs" on which drivers strove to doze despite the wintry blasts. The lugubrious black horses held their long wet tails between their legs, sullenly patient and submissive. Death was in the old brick, and the funeral services soon would begin. Outside the kitchen door

crouched the dead man's favorite hunting dog.
He had barked all the night when his master
died, but had been silent and sad-eyed ever
since. The Norway spruces in the front yard
drooped their branches at times; they seemed
to betoken grief when not battling the unsympathetic north wind. Every few minutes the
kitchen door would open, and black-garbed
men, stiff and uncomfortable looking, would
peer out as if to see if any more carriages were
coming. The services were about commencing
when some one noticed an old-fashioned broad-
tread buggy pulled by a huge draft horse plow-
ing its way along the river road in the direction
of the mansion. "Better wait a minute or
two," said one of the sons of the deceased;
"looks as if more were coming." And the
volunteer choir laid down their hymnals. It
seemed an interminable time before the top
buggy drew up in front of the brick mansion.
An old man, white-bearded and of military
bearing, got out, and walked up the path. One
of the sons of the deceased came out of the
side door, and with serious face, greeted the
aged visitor saying, "How are you, General?"

The old man replied, "Too bad about the
Major; we shall miss him very much." Then
the two men went in the house, and the services began. Of all the mourners none was
more sincere than the General. His friendship
for the late Major had lasted over fifty years,
when they were companions-in-arms in the old
Battalion Days. These Battalions, which were
the forerunners of the present National Guard,
wielded a potent influence and turned out some
well-equipped soldiers. Officers and men from
these early organizations proved highly effi-
cient in the Civil War. Many wondered how
officers who lacked the West Point training
displayed such innate military knowledge.
There were some things that West Point didn't
know that the old Battalions taught. The
companies and "regiments" bore distinctive
names, such as the Brush Valley Blues, the
Sugar Valley Greys, the West Branch Light
Artillery and the like. Their uniforms were
as distinctive as their names. Local pride ran
high, and sometimes during reviews or sham-
battles real bloodshed was narrowly averted.
They were like the present National Guard

plus fifty per cent. more snap, minus fifty per
cent. of tiresome routine. The Civil War
marked the passing of the Battalions, and until
we have another war of like magnitude the
efficiency of the new regime cannot be tested.
It was nearly sixty years ago when the famous
review took place at Williamsport that was
participated in by most of the Battalions in
the central and western parts of the Commonwealth. The Governor and his cabinet, several
United States Army officers, prominent veterans of the Mexican War, and a foreign diplomat or two from Washington made up the
reviewing party. There were also the families
of these worthies, and the wives, mothers, sisters and sweethearts of the Battalion officers.
There were also the " multitude" who came
out of patriotism, curiosity or relationship to
the " rankers" in the Battalions. The spec-
tators in their quaint costumes were almost
as picturesque and showy as the soldiery themselves. The grand pageant was held on the
" flats" below town, being blessed by an unusually clear, sparkling day. The gay uniforms and side arms gleamed in the sunlight;

the grandeur of it all was imperial rather than democratic. But underneath the gaudy show, there was a solid basis of democracy, as that wide and sickeningly foolish social gulf which now separates officers from " non coms" and privates, did not exist. All were drawn from the same wood; distinctions of rank were temporary to the parade-ground and armory. No sham battle took place this day; it was a general gathering together or muster of strength, and not a display of " Dutch bluster." The General of later days, and the future Major, whose funeral it was his duty to attend, were at the time of this grand review both young lieutenants—the Major in the Sugar Valley Greys and the General in the West Branch Artillery. Earlier in life they had been classmates at New Berlin. Both had brought their sweethearts and families to see the display, which was the grandest event in the annals of Central Pennsylvania military history. The Major's sweetheart was a serious-minded girl, whom he afterwards married, while the General's was a bright-eyed, daring girl, one of his many romantic attachments, but she was not

the person he eventually wed. She was devoted to him, absolutely, and why marriage
failed to crown their romance, is only another
of the unfathomable mysteries of courtship.
Many as had been her admirers, she was cold
and haughty with them all until she met the
young lieutenant of the West Branch Artillery.
With him she was a different girl; her great
love had subdued her defiant, spirited nature.
Among her past admirers was a captain in the
Oak Valley Dragoons, the gayest-looking organization that existed in Pennsylvania. Re-
cruited from among the sons of prosperous
farmers in one of the richest and most beautiful valleys, they represented in the main, fine
types of manhood. Their mounts were home-
bred horses, big, powerful beasts of a kind that
are produced no more, and more's the pity, in
our State. They were the final outcropping
of the now extinct Conestoga breed, but the
admixture of Morgan and thoroughbred blood
gave them a fineness and suppleness not possessed by the true Conestogas. This captain of
the Oak Valley Dragoons, though repulsed long
ago in his assault on the heart of the Artiller-

ist's dashing sweetheart, was grieved none the less when he saw her at the review as the guest of another officer. She should have attended the review with him, he fancied, because she lived in Youngmanstown, just across the mountains from Oak Valley. He rode his powerful red roan stallion up close to where she was sitting and bowed obsequiously. She didn't pay much attention to him, which nettled him completely. This was augmented when he noticed the lieutenant in the Artillery in close conversation with her. The Dragoon was a small, oddly-built fellow, and would have been no match for his rival from the West Branch in a scuffle, so revenge must lie elsewhere. With furtive, restless eyes he kept watch on his rival; he knew he would even the score before sundown. He was especially angered when his horse ran away and had to be stopped by one of the artillerymen in full view of his cold-hearted charmer from Youngmanstown. This was an added reason for revenge. He must show her that artillerymen were far from perfect; they also made mistakes in tactics and horsemanship. As the day progressed and the

faultless evolutions of the artillery won much
applause, the heart of the Dragoon captain
boiled hotter and hotter with hate. The Dragoons made a fine showing, and were loudly
cheered, but he, their captain, had made a fool
of himself by letting his horse run off; no
enconiums could counteract that. It might,
if the artillery also displayed some unhappy
blunder. It seemed a long while until he could
turn the tables. At every period of rest he
sat moodily on his charger, perhaps brooding
over that strange decree of Fate that compels
one who would make another ridiculous to first
show off foolishly himself. This part of his
bargain with Fate had surely taken place; the
revenge part must come soon. The afternoon
was practically over, and many of the spec-
tators who had come from more distant points
had departed, when the chance presented. The
artillerymen were at parade rest and the Governor with his distinguished party were shaking hands with some of the military authorities
in charge of the display, preparatory to entering their coaches to drive to the Canal landing.
The lead horses on one of the gun-carriages

had been restless all afternoon. They were a
young pair of farm-bred animals, and lacked
the docility that comes from frequent " bap-
tisms of fire." The young lieutenant, dismounted, was standing by their heads, talking
to them gently, until their outrider, who was
adjusting the trace-chains, returned. Just
when it seemed that they were calmed, the
young officer turned away from them to wave
to his sweetheart, who was remaining until the
last soldier would leave the field. When his
duties were finished, it was planned that the
West Branch hero would escort her to the
packet. From afar the captain of the Dragoons
noted the artillerist waving to his beloved;
the restive horses standing heads free; the outrider busying himself with the trace chains.
Suddenly discovering that he had an important
message to deliver on the opposite side of the
field, and that this rest-period was a good time
to deliver it, he spurred his charger into action.
The big grade Conestoga stallion plunged forward, and his rider headed him for the narrow
lane between two of the gun carriages of the artillerymen. As he neared the restless colts

standing at the lead of the young lieutenant's
outfit, the big roan swerved violently, bump-
ing into the mettlesome colts with considerable force. The rider was so close he may
have—so the lieutenant always believed—dug
a spur into one of the frightened animals. At
any rate, they reared on their hind feet and
started out at a run, dragging the second pair
after them, and upsetting the outrider who
was at work at the traces. The rider of the
second pair, though a strong mountain boy,
felt his arms as weak as India-rubber when it
came to stopping his mount. The young lieutenant had turned quickly and sprang at the
frightened beast nearest to him, but he was a
second too slow, the gun-carriage and the four
horses topsy-turvey were careening across the
field headed for the Governor, his guests and
the ladies. There was a wild scramble, and
men, women and children tumbled over one
another on the grass and among the benches.
Some of the women screamed, others fainted;
confusion reigned, a calamity seemed imminent. Several women hung to the Governor's
coatsleeves, dragging him, ponderous individ-

ual, to the earth. Some persons, quick enough
to disentangle themselves from the struggling
mass, ran to the right or left, escaping to
points of safety. The young lieutenant whose
inattention might have caused the runaway,
was dumbstruck; he feared for his sweetheart; he lamented the disastrous outcome of
the glorious display. He would be blamed,
ridiculed, discredited. Suddenly a young officer in the uniform of the Sugar Valley Greys
and mounted on a rangy black thoroughbred
was seen sweeping across the field, diagonally
towards the runaway gun-carriage. He had a
long distance to go, but he timed his pace to
a nicety. The runaways struck his mount
broadside with terrific force, and in an instant
there was a mass of upturned hoofs, and tails
and wheels, and dust, but the danger was
past. It was fifteen minutes before the hero,
and the artillerymen, were extricated from
the awful tangle. The lieutenant of the Greys
was taken out unconscious; the extent of his
injuries could not be ascertained at first. The
lieutenant of the West Branch artillery was
by his side constantly, as was his sweetheart,

and the dashing young belle from Youngmanstown. The Governor accompanied the stretcher
that bore him to a nearby farm house. Several
surgeons examined him and predicted that he
would recover, as apparently no bones were
broken. His escape from death or permanent
injury was little short of miraculous. The
artillery lieutenant, the girl from Youngmanstown, his sweetheart and several members of
his company, remained with him for a week.
At the end of that time he was able to be
moved to his home. He recovered completely
and in six weeks was working on his father's
farm above Logansville as if nothing had happened. But the friendship that had begun in
the old academy at New Berlin, and grew
warmer when both met as brother officers in
the Battalions, had found a lasting bond when
the lieutenant of the Greys saved his companion's happiness and honor at the risk of
his own life. The " Hero of the Greys" remained in the Battalions long enough to reach
the rank of Major; then he retired, as he went
across the mountains to live. The young lieutenant of artillery became Major General com-

manding all the Battalions. The captain of
Dragoons took to drink and dropped out of
sight. The two friendly officers fought bravely
in the Civil War as commissioned officers, each
having been wounded several times. After
the war the warm association continued, and
the old companions-in-arms met whenever possible to renew former times. When death
overtook the Major, at a ripe old age, at his
comfortable mansion by the Susquehanna, the
General's drive of twenty miles up the valley
to pay a last tribute to the deceased, was his
final but permanent mark of honor and gratitude.

XXIV.

THE SWORD OF PINE CREEK

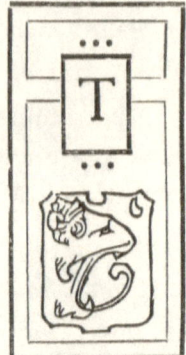 HERE are certain localities that Romance chooses from generation to generation to be the scenes of its little episodes. Other places, maybe grander or more picturesque, are ignored. The mountain pass between Livonia and Sugar Valley is one of the favored spots of Romance. It was here that the unhappy love affair of Francis Penn, grand-nephew of the founder of Pennsylvania, and the beautiful Indian maiden Marsh Marigold, had its ending. It was also the scene of the culminating point of the romance of Captain Morgan Evan Morgan, of the British line, and the attractive half-breed girl, Atoka Strahan. It was sunset last summer when we drove across the mountain, discussing the sad fate of Marsh Marigold on the way. The sky was pale orange color, shot with umber and mauve, and every tree and bush stood out distinctly

414

in the final foray of light. Down in the hollow
was a large lumber camp. We could hear the
bark-peelers singing their happy songs; supper
was just finished; they were care-free for the
night. I remember saying, " Isn't it strange
that the shanties are built exactly where the
great Indian encampment was located?" My
companion replied the reason for that wasn't a
coincidence, but the fact that both Indians and
bark-peelers wished to live close to the big
springs. High in the elbow of the mountain,
close to never-failing springs, it was no wonder
that the redmen put up a gallant fight in their
natural fortress. Perhaps its inaccessibility
is the reason why much of the hemlock forest
has survived in this glen long after it had been
removed from the adjacent hollows. It was
moonlight this spring when we drove across
the mountain discussing the romance of
Morgan Evan Morgan and Atoka Strahan. A
new moon of polished silver ruled in a sky of
silver grey, shedding rays which lighted the
lumbered-off vistas and roadways with an eerie,
unearthly light. The tall hemlocks looked
taller than they really were, all the world like

ghostly warriors with grey war-cloaks when
the moonlight shimmered down their sombre,
impenetrable facades.   Down in the hollow
bright yellow lights gleamed from the windows
of the lumber camp; it was still too early in
the season for the bark-crew to be on hand and
sit outside singing songs after supper.   We
sang a bit ourselves—snatches from the martial melody of "Bonnie Dundee," when not
speculating on the fate of Morgan Evan
Morgan and his Atoka.   Truly, it was a night
of nights.   It was in the hollow where the
camps are now located that Chief Arrow-Wood
maintained his stronghold.   He had fought
his enemy, Chief Rock Pine, who ruled over
Brush Valley, to a standstill.   Rock Pine tried
to dislodge him for five successive years and
then gave up saying, "He is my vassal, even
if I can't chase him away."   Over in Sugar
Valley Hyloshotkee, then in his prime, suc-
ceeded in limiting his operations to the south
side of the valley, where he grew his Indian
corn, hemp and potatoes along the foothills
unmolested.   But his stronghold was in the
elbow of the big mountain, close to the never-

AUSTIN, PA., BEFORE THE FLOOD OF 1911

Photo by W. T. Clarke, Conrad, Pa.

failing springs. One reason why Arrow-Wood
was so tenacious of his mountain retreat was
that he had been " moved on" so many times
that he had become tired of it. He was a son
of a King of the Delawares, and had been born
on the western borders of Lancaster County.
Treaties, war and invasion by the whites had
driven him steadily westward. When he
reached his eyrie in Bull Run Gap overlooking Sugar Valley he told his family
and clansmen that he was done moving.
" I will die here," he said, and he was
true to his promise, as old age carried him
off, in his lodge-house by the never-failing
springs during the autumn of 1761. In his
early youth in Lancaster County, he had married an Indian widow named Love Vine, whose
first husband was a Scotchman named Alan
Strahan. The first marriage was short-lived,
as the Scot was ambushed and murdered by a
strolling band of Lenni Lenape. Six months
after his death an infant girl was born, whom
her mother called Atoka. Arrow-Wood, per-
secuted and buffeted, chanced to camp where
Love Vine was eking out a solitary existence.

He fell in love with her, but principally loved
the infant girl; she was so winsome and cap-
tivating. Rumor had it he married the mother
so he could bring up the baby. With his wife
and ready-made family he gradually drifted
west, pushed on by the relentless force of the
whites. Several other children were born, but
they could not compare in attractiveness with
Atoka. When the French and Indian war
broke out, many of the Indians in Central
Pennsylvania, among them Arrow-Wood, sided
with the French. They had been the first
white men on the scene; they had used the
Indians well; if any white men were entitled
to the soil the Frenchmen were the ones. After
Braddock's defeat in 1755 the redmen became
emboldened, and were the aggressors in many
conflicts with the settlers. Massacres were so
numerous that the provincial government
erected a chain of forts to protect the outlying
settlements. Among these was Fort Augusta,
which stood at the old Indian town of Shamokin, now Sunbury. Immediately after it
was built friendly Indians, mostly squaws and
young girls and boys, began to frequent the

stockade, to trade with the soldiers and
settlers who made headquarters there. Among
them were Love Vine, her daughter Atoka, and
the former's younger children. Captain
Morgan Evan Morgan, a young Welshman, who
was stationed at the fort temporarily, await-
ing orders to be sent to the Ohio region, took
a kindly interest in the horde of visiting Indians, and often made purchases from them
" just to help them along," he said. He took
particular notice of Atoka, who was about
seventeen years old at the time. She had been
born in 1739, about the period when Reading
was being " mapped out." Her appearance
was so different from any of the other Indian
girls frequenting the fort, that the young officer set out to make inquiries concerning her.
Through Thomas McKee, the Indian trader, for
whom McKee's Half Falls received its name,
he learned that her father had been a Scotchman. This accounted for her dun-colored hair,
and eyes that approached the hazel more than
the brown. Her smooth complexion was
tawny, and not copper-colored, like her race.
The broad cheek-bones and full lips betokened

her Indian blood more than anything else. Except for these features she might have passed for a sun-burned European. She was tall and supple, and her shapely hands were skilled in making pottery and basket-weaving. Coming from roving stock, she spoke several Indian dialects, as well as a few words of German and English. Captain Morgan, tall, dark and distinguished-looking, made an impression on her, as she had on him. He bought all her baskets and utensils, praised her work, and said as many pleasant things to her as his limited polyglot vocabulary allowed. He saw to it that all the Indians in the neighborhood were well treated, which made the squaws desire to tarry longer than was their wont. Everything became so pleasant—thanks to his interest in Atoka—that some of the older officers dubbed him "Morgan, the Peacemaker." In the midst of this premature millennium came the news that an estimated force of 1500 French and Indians were coming down the West Branch to attack the Fort. The garrison tried to keep the news from the squaws, but they heard it somehow and all of them, including Love Vine and Atoka, departed for the wilderness. It would have been giving real cause for offense to detain them. Soon after they had gone, Captain Morgan and eight trusted men were ordered up the river to re-enforce the garrison at Fort Number Seven, which stood several miles above where Tiadaghton or Pine Creek empties into the Susquehanna, and which had been once occupied by the French. Fort Horn was later built on this site. A week slipped by after their arrival at Number Seven, and no hostile Indians nor Frenchmen were heard of. Morgan told his men that he wanted to go on a secret reconnoissance; he had some intimations of the approach of the foe that must be investigated. He started off one fine morning, and none dare gainsay him. His brother officer at the fort, Captain James Lane, was an Irishman, who was decidedly jealous of the new arrival. He was glad to see him go on the scouting trip. " The young fool will be killed," was the comment he made on it. Early the next morning a visitor appeared at the stockade in the person of Toadflax, a friendly Indian living on the north side of the

river, who occasionally carried out hunting
and fishing commissions for the soldiers. " I
have some strange news for you," he told Captain Lane. " Morgan came to my tent yester-
day and bought an Indian hunter's outfit; I
painted his face like a redman; he crossed the
river and started out Love Run. I followed
him to the south side of Sugar Valley, where I
saw him join several members of your hated
Arrow-Wood's band and go away with them.
The man is a traitor, I am sure; he is betray-
ing your garrison to the enemy. As proof that
what I say is true I can show you his uniform,
which he left with me. He only took his
sword with him." Captain Lane was genuinely
indignant; if he had joined members of Arrow-
Wood's band he was a traitor, and as such
must be caught in the act, and killed to atone
his baseness. He called for volunteers to trail
the villain, to which every man in the fort
begged the chance to distinguish himself. Two
Irishmen, Pat Mucklehenny and Shane Mc-
Micken, who knew the woods well, were selected
as the most trustworthy. Accompanied by
Toadflax they crossed the mountains and went

as near to Arrow-Wood's fortress as safety
would permit. But they found no traces of
Captain Morgan. On their way back they met
a squaw, and tortured her until she confessed
that she had seen the Captain, dressed as an
Indian, but carrying a sword, moving in the
direction of the north, that same morning.
They were evidently hot on the trail. When
they reached the Susquehanna they met two
friendly Indians, who said that they had seen
a tall, queer-looking Indian crossing the river
in a canoe, just above the mouth of Tiadaghton.
The pursuers made an improvised raft, and
followed. Meanwhile Captain Morgan, whose
worst offense had been a lover's fib to a brother
officer—he had merely slipped off to meet Atoka
clandestinely—was heading for the fort in a
roundabout way. He naturally used the disguise, as it would have looked strange if he
visited Arrow - Wood's territory in a British
uniform. Toadflax had told an untruth when
he said he saw him meet several members of
the hostile chieftain's band. He had merely
seen him meet Atoka; they had strolled away
together. Captain Morgan was no traitor, but

was very much in love, and love is blind to danger. After a delightful visit, every moment of which seemed elysium, especially the moon-lit evening they spent together on a ledge of rock above the gorge, not far from the Indian fortress—it must have been a night like when the writer drove through the pass last summer —the young lover started for the north, intend-ing to return as quickly as possible to the fort. He had to cross the river to get back his officer's regalia; he could not return in his disguise. When he arrived on the north bank of the river he followed the creek in the direc-tion of Toadflax's encampment. A quarter of a mile up the stream, his keen eyes detected a party of strange Indians, fully armed, skulking along the eastern shore. They had evidently seen him; but he would assume an indifferent air; maybe the danger would pass. They might think him a friendly Indian. Turning off from the path he drew his sword from the scabbard—it was the only thing that "gave him away"—and drove it into the soft earth up to the hilt, in the centre of a bed of wild parsnips. Unbuckling the belt, he rolled it up with the

scabbard and hid it under a giant pine log
that had gone down in a windfall. Then he
returned to the path, and looked across the
creek, as unconcerned as you please. The
strange Indians did not make a move to molest
him, so both parties kept on their respective
ways on the opposite banks of the stream. As
he neared Toadflax's encampment the sharp
report of a firearm rang out in the calm afternoon air. Captain Morgan fell in a limp mass
among the reeds, shot through the back, and
bleeding copiously from the mouth. As he lay
there Captain Lane, with a smoking musket
in his hand, accompanied by his evil geniuses,
Pat Mucklehenny and Shane McMicken,
emerged from a thicket. Lane put his booted
foot heavily on the prostrate form and orated,
" We have run you to earth, vile traitor; we
have seen you accompanied by your hostile
band, bound to betray and destroy us," and so
on at great length. Morgan's pale face turned
over; he gazed at Lane with his marble-like
eyes, and tried to raise himself on his hands.
Evidently he wanted to speak, as the rich red
blood gushed more freely from his mouth. He

was a hideous figure, covered with war-paint
and blood in ill-fitting Indian attire, as he
sank back, gasped, gulped and expired. That
night, they say, the wolves made him their
portion. His neglected bones became a trellis
for the wild morning glories; a Carolina par-
rot nested in the skull. Lane and his comrades were highly rewarded by the British
government; even Toadflax was given a farm
and told to always be a " good Indian." As
for Atoka, she sat on the high ledge of rock
which overlooks the beautiful pine-crested valleys, and watched and waited. Her lover
did not come, she never knew why. The wild
pigeons flew from the north like trails of dark
smoke. They must have flown over Morgan's
camp. But not one of the uncounted millions
brought a message. Like a fragile flower
plucked and left out of water she faded and
drooped, until one day she wandered off into
the forests, doubtless dying of exposure. Her
disappearance hastened Arrow-Wood's end, for
he loved her more than his own children.
Nearly a hundred years later, about 1850, John
Callahan, one of the respected farmers along

Pine Creek, while grubbing roots, uncovered
Morgan's sword. Much was said, guessed and
written about it—it was called "The Sword
of Pine Creek." If it hadn't been for some of
the older Indians living on Nichols's Run the
whole affair would have remained a mystery.
They knew the sad story, and on occasion related it.

Metalmark Books is a joint imprint of The Pennsylvania State University Press and the Office of Digital Scholarly Publishing at The Pennsylvania State University Libraries. The facsimile editions published under this imprint are reproductions of out-of-print, public domain works that hold a significant place in Pennsylvania's rich literary and cultural past. Metalmark editions are primarily reproduced from the University Libraries' extensive Pennsylvania collections and in cooperation with other state libraries. These volumes are available to the public for viewing online and can be ordered as print-on-demand paperbacks.

LIBRARY OF CONGRESS CATALOGING-IN-PUBLICATION DATA

Shoemaker, Henry W., 1880–1958, author.
The Indian steps : and other Pennsylvania mountain stories /
Henry W. Shoemaker.
p.   cm
Summary: "A collection of literary folklore from central Pennsylvania,
originally published in 1912"—Provided by publisher.
Includes bibliographical references and index.
ISBN 978-0-271-06366-9 (pbk. : alk. paper)
1. Pennsylvania—Social life and customs—Fiction.
2. Mountain life—Fiction.
I. Title.

PS3537.H95I53 2014
813'.52—dc23
2014011615

Printed in the United States of America
Reprinted by The Pennsylvania State University Press, 2014
University Park, PA 16802-1003

The University Libraries at Penn State and the Penn State University Press,
through the Office of Digital Scholarly Publishing, produced this volume to
preserve the informational content of the original. In compliance with current
copyright law, this reprint edition uses digital technology and is printed on paper
that complies with the permanent Paper Standard issued by the
National Information Standards Organization (ANSI z39.48–1992).

www.ingramcontent.com/pod-product-compliance
Lightning Source LLC
Chambersburg PA
CBHW020649110726
47901CB00001B/115